ABOUT THE AUTHOR

Tyler Darling was raised in Coconut Grove, Miami, Florida. She has traveled a road most of us would not venture down. As she says, "I was either very lucky or blessed with guardian angels to have survived."

Tyler has two sons, two grandchildren, and as she puts it, "My four fur babies!" Ms. Darling has lived in many exotic places, e.g. Malaga, Spain; Montréal, Québec; the island of St. Lucia; Vancouver, British Columbia, to list a few. She has lived in or visited all but seven of the United States.

Her spare time is filled with training dogs, reading and music. She is an avid student of other cultures. In fact she has hosted twenty-seven foreign exchange students, mostly from Eastern Europe; one at a time of course, for a period of a year. She volunteers with Hospice and the United Cerebral Palsy Foundation

ACKNOWLEDGEMENTS

John Wills, the world famous and highly published author of *Haiku* encouraged me to put pen to paper. It was my dear friend John, who titled this book. I hope he can read it in heaven.

***

"Remember, he can read it in heaven." said Father Tierney of the Gesu Church of Miami, Florida. I did as he said, thus the book…Woman of a Thousand Faces.

***

Without the love and continuous encouragement of my *sister of the heart* Linda, this story might not have been told. "Remember he can read it in heaven." she would say year after year. Linda is in heaven now; I know she is *over the moon* to see this story in print. I love you Linda!

***

And Mame, who is not jaded by the suffering of my Caleb and the others in her care. She is the epitome of compassion, caring and support to my son and me. I love you Nurse Mame.

***

To Israel. Anytime I called you in a frantic and frenzied state of confusion about a health issue with my Caleb, you calmly and oh so patiently got me all the answers I needed to go forward with surgery or some other procedure. I love you Israel.

***

I am extremely grateful to "KC" in California, for her endless hours of proofing and steering me in the right direction when I lost focus of the story of Gabbi.

***

And to you my *Mr. TNT*, every time the pain of writing this became overwhelming, Grammy heard your sweet voice and saw your smiling face. I love you *to the moon and back!*

***

To my dear Canadian friend, Mary B., who loved and believed in me for all of these years, you will always be in my heart.

***

And to my four fur babies who entertained themselves for endless hours allowing me the time to tell the story of Gabbi.

***

Thanks to Janet, my artist friend for her professionalism in pulling together the vision I had for my cover. Find her at <u>fuzzballs@videotron.ca</u>

***

And then there is Karen; a friend through the worst of times and the best of times. Karen made a tiny office out of a closet in my home where she sat hours a day, typing as I dictated. This I know, Woman of a Thousand Faces, would not have made it to print without her devotion. You worked your magic girl!

***

And last but not least, I am thankful for my faith, family and friends.

DEDICATION

To my sons: Brett, who gave my life purpose, joy, love, and companionship. I love you to the moon and back.

Caleb, you are my living angel. I pray when we are together in heaven I will be able to hold you; your body free of pain; a mind as bright and clear as your brother's. But most of all son, it's in heaven that you will have the ability to hear my words and feel their meaning. I love you son! And then Caleb to finally hear the words I've never heard from you; the words that all mothers live to hear...*I love you Mommy!*

Woman

of a

Thousand Faces

by

Tyler Darling

Dear Iris
Love & Hugs

Tyler Darling

Tyler Darling Books www.tylerdarlingbooks.com

Published by: alis volat propris

Sold by Amazon Digital Services, Inc.

Language English

Credit cards accepted through PayPal (Visa, MasterCard, American Express, Discover and eCheck)

Prologue

The priest grasped my shoulders after giving Caleb his last rites, looked with his piercing ice blue eyes into mine and said,

"Don't waste your energy crying. Put on paper everything a mother would share with a growing child, after all, *he can read it in heaven.*"

Everything? The terrifying day in Bimini that changed our lives forever? The gun. The strange accents. The sound of shattering glass as I hid behind the pseudo-security of the nursery door. The chest clenching fear. The bloody scene at the dog track in Hialeah? The handcuffs. The three burly policemen. Ray being hauled off.

They'll love the stories of our cozy first home in Miami; the sprawling ranch in Wyoming; the villa in the Bahamas and the extravagant gifts Raymond showered on us.

In the wild, a mother will kill or be killed to protect her young. What about a modern mother; a mother raising her children in a so-called civilized society? What will she do to assure the health and safety of her offspring? Will she lie, suffer countless indignities, compromise her values, even do the unthinkable to keep her babies together and protected?

I've made my decision. I *will* tell my sons the truth about me, about our lives together. My first born son Caleb is severely brain-damaged. He may never be able to process the information I share with him; he's my best friend, my confidant. I tell him my darkest secrets without fear of judgment; share my greatest joys.

Will Sean love me even more, when he realizes the strength of mind and character vital to save him from this insanity?

Father Tierney understood my need to share with my children; let the chips fall where they may. I want them to know the whole story; every tumbling domino that affected our destinies.

PART ONE

Chapter One

"I need a confidante! If I'm making a mistake confiding in you it won't be my first, but it could be my last. Juliet you are the only one I trust."

"I called you over this afternoon because I'm about ready to burst. I've known you for two years, but you haven't known me; I'm living a lie." I could see her start to talk; I put my hand up to stop her.

"Of course you can trust me! Look, you've got a voice as clear as a primary color, but if you don't start talking now and tell me everything, I'll squeeze your bloody neck and you'll never sing another note."

"Hold onto your wig girlfriend, you're about to take a journey. I'm living in the witness protection program and I *am* leaving its protection."

"What?" Juliet exclaimed.

I could see the puzzled and shocked look on her face. "No Juliet! Listen. It's as bizarre to tell as it is to hear. Uncle Tommy is the pseudonym, codename, for my contact in the FBI. I'm telling him that I am leaving Nashville and this twisted role they created in an attempt to save my life. I can't do it anymore. To this point, my whole life has been bogus. It's time for me to take control. *Oh wild and crazy friend,* my life is complicated. It's not at all what it appears to be. And if I tell you the truth…"

"No honey, I don't. I'm living it and I don't understand it. But after reading everything that's in the envelope, you might have a better understanding as to why this has been a living nightmare. My boys are bone of my bone, flesh of my flesh; I've sold my flesh for them. *And* I've left the only man I ever loved to protect them. I will create a life for them. Miami is like my second skin; it's home."

As she sat fingering through the pages and reading the articles I asked her "Do you want another drink?"

"You bet I do. I'm sitting here shaking and it's not even my life."

"Okay, you keep reading and I'll make you another."

While Juliet read the pages that explained so much and answered so many questions, I snuggled with Leski on the sofa.

"Wow Katrina, I feel like I have just had an out of body experience. Believe it or not I find myself at a loss for words, and I never thought that would happen to me in *my* lifetime."

As she stood up, I walked over to her. She hugged me close and cheek-to-cheek she whispered in my ear, "Katrina, my friend, no matter who you really are, *I know your heart.* I love you and I'll do anything you

"Look girl, you've only been walking this earth a twenty few years; do you have an early check out wish? What truth? What the hell is going on?" Juliet rushed on. "Start at the beginning. You're right, I'm your crazy eccentric friend; the singer, entertainer, world explorer, who happens to dig the hell out of you, Katrina. Open up girl. I sensed all along you were a walking mystery. *Hey*! Is Katrina even your real name?"

As I got up from my uber comfy sofa, I slipped my hand under the cushion, retrieving a manila envelope from its hiding place. I handed her the envelope and instructed her, "Juliet, don't open this until I finish telling you the story. What's in here will help you understand further why I'm in Witness Protection." I walked over to my little bar thinking, her drinking habits are on the upper end of social; I'd better make her a Tequila Sunrise.

"By the time I finish this cocktail, some of the shock will have worn off. Start at the beginning and tell me how you landed here." Juliet sighed.

I proceeded to tell her of my beginning, and life in the orphanage and…three hours later I said, "All right, Juliet. I've filled you in; you've had a cocktail, *now* you can open the envelope."

Running her hand over it, she looked up at me and said, "Do you really expect me to digest everything you told me in an afternoon?"

ever ask me to do. Wait a minute! Have you done what the priest told you to do?"

"Priest?"

Breaking our embrace, standing eye to eye she said, "Yes, remember Father Tierney? He told you someday Caleb could read it in heaven. Start writing, put it all down." she said with urgency. "I'll help any way I can. Katrina, your story could help a lot of young women, you're not the only dumb virgin who fell into harm's way. These stories need to be told. Write it down, especially for your boys."

"Now, if you're going to leave Nashville and witness protection girl, you'd better have a plan."

"Bingo! I've got one. I've saved enough money to buy a house; a really big house. I'm going to open a nursing home. I'll convert the house so it'll be wheelchair accessible. I'll hire nurses and staff." I was rushing as the adrenalin coursed through my brain; I couldn't talk fast enough. "That way I'll have both of my sons with me."

Juliet asked, "Why a nursing home? What do you know about running a nursing home?"

"Absolutely nothing. But I'll hire the best. *And* I have one of the best role models in the whole world."

"Who's that?" Juliet asked.

"Remember I told you about the orphanage and Aunt Esther?"

"Yea."

"Well, Aunt Esther didn't have training but when her husband died leaving her with infant twin daughters, she did what she needed to do to save her family. She's my inspiration and role model. In fact, the nursing home will be filled with as much love and caring as Aunt Esther's orphanage was."

"Look you flamboyant blonde bomb shell, do you really think Ray is gone forever? Aren't you scared that he'll resurface and do you harm? I need you to promise me that you will have an escape plan; just in case they come looking for you. You know, like keep money and your passports and important papers in a jar and bury them in the yard. Remember banks are closed on weekends." she said adamantly.

"Okay, I promise. What a great idea!"

"Leski, my big beautiful Russian Wolfhound, do you hear what Juliet's saying?" she looked up at me with those huge almond shaped Borzois eyes. I'd swear I saw a twinkle in them; like she was saying to me, "Don't you worry Mom; he'll never make it past the front door!"

"Juliet, I feel like a mother wolf and Leski is my wolf twin. When threatened, we will protect the pack, just like in the wild. I know that everyone is not an animal person and may not understand the symbiotic relationship that I share with Leski. But I know you can Juliet."

"Do you think Ray is a sociopath?" she asked as she traced the top of her cocktail glass with her forefinger; her mind was obviously on the urgency of the life and death matters at hand.

I looked down into the deep, rich, ruby red port that I had poured for myself. "That's a deep question and I struggle with it. Certainly he displays the pattern. When I looked the word up in the dictionary, it was *his* picture I saw."

"But you said the FBI thinks he might kill you. That's why you're in Witness Protection. They took this very seriously, and I think you need to as well."

"Look Juliet, I've survived near death; I'm not afraid of dying if that's the destiny laid out for me. If he kills me, I'll stroll the streets of heaven with panache." I said as I threw my hands up into the air.

"I'm tired of the ghosts of my past controlling my future. God didn't make me a flawed woman; it's just my flawed choices that have made my life hell so far. I have a lot to prove to my kids *and* myself. I may have been victimized, but *I refuse to be a victim."*

"But what *about* your kids? He may harm them like in the movies, you know, to get back at you."

"You're right. He could do that very easily if he's a sociopath. That's why I'm keeping our fictitious names."

"And Caleb? You can't possibly take care of a severely brain-damaged child."

"Well, I've spoken to Sunrise Care Facility in Miami; they said there is room for him there. We've worked up a financial plan that I think I can meet until I get *my* facility up and running. It will probably take a year. During that time I'll convert my pain into the creation of a new life for my kids and me. *My* family!"

"Oh Katrina, there is just so much for you to think about, and plan. It sounds like you are really going to do it. Remember, I'll help you in any way I can. Right now, I need to go home and take a long hot bubble bath."

We walked to the door and with another hug, she was gone.

My burning desire for family, the need to belong overrode my instinct for self-preservation. Sure, they could find me and kill me; but hell, I've spent the first chunk of my life desperately trying to create a family. First, with the father of my children; a dark, dangerous and devious man. And then an alcoholic who nearly beat me to death."

It had to stop. I *have* two children. The light finally came on. I *have* a family of my own.

Chapter Two

Yum! Grapefruit juice and vodka; a decadent indulgence, at this hour of the day. This Miami girl loves her juices. Just one, to give me the bravado for what was coming next; *the questions.*

As I sat waiting for the waning sun, I settled into my rickety rocker, on my rickety veranda. The effects of salt water and stifling heat, crippled the porch slats, reminding me of Nanny's hands; gnarly and crooked as she aged. Without warning, a black cat ran out from a stand of Areca palms. I didn't see a mouse or anything else. My chest tightened and my hands trembled, jarring me back into reality. *Black cats and Raymond; synonymous with evil and impending doom.*

"Shoo cat, run and take the evil with you!" I hissed.

Would we ever really be safe? How many times will I have no option, but to yet again, reinvent myself?

I reached for my liquid courage and returned to my bedroom. It was nearing the time for our ritual. I'd put on my happy face, ready to spin yarns for my angelic son, who was oblivious to the dangers I'd gotten us into.

Sean, my second-born son, was four years old. He would use the little stepstool to climb onto my big old four-poster bed, scoot over to me and cuddle up.

"Mommy, can we have story time? I'll get the box."

He'd pull up three big picture albums and sit in the middle of the bed. His blond hair was cut bowl style, like the little Dutch boy on the paint can. Sean's azure eyes were crystal clear and filled with wonder. I'd tell him stories that related to the pictures in the box. His questions were always the same, "But why?"

The albums were filled with snapshots that had never been mounted on the pages. Each picture told a story: Montréal, Miami, Wyoming, the Poconos, and the Bahamas. On and on. My life was laid out before me. Murderers, drug runners, beatings; had all of this really happened to me? It was hard for me to wrap my mind around it; hard to believe I'd survived.

Sean liked to pick up a picture and ask me about it, then wait for me to share an adventure. On this day he dug into the pile with two chubby little fingers and came out with a snapshot.

"Is this you, Mommy?" he asked

There were no secrets between us. That is to say, if he asked me specific questions, I'd answer as age appropriately and honestly as I could. Those questions never asked, would remain my secrets.

The woman in this picture *was* me; the man, his father. Memories aren't always happy, but I owed it to this child to answer every question about the family he once had. This wasn't going to be easy.

"Sure is. That's me when I was much younger and that's your daddy, Raymond. This picture was taken at the golf course on Old Baldy Mountain, near Saratoga, Wyoming."

"Something's funny Mommy; there's something wrong about this picture."

"Really, like what?" Uh oh, I thought. Take a deep breath.

"Well, see those trees? There's no coconuts."

This must have been divine intervention. I looked up towards the ceiling and winked, thanked God for sparing me *this* time. I could answer this one! I rolled over and tickled Sean's tummy, kissed the sweet folds under his neck. "No coconuts! No coconuts!" I said as he giggled.

"You're right honey. They don't have coconuts in Wyoming. We live in Florida; here we have coconuts. I think in Wyoming the trees have acorns."

He seemed to sense that the next picture was important and he handed it to me carefully. "Okay, Mommy, who is this baby?"

Hold on Gabbi, I thought. Keep it light. Don't frighten him. Putting a smile in my voice, I answered. "That baby is your brother."

"My brother?"

"Sean. Mommy had a baby before you were born. His name is Caleb."

"But he looks like a mummy; like in that movie?"

The brain hemorrhage had caused Caleb's head to swell up. The bandages gave his head the appearance of a light bulb wrapped in gauze.

Breathe Gabbi. "Yes, he does honey. You know, your brother is very special; he lives in a hospital."

"Oh, is that why he doesn't live with us?"

"That's right sweetie."

From there he picked up a picture of us fishing in the Keys. "Here we are, on vacation Mommy."

It would be easy to remove all the pictures of Caleb and spare myself future gut wrenching sessions. But that wouldn't be honest, and Sean would have to know at some point. No, I'd answer each question as it came up; just the answer. No more, no less.

We tickled and rolled and played in the bed. Soon it would be Sean's bedtime. As I moved the carton of pictures back into the closet, I knew it was just a matter of time before I would have to fill-in with more details.

After tucking Sean into bed in his own room, it was my time to enjoy the quiet hours; to reflect on the day. Often while lying in my bed, before falling asleep, I would grab the pillow that Sean had just been lying on. It still held his sweet scent. Shortly after closing my eyes, I'd fall asleep. At times, sleep could be disturbing; tonight would be one of those times. My dreams of Caleb were vivid.

***

Another night, another question.

"Mommy, what were you like when you were little?"

My heart pounded. How much should I reveal about my childhood? These questions brought up a lot of pain.

"That was a long time ago sweetie. I'll tell you what I can remember, okay?"

He nodded and smiled.

"I remember living in Miami, in a large house made of wood. There was a front porch. We had a black nanny."

"What's a nanny?"

"My nanny was fluffy and soft. She wore a white apron and cooked us Aunt Jemima pancakes. She let us little kids watch *The Lone Ranger* on Saturday mornings. Best of all, she loved me. I guess you could say a nanny is like a mommy."

"Okay." he said and was quiet for a moment. "What little kids, Mommy?"

"Well, I lived in a kind of orphanage. A place where children lived if they didn't have a mommy, or if their mommy worked so much she couldn't take care of her child. Aunt Esther was the woman who owned that house. Living with her and my nanny were wonderful years. On weekends she would load us kids into her car. It was a big, shiny silver Buick convertible. We were with her the day she picked it out at Dixie Buick. One of the kids said he liked the black one. But she told him it was too hot in Florida to have a black car."

Esther was a retired kindergarten school teacher in Coral Gables. She proceeded on that day to explain the effects of the hot, blistering Florida sun on a dark colored car. For one thing, the paint would oxidize. For another, the car would be too hot to even ride in.

I went on, telling Sean about life with Aunt Esther, how we would pile into her Buick and head for the Crandon Park Zoo and Matheson Hammock Park, near our home in Coral Gables. We'd be all dressed up. It was like a religious trek for us on weekends. I remember that as she drove, Aunt Esther would click her false teeth together and we kids would snicker. I was always frightened by the blood red lipstick that seeped into the tiny lines around her thin lips. That was a scary sight for a little kid.

I loved the elephants at the zoo. I'd head directly to the holding area to see my best friends in the world, the "Ellies". For many years I thought they were mine! I made up fantasies all week about what *my* elephants were doing. I couldn't wait for the weekends to go back to the zoo and hear their stories in our secret elephant language. Those passive giants and I stared into each other's eyes; I wanted desperately to share all of the events from the past week. And they would talk to me. They'd tell me about the bullies who stole the peanuts that visitors threw to them.

Swaying their humongous bodies to and fro, they told me how the older elephants pushed them, preventing them from shuffling closer to the cold metal fencing and catching the flying peanuts. I'd tell them through our secret Ellie-speak about the boys at Aunt Esther's orphanage. They bullied me, pulling on my ponytails, wrenching my head back, taking my dessert from me when Nanny wasn't looking and threatening to beat me up if I yelled out.

The elephants' eyelashes protruded far out from their eyelids, resembling the long strands of errant hair left in my hairbrush after a brisk brushing by Aunt Esther. I yearned to slip into their enclosure and find a safe, hidden area where I could curl up and nap, away from the cruelties of siblings and adults. We'd comfort one another until we were discovered by the zoo keepers. I dreamed of a time when we would provide shelter and safety to each other, commiserating about the trials of our collective lives.

All during the week when Nanny put a pot of honey on the table for the homemade biscuits, that scent triggered my memories of my Ellies! You wouldn't have thought that those enormous animals would have such a sweet smell as honey, but they did.

In the evenings while watching cartoons in the parlor I'd take my blankie, curl up on the old, worn leather chair and fall asleep embraced by my elephants! Well, in my imagination anyway.

***

"On Saturday nights Nanny took us upstairs to be spit-shined for Sunday morning church."

"Oh no, your nanny spit on you?"

"No, honey, that's just a saying." I laughed.

We were bathed. Our hair was shampooed and then rinsed with White Rain conditioner. After drying us off Nanny sat us up in the middle of the bed. There was a large bag made of brocade; I guess it would be called a carpetbag. We could only imagine what sorts of treasures were in it. One by one she pulled out long white strips of cloth cut from old sheets.

Next she would pull a rat-tail comb out of the bag. She'd section our hair, roll it around her large wrinkled fingers, and tie it up with the rags. Those gnarly, spooky-looking fingers touched us gently and lovingly and never hurt us, not even once.

Sunday mornings, Nanny would untie all of the white rags in our hair, which she had put in to create curls. We were dressed in our matching finery, complete with Mary Jane shoes. After checking us from top to bottom for cleanliness and tidiness, she marched us downstairs to the front parlor. There we would sit and wait for Aunt Esther to drive us to church. We were lined up on the big sofa, not taking a chance that one of the boys would sneak out into the back yard and get dirtied. Or, that one of the girls would sneak into Aunt Esther's Red Crocodile handbag, exploring; hoping to find one of her red lipsticks thinking that would be a perfect addition to our Sunday finery; or maybe find her sweet smelling Wild Rose Cologne.

Aunt Esther had twin daughters, Elizabeth and Cassandra. Their father had died when they were little. With two babies, a huge home and little money, Esther took children like me into her home. Her pension wasn't enough to maintain six bedrooms, three bathrooms, a front parlor, formal dining room and a huge working kitchen.

Elizabeth, Cassandra and I looked a lot alike, with our blue eyes and blond hair. We were dressed alike every day. We loved the attention given our golden curls, pastel dresses and Mary Jane shoes at church on Sunday.

There were days when it was too hot to stay inside, so we'd go outside and play in the soft, refreshing afternoon rain. Jumping puddles and looking for rainbows would take us into the cool of the evening, when Nanny would set up the long wooden picnic table for our dinner. We ate outside under the umbrella of the huge old banyan tree. I always felt safe under the canopy of that tree.

"See these two little pock marks on my face? They're from when I had the chicken pox. Aunt Esther had me sleep downstairs separated from the other kids. She kept the room dark. The doctor told her the light was not good for me. I was so lonely in there until Nanny would come in and read me stories from Uncle Remus."

"I know Mommy. It's about Br'er Rabbit and Br'er Fox. Those are the same stories you read to me!"

"Yep." I said. "She also read me Little Black Sambo. Nanny made me feel loved."

"Just like you make me feel when I'm sick, huh?" he chirped.

Many details of my life weren't appropriate to share with a small child. I didn't want to tell Sean about how I cried myself to sleep every night during the years with Aunt Esther; how I waited for the sounds of my real mommy coming to me, how the faded wallpaper that covered the old plastered wall—cabbage roses in shades of pink and green—became blurred through my tears.

There was a huge gardenia tree outside my bedroom window. In those days no one had air-conditioning. The night breeze would carry that sweet scent into me. It had a calming effect. Finally I'd fall asleep, my thin cotton pajamas soaked in sweat. Lying there all alone I waited for my mother, listening, desperate to hear her footsteps in the hall.

Chapter Three

Finally my mother did come to Aunt Esther's house. There was a stranger with her.

"Honey," she said, "this man is going to be your daddy. You'll be coming with us! We're moving to Virginia. This is your new brother, Eric. Isn't he cute?" Mother held the boy's pudgy little hand. The sight of her holding the hand of a little toddler with a head full of blond curls was a shock.

The room began to spin. I couldn't make it stop, but I could see the faces of everyone staring at me. No matter how I wished for it to stop, the spinning sensation continued. I don't remember falling to the floor. When I awakened, my mother and *that* man were looking down at me. The look on her face was concern, but I wasn't sure it was for me. I wondered if she was seeing me as a threat to her newfound life. Did this mean I would lose Nanny and Aunt Esther? I was terrified and conflicted. Did I want to go or stay? My stomach churned.

"Please don't let this happen," I pleaded with Nanny. She looked as bewildered as I felt. I cried and ran away from my mother, back to the safety of the huge old banyan tree, to hide under the gnarled old roots. Now that sacred, sheltered space had a different purpose. Before, all of us children at Aunt Esther's would use that tangled mass as a hiding place, while laughing and yelling out, "Hide and seek. You're it!" But on this day there was no joy in my heart as I shivered beneath the old tree.

***

Sarah, my mother, married Joe and I went to live with them. Joe was in the navy, and our blended family moved many times. I had been in six schools by seventh grade. Joe legally adopted me. With the stroke of some judge's pen, I lost all ties to my real daddy. I lost my real aunts and uncles and cousins. It was as if the former me had never existed.

I had lived with Aunt Esther in Miami for five years. With her I had security, love and a sense of family. I had roots at Aunt Esther's. My mother had stayed there with us off and on, but I was without her most of the time. She never told me where she was or what she did during those years.

Probably because of some sort of privacy agreement, Aunt Esther never spoke about my mother during my years with her. She never said, "Gabbi, your mother is away working right now but she'll be back this weekend to see you." Nothing like that was ever mentioned.

My mother rarely spoke about her family, her childhood, or my birth father. She grew up in Port Jefferson, New York, with a father who was a prominent golf pro and millionaire. My grandmother, I am told had drinking issues. Because of that, most of running the house and caring for her siblings fell on my mother's shoulders. When her family took the Queen Elizabeth II to Europe every summer, again my mother had all the responsibilities of caring for the family.

Over the years, I'd heard from an uncle that my mother married a boy from the wrong side of the tracks as a way of escaping her unhappy home life. She became pregnant. The only other information I was ever given was that she realized she had made a mistake, so she placed me in a foundling home in Miami.

Five years later she met Joe, a young sailor in his dress whites, at the Miami International Airport while waiting for a plane. He was balancing an infant boy on his lap trying to get him to drink milk out of a glass. I guess my mother saw that as an opening to make conversation. It seemed to work; several months later the sailor with the son and the woman with the daughter got married.

It pained me for many years that she wouldn't tell me about her life—or my life—before she met my adoptive father. But as an adult I grew to understand that it hurt her too much to bring up why she left her home at seventeen, or why she left my father when I was only weeks only.

How, I wondered, did she choose to move us from Long island, New York, to Miami, Florida? How did she find out about Aunt Esther's foundling home? When she disappeared during those five years, where did she go? I had vague memories of seeing her now and then—hazy, dull memories.

***

Joe had been stationed at the Key West Naval Base, ninety minutes from Cuba. While he and a bunch of his buddies were partying in a Cuban Bar, he met a hot-blooded native redhead. They had a child, a boy. I have no more information, except that Joe did marry the woman so she could come to the States. One day, she left the boy with a babysitter and disappeared, never to be seen again.

Joe's son, Eric, and I were raised as siblings. He was two years my junior. I resented him in our early years together, but I grew to love him. We played and interacted as real siblings.

I spent years trying to find my birth father, having discovered his name in an unlocked silver box under my mother's bed. I asked Eric if we should look for his mother too, but he said he couldn't care less.

My growing up years from age five to seventeen were difficult. When Joe retired from the navy, we moved to Cherry Hill, New Jersey. They bought a home in an upper middle-class Jewish community. Mother converted to Judaism. In Jewish tradition the children are raised in the mother's faith. And so another part of my heritage was changed. I became a Jewess. We went to synagogue every Friday night. We celebrated Hanukah, not Christmas. I did love learning about Judaism, but I hated not having Christmas. I missed the trees and presents.

Joe was a very rigid man. There was no gray area in his way of thinking. Anyone who disagreed with him about religion, politics, education, or any other topic was wrong. Period! He was very bitter and told me for years that life was "no bed of roses". He said I would need to study hard, earn a college degree, get married and have 2.2 kids. In his view, that was the correct way to live.

I was probably one of Joe's biggest embarrassments in life. In his eyes, I brought shame to our home. I was a hippie. My world was one of laughter, love, peace, harmony, understanding and forgiveness. I was a thorn in that man's side from day one.

I've never understood how his "tickle-tickle" game, figured into his self-righteous, straight-arrow ways. He was not the perfect man he wanted the world to think he was. He gave in to a deep, dark drive. A pervert lurked inside him and I was on the receiving end.

During the years in New Jersey, I clung to my mother. I can remember her *demanding* I go outside and play. I'd been uprooted from the security of Aunt Esther's, so I latched on to Mother. I was terrified that if I went out to play she'd be gone again when I came in. Either she never understood that about me, or she simply didn't care. I was forced to leave the house and find things to do besides hang around her.

In junior high school, my body developed quickly, and I turned into a curvy young woman. Joe's fondling became a morning ritual. I felt terribly ashamed and was sure if my mother found out I'd be discarded. I was positive she loved him more than she loved me, and that I would be seen as a home wrecker. I told no one what was going on.

Music was the only thing that held me together. My teachers encouraged me to join the chorus and choir. I performed in all the school plays and was involved in all sorts of talent activities. I was also selected to sing with the madrigal singing group, and we traveled throughout the state during the Christmas holidays.

In ninth grade, a boy from chorus asked me to audition for a folk music group he was starting. He said I reminded him of Mary Travers of Peter, Paul and Mary. I got the "gig", which was a lifesaver. Finally I had the answer of how to be away from home as much as possible to escape the verbal and sexual abuse of my adoptive father.

There was always a need to practice for a school activity. On weekends I performed in local coffee houses. My little band of five, the Cavaliers, sang for the USO. We performed at McGuire Air Force Base and Fort Dix Army Base. Because I was so young, a chaperone was assigned to escort me when we got to the bases and stayed with me until we left.

The idea of dating in high school made me feel ill. I just could not allow a boy to kiss me. It made me physically sick to be put in that position. Some of the boys from my synagogue would invite me to the movies. I went, but they always wanted to end the evening with a kiss. Since I never complied, I didn't do much dating.

After graduating from high school, my goal was to leave home and escape Joe's abuse. Without my parents knowing, I composed a letter to a hotel in the mountains of Québec, where my family spent two weeks skiing every year. I asked for a job, reminding them that my family had stayed with them for many years. I was amazed when they responded and offered me a position as the social director. They said they also wanted to offer my singing and guitar-playing talents to the guests at the lodge.

This letter represented a guarantee that for the first time in four years I would not have to protect my breasts from my adoptive father every morning after the alarm clock went off. I was ecstatic.

***

The Hotel Marquise became my sanctuary, and I made friends there. My job in the afternoons was to offer organized sing-a-longs. I would play my guitar and sing folk songs in front of a roaring fire. Each afternoon the Jesuits prepared the fireplace to provide warmth and ambience for the guests after their long day on the slopes.

I soon felt that I had evolved from a naïve teenager to a young woman making it on her own in the real world; a world that was nothing like Joe had described it.

Several months into my new life, I headed for the slopes on my day off for an afternoon of skiing. As I stepped onto the lift, a tall, handsome man—a Paul Newman look-alike with sandy hair and piercing blue eyes—approached me.

"May I share this lift with you?" he asked.

"Sure," I said, catching my breath and wishing I'd spent longer on my makeup that morning.

"Is this your first time?"

I didn't know how to respond, so I just shook my head and looked up at the mountain. I'd never had young man smile at me like this, and I'm sure I had a surprised look on my face.

"I'm Raymond," he said as we took off.

He really was making conversation with me. Stunned, I said, "I'm Gabrielle. My friends call me Gabbi."

Without a seconds hesitation he asked, "May I call you Gabbi?" And again I just nodded.

He didn't have a very thick French accent. I was relieved; here was the prospect of actually making an English-speaking friend. But I knew he was French; his English was thick with French flavor. Most of the people I had met at the hotel were French-speaking. They knew enough English to mingle with guests from the States, but that was the extent of it. My limited French compounded the problem of connecting with my peers in any intimate way, so my friendships remained superficial. I guess I was lonelier than I had admitted to myself.

After finding out that Raymond was from Montréal, here on vacation with his brother and staying at the Hotel Marquise, I spent the entire day with him, even having my first hot-buttered rum with him that night in the hotel bar before heading back to my room. It seemed like my first real date, and my head was spinning. It was hard to sleep as I replayed every minute of the day in my head.

***

Most nights after the guests were in the grand ballroom dancing, Ray and I would bundle up for the long walk into St. Agathe. He made sure I had wool socks under my mukluks. I was shocked one morning when he handed me a large box that said Authentic Mukluk Moccasin Boots. They were handmade by native Canadian Indians.

Before we left on those outings, he also made sure I wore thermal long johns under my slacks, a heavy sweater, gloves, a scarf and a warm alpaca hat. The friends we'd made joined us as we walked. I learned that when it's forty below zero with five feet of snow on the ground, people don't drive.

I'll never forget those nighttime excursions. The entire world looked like it was made of crystal. The humongous evergreen trees glistened, heavily laden with ice. The moonbeams twinkled from a wolf moon. The atmosphere was pure, free of smog or dust yet it appeared we were walking in a fog. This fog was the result of taking air into our bodies, warming it and exhaling it into the below zero atmosphere.

Raymond and I held hands, running and sliding. The burning flakes of snow landing on our cheeks prompted us to go as fast as our frozen feet would allow. Everything on those nighttime pilgrimages was white or green. The hardwoods and evergreens fought hard not to snap in half under the weight of the snow during those Canadian winters.

There were times when I thought my heart would burst from joy. I had friends. I had a man who treated me special, telling me how beautiful I was, what a great singing voice I had.

At the only diner in town, we usually ordered poutine, a popular Canadian comfort food. It consisted of a generous mound of French fries, dripping with melted cheese curds and brown gravy. There was always laughter; I felt uninhibited and interacted as if I were an equal. *That* was a first.

***

After working at the hotel for four months, I became aware of a number of problems. My room in staff quarters was located on the third floor of the huge old wooden Victorian structure. Ray decided I wasn't safe sleeping up there with the others. The group was made up of kitchen and dining room staff, entertainers and cleaning people.

"Gabbi", he said. "I want you to let me sleep in your room tonight. I just don't trust those guys with you up here alone. There's no lock on your door and there doesn't seem to be any heat up here."

"I know. Come see this." I grabbed his hand, happy to have someone looking out for me. "Try to open this fire escape door." I said, motioning toward a heavy door at the end of the hallway.

The carpet on the floor was threadbare, and the floor planks under it creaked as Ray made his way to the door.

"Well, first of all, look at all the ice." he said. "The door doesn't even meet the jamb anymore. Ice has built up in the cracks."

As he grunted and pushed his shoulder against the door, I could see it would never budge, even with his force.

"Baby, this place is a fire trap and it's not likely to change anytime soon. I've overheard talk in the dining room that the owners don't have the money to even pay for the grocery orders."

"I know." I said. "The staff hasn't been paid in two weeks. I've been selling some of my clothes. I've almost given things away just to make enough money to buy things I need in St. Agathe. But I can't tell my parents! They'll come and get me."

There was no way I was going back to New Jersey.

***

Ray slept in my room that night, hugging me and making me feel safe. But, the next night was a different story. His gentle kisses were warming and caused tingling sensations up and down my body. For the first time in my life, I wasn't afraid to be touched. I *wanted* more.

I was stiff at first, thinking about my adoptive father pawing at my breasts. But Ray was so tender and I could feel his heart beating against my chest. He moved slowly and deliberately; never rushing or touching me in a rough way. He must have sensed my lack of experience.

Surprisingly, rather than feeling exposed or vulnerable lying there naked, I felt free and alive. After my orgasm—my first—I could have gone on making love with him all night long.

Raymond had opened Pandora's Box. He'd awakened my sexuality; lit a fire deep inside of me that was insatiable. Later that week, it was a bit embarrassing when he had to beg me to let him sleep, laughing of course. But each time we made love, I'd curl up in his arms afterwards and he would talk to me in French, in a soft, low voice. I had no idea what he was saying, but it was so romantic and I felt safer than I'd ever felt.

I never worried about him leaving me at the end of his vacation. I was sure we were in love and that he would ask me to marry him. After all, we'd had sex! That's how utterly clueless I was to affairs of the heart.

***

"I'm moving you out of here Gabbi." Ray announced one morning after breakfast.

"What are you talking about? Move me where? I can't let my parents know anything about what's going on up here. They'd kill me!"

"I have to get back to work Gabbi, and I'm not leaving you here. *This* is an impossible situation."

"But--"

"No buts, pet. I've called my mother in Montréal. I'm taking you to her house until I figure things out."

My mind raced. Ray wanted to take care of me; I was really loved! The past two weeks hadn't been a fairy tale. In my naiveté, this must be *real love*.

Chapter Four

I packed my things and left the hotel with Ray, telling the owner there'd been an emergency at home. Ray said I could send them my resignation letter from Montréal. I would apologize, but say that I couldn't come back due to an illness in the family.

Ray's parents had a large, rambling old house in Montréal. It seemed like a boarding house there were so many people living there; several of Ray's brothers, their wives, four children—and Ray. I couldn't understand why he would be living at home if he had a successful import business, which was what he'd led me to believe. But I didn't ask; I guess because I was still up in the clouds with happiness over being wanted by this man.

Ray's mother, Bridget, welcomed me and didn't seem fazed at all about Ray showing up with an eighteen-year-old American girl in tow. She told me to call her Nana, which everyone had started calling her after the first grandchild arrived. Because she was a strict Catholic, I was directed to a guest room on the third floor, which they referred to as "the garret." I imagine she guessed that Ray and I were sleeping together, but that wouldn't mean she'd let it happen under her roof. Ray's room was on the second floor, and not a night went by that he didn't slip upstairs and into my bed. We'd tickle and giggle and make love—all the while trying not to raise our voices above a whisper.

I began combing the want ads for a job, but Ray said he wanted us to fly to New Jersey so that he could meet my parents; employment for me would have to wait.

Within weeks of arriving at his home in Montréal, Ray and I traveled to New Jersey. On the flight it was a good thing I had on my seat belt when he announced that he wanted us to get married. My face must have turned purple; the chicken salad I was eating lodged in my throat.

"Why do you look so surprised, baby?" Ray asked, laughing. "Why do you think we're going to see your parents? Don't you want to tell them in person?"

"Well…um," I stuttered. "Um, yea. I guess so."

We stayed at my parents' home for several days. During that time it was obvious they were sizing Ray up. I put off telling them I was engaged until the end of our visit and by then, they'd formed their opinion— and not a good one.

"Gabbi," mother said, "your father and I want Ray to get a job here and a place to live for a year. If after that if you still want to marry him, we'll give you a beautiful wedding."

We were sitting in the kitchen where I had done homework and shared family meals as a kid. I folded my arms around my tummy and thought, *Oh my God! Can't you see we're in love? And I'm probably pregnant?*

But those words never passed my lips because Ray immediately spoke up.

"That's an excellent plan, Sarah. We'll fly back to Montréal tomorrow and I'll make all the arrangements."

***

Back in Montréal, weeks passed with no further mention of our getting married. In fact I was ignored whenever I broached the subject. Ray left the house every day and often came home late at night. He never talked about his business or offered to take me to his office. We made love every night, but at other times around the house he was quiet.

I couldn't sit around all day chatting with Bridget and watching her work; she wouldn't let me lift a finger. So one day I took the bus downtown and got a job as a receptionist at an insurance company.

"You don't have to work Baby," Ray said when I told him that night. "I just need you to be here when I get home." He didn't seem angry, just distracted.

***

Ray's mother was French Canadian. His father, Victor, was from Massachusetts. Bridget had given birth at home—to fourteen children, Ray was the third. Twelve survived; nine boys and three girls. This explained why Bridget looked much older than she was.

But she was funny and always jovial, and I loved spending time with her.

Victor was a CPA by vocation and a chronic gambler who squandered the family's money on an almost daily basis. But Bridget seemed to always find creative ways to keep everyone fed. I learned from one of Ray's sisters that over the years there had been times when Victor bought the family a new home, but would soon lose it due to gambling debts. They had moved repeatedly.

Part of the social program provided by Canada for its citizens was a stipend for each child in the home. On the days that such checks were expected Bridget would send one of the grandkids to the mailbox. She would immediately grab her coat and her black fake-leather handbag and rush off to catch the bus to the grocery store.

The phone was often disconnected; each time, she would have the service put back on in the name of one of the children whose name hadn't already been used as an account holder. For an uneducated woman she was smart in lots of ways and she somehow managed to keep the household running. I respected what she did with the life that had been presented to her.

Ray's father, on the other hand, was a ne'er-do-well, and I did my best to avoid him. He seemed to think that his sole responsibility to his family was to go to work every day, stop on the way home at a corner store, and buy racing forms. This college educated man was of the belief that his exceptional ability to work with and understand numbers could make him a millionaire by gambling. So there he'd sit at the large kitchen table with his sons surrounding him as he played with numbers on a yellow legal pad. I have visions of that wiry little man with gray hair and horn-rimmed glasses smiling fondly at the boys as they sat with him; clearly they worshipped their father and wanted to learn his so-called "system".

System; a term commonly used in the gambling world for figuring the odds and having a sure fire winner in every race. He'd leave for work every morning in what appeared to be the same gray tweed suit tailored by an Englishman with the same gambling affliction. They had a business man's agreement. The tailor kept Victor in custom suits, while Victor kept the tailors books, showing a pittance in profits for the government while leaving mounds of profits for gambling. Of course there were other merchants and other deals. These relationships were built on need, sickness and conspiracy. Not once in all the years, not even on weekends did the "old man", as his sons referred to him, ever wear anything less than a tailored shirt, a vest made of Scottish wool, that always made me feel itchy just looking at it and tailored pants. When he'd come home from an evening of gambling, his sons would greet him at the front door, all bending over to hug this mild man; anxious to hear the tales he'd share.

***

In the three months I'd spent with Ray's family, I realized I was pregnant *and* living with hardened criminals; several of Ray's brothers had spent much of their lives in prison. I'd heard talk of robbing, drug running and other illegal activities. I witnessed the "wives" of Ray's siblings struggle daily to raise their children and maintain homes. They wondered with every knock on their door if it was the Mounties looking for their "husbands", or worse, delivering news that their husbands were dead from some criminal activity gone wrong.

One evening I went to the movies with Ray's sisters. The movie was *Bonnie and Clyde,* with Warren Beatty and Faye Dunaway. On the ride home the sisters laughed about how the movie mirrored their own lives. I sat quietly, my mind racing. How had I gotten myself into such a world? Everything here was foreign to me, not just the country and the language, but this family I was now involved with…they were actually laughing about the times when their husbands or lovers had been in prison.

We were all now sitting at the kitchen table, the bare bulb light glaring above us. It was all I could do to keep myself from jumping out of my chair, grapping my coat and escaping this *twilight zone.*

It got worse.

Ray's sister Haley turned to me, still laughing and said "Wait a minute. Didn't you know any of this?" Seeing the look of absolute shock on my face, she continued. "Yea, Ray's been in prison three times!" She jumped up and began rummaging through a kitchen drawer filled with newspaper clippings. She proudly thrust one in front of me. There it was, in black and white, Ray's name. Arrested for counterfeiting.

Emmett's pregnant, flaming red haired girlfriend read the confusion and terror on my face. She took my hand and said, "You should know that Ray was in prison for pandering, counterfeiting money…"

"Wait! What is pandering? What is that?"

"Pandering…well, he took young girls across the border to work as hookers. Yep, that's why he always has big rolls of doe, re, me in his pockets; none of our husbands work a 'Square's' job."

"Alright! That's enough! You've scared the girl *enough!*" said Rita.

I was pregnant, and very sick. I just can't let them know that I am terrified. I can't be sitting here. *What have I gotten myself into? I looked down at my stomach, feeling the baby kick and prayed to God that it wasn't a girl to be born into this life of mobsters and degenerates. Yep, I'd made my bed. How could I not have seen that Ray was as involved as his brothers in the underworld wheeling and dealing?* I was devastated and began planning my escape that night.

***

It was February; snow swirled in the wind, like little funnel clouds. Raymond and I were standing in front of the bus station in downtown Montréal. He touched my rounded tummy softly as I looked into his eyes. I was leaving him, headed for Miami and my beloved Aunt Esther. I prayed she could help me sort out the mess I'd made of my life; help me decide what to do next. Ray's eyes were dull; he didn't look upset, which made me wonder if he had ever cared about me at all.

"Are you sure about this Gabrielle?" he asked, his voice flat. "You know, no other woman in my life has walked out on me. What makes you think you can do it and succeed?"

I took a deep breath. "You and your brothers are bums, criminals. You've been in prison. You sit with your father and plan what horses at what tracks across Canada to bet on. Do you really think that's a job? And I know you don't have a business. I've seen you making lists on little pads with stubs of pencils, making charts on each horse. I've seen legal tablets with plans for making counterfeit money; where to buy the paper and ink, and who can do the printing."

I paused but he said nothing, just stood there looking down at me as if I were a silly little thing. I went on raving. "My father worked Monday through Friday. *That* is what a father does. How can I not leave? *I'm pregnant!* This is *our* baby! I have a responsibility now. Don't you get it? Your world is no place to raise a child."

I took another breath, squared my shoulders and said, "I don't know what to do or how to do it, but I'll learn. I'll get a job, find a place to live." My voice sounded strange to me; I couldn't believe I was saying this.

Announcements were being made over a loud speaker, but they were in French and I couldn't understand them. I looked at my watch.

"It's time to get on the bus," Ray said. His face was vacant, as if I hadn't just railed at him. He leaned down and held me. I began to sob.

"Are you going to join me in Florida?" I whispered in between sobs. "Are you going to change for me? Will you be a proper daddy?"

I pulled out of his arms and turned my face up to him, waiting for him to laugh at me. Instead, he said, "Yes, my pet. I will come to you."

I was shocked, but for some reason I believed him.

I knew I could create a life for my baby and me, in Miami. That's where I spent my childhood, with Aunt Esther and with so many wonderful memories.

I took a deep breath, brushed away tears and took the four biggest steps of my young life. The metal hand grip I held to board the bus was cold and hard. A sign of what my new life held in store for me? I climbed those steps. Few things in my life would ever feel safe or comfortable again.

***

Whatever courage I'd mustered to save money for the bus ticket, pack my bags and leave Ray, seemed to melt as I boarded that bus. I was terrified and sat literally trembling. I was going to be a mother. The fluttery feelings in my womb were a frequent reminder of that fact. I was swallowing over and over, feeling that I was going to be sick. I'd had morning sickness for three months, but thought it had finally passed. There was an Indian family also traveling on the bus; they had bags filled with food that released a cloud of curry-scented air, which aggravated the morning sickness, increasing the waves of nausea, making the trip pure torture. But fear was probably the main reason for my nausea. Yes, I was going to a familiar place where I was loved, but my future was a total unknown. All I knew for sure was, that I had to grow up, become an adult; a *dependable* adult.

I tried with all my might to pretend that the bus seat was, in fact, the soft armchair that was in my bedroom during my teen years. As long as I was curled up in that chair, I felt peaceful and safe.

I drifted off finally and didn't wake up until we pulled into the bus terminal in Newark, New Jersey. There we could get out and buy snacks and stretch our legs for an hour. That wasn't to be. It was 1967 and black people were rising up across the U.S., demanding desegregation. On this day, they happened to start a riot in the Newark bus station.

Young men—both black and white—were throwing stones and cans at the buses and suddenly then banded together and began rocking our bus.

Our bus driver sat there for a few moments, taking in the scene. All of a sudden he jerked open the door and yelled, "I'm getting off this bus. You're all on your own!" With that, he bailed out.

My body felt cold, but I began to sweat. More men had joined in, and the angry crowd outside our bus had turned into a mob. I was scared to death, but was frozen in my seat. "What should we do?" I asked the elderly black man sitting next to me.

He didn't answer. I think he was as frightened as I was. I began to cry. The old man's shirt was tattered and soiled. His brown trousers were worn thin and a frayed piece of rope was serving as a belt. I didn't care how unkempt he was. As he touched my shoulder I looked into his eyes and saw compassion.

With words, he told me I wasn't alone, while his eyes said *I will protect you.* He instructed me to get down on the floor and wedge myself between my seat and the seat in front of me. With his finger to his lips he implored me to be quiet. *Sshhh, don't make a sound, he gestured.*

I did as he told me and hulked down between those seats for what seemed an eternity. Finally, the old man tapped my shoulder; then with a gentle squeeze he said,

"We have a new driver. We're safe. You can get back in your seat."

It had been dusk when we pulled into that station. Now, as I looked out the window, it was totally black. I grabbed my "angel" and clung to him as if I had just been plucked from near drowning. This was the first time in my life that I had thought I was going to die. The tears flowed.

***

In Miami, Aunt Esther was waiting for me at the bus station with her daughters, my old playmates from childhood, Elizabeth and Cassandra. They hadn't heard about the nightmare in New Jersey, but I didn't want to spoil our reunion by talking about it. I just bucked up, shook it off and, hugged them.

It had been thirteen years since I'd been at Aunt Esther's, but it was as if it were yesterday. With her arm around my shoulders Aunt Esther said, "Well, Gabbi dear, the girls have set up your old bedroom for you."

Time had made no distinguishable changes in that bedroom. The wallpaper with cabbage roses was still there, and the gardenia scent hung in the air. The pale pink, threadbare chenille bedspread looked familiar and comforting. I walked over to the window as a rush of emotions swept over me. Until this moment I had tried hard to be strong. But in *this* bedroom I had the freedom to let go and feel the terror of the past thirty-six hours. I was exhausted.

Somehow the scent from the gardenia tree gave me the feeling of an old, loving friend embracing me saying, *"It's okay; I'll hold you while you cry."*

I collapsed onto the bed; Cassandra covered me with a light summer blanket. Elizabeth ran to get a cold, wet washcloth to wipe my brow. Morning sickness had taken over my life again, it seemed. Aunt Esther hurried to the kitchen for what she said would be the remedy. She returned with a tray. On it was a juice glass that I recognized as the same glass I had used as a child here, so long ago. It was filled with room temperature ginger ale. There were four saltine crackers evenly spaced on one of Aunt Esther's Rosenthal dessert plates. The border was painted with tiny, delicate pink rosebuds. It always fascinated me as a little girl how translucent these special plates were.

Having handmaidens and being pampered was delightful. For a few days, I enjoyed as much of the TLC as I could get. The trauma of the bus trip from hell and leaving Ray had left me drained.

I awakened nestled in the safety and security of my childhood bed. I lay there watching the dust particles as they danced in the rays of sun streaming in my window. The dust motes took on a life of their own. I imagined them to be a group of silly, carefree children circling round and round, singing. Something about this room transported me right back to my childhood.

"Swing your legs over the edge of the bed, put your feet on the floor, and then sit your body up." Aunt Esther instructed. "Always touch your feet to the floor before sitting up. It's an old wives' tale that works! If you still feel nauseated lie back down and eat some of these dry soda crackers."

It did work; I was beginning to feel life coming back into my being. The morning sickness was fading.

I stood brushing out my long blond hair while gazing into the old hazy mirror, in obvious need of re-glazing. For a fleeting moment the reflection was not a shiny-faced, vibrant young woman. It was an older woman, a tired soul with deep lines in her face. At first I thought, Oh God, is this a glimpse of me in the future; some warning from another dimension? No, no; it's only the worn-out old mirror, my Pollyanna side said, everything will be fine. But lately I found myself wondering if that image had been a heads-up about what was to come.

***

It was time to begin planning my life. I started down the steep stairs to the kitchen, but I had to grab the banister as a strong wave of morning sickness swept over me. One foot in front of the other, I thought, one step at a time.

"Good morning, Aunt Esther." I said and smiled as I hugged her neck. I turned my cheek just in time to avoid getting red lipstick on my face. "Well, I need to find a job."

Esther was sitting with her elbow resting on the kitchen table, spinning her rings on her fourth finger, around and around. This was as much a habit for her as finding her false teeth in the morning. They'd been resting overnight in a cup of water with baking soda. As I turned from this wonderfully familiar sight I felt a rush of memories flooding over me. There outside the old, screened kitchen door stood my aged and weathered friend, the banyan tree. As if shaking off a demon, I wouldn't allow those memories, no matter how good or bad, to consume me at the moment. I had a much more important task at hand.

"What type of work are you qualified to do, Gabbi?" Aunt Esther asked.

"Qualified? What do you mean? I'm just going to get a job!" I exclaimed.

"Come sit with me, dear." she said, reaching out to pull me over to her. "Look, honey, here's today's *Miami Herald*. Open it and go to Job Opportunities. What jobs are you qualified to do, dear?"

"Aunt Esther, I haven't been out of high school very long. I don't know if I'm qualified to do anything."

"Gabbi, let me see the paper. You have qualities that don't come with a college degree."

I passed the paper back to her. Aunt Esther's sympathetic tone was comforting, but never to be confused with "Oh, you poor, weak, incapable girl."

As if reaching into her own life experience, she said, "Gabbi, you're a girl. You're almost a woman and soon to be a mother. This is an important time for you, stepping into life and accepting your responsibility. There'll be no going back. Life need not be dreadful. You've been taught tools of survival, and you'll be just fine. I'm sure of that, dear."

"Like you, Aunt Esther. You're my hero; raising Elizabeth and Cassandra without a father, working to care for all of us kids, earning the money to keep your home. If I'm to be a single mother I have you as my guide."

"All right, let's see. Here's something Gabbi. Listen to this: 'Salesperson needed for boutique. Must have strong people skills.' That's you Gabbi!" She beamed.

That afternoon, after a brief interview, I was given the job at Clarisse's Boutique on the Miracle Mile in Coral Gables. A couple of weeks later with my first pay check in hand, I asked Aunt Esther to drive me to the airport. I purchased a ticket: Montréal, Québec, to Miami, Florida. I asked her to take me straight to the post office. "The sooner I can get Ray this ticket, the sooner he can come be with me, Aunt Esther."

She smiled and glanced over at me, but she didn't say a word.

A week later I again asked Aunt Esther to take me to the airport. This time I was going to meet Ray's flight. I didn't know which was worse that morning, the butterflies of excitement or the morning sickness. Neither of those could touch my feeling of total despair as I waited at the gate; one passenger after another disembarked until the plane was empty. No Ray.

Again, Aunt Esther didn't comment.

Back at Esther's, after gathering my courage, I called Ray to find out why he hadn't been on the plane. "Baby, I'm sorry." he said, his voice all sweet and sticky. "I had to cash the ticket in. There was a horse running at Aqueduct that couldn't miss."

Through my tears I asked, "What does this mean, Ray?"

"Well, Pet, it means the horse lost and I don't have the money to buy another ticket."

***

After saving for a month, the next ticket I bought for Ray was nonnegotiable. Montréal at that time of year was gray, gloomy, and snow-covered. Ray had no job, no new snow bunny to keep him warm, and an airplane ticket that couldn't be cashed in. What was a fellow to do? Stay in that bleak environment or head for subtropical Miami? He didn't have to think twice; he got off the plane this time.

Chapter Five

On Ray's first morning in Miami, he was greeted by the sound of songbirds, the scent of gardenia bushes, and the sight of grapefruits hanging large and plump from the boughs of the grapefruit tree.

"Get up! Get up, Baby, hurry!" he was nudging me and pulling on me to get out of bed. He'd had a revelation. "Grapefruits grow on trees! They have grapefruits growing on trees here." he said, wide-eyed.

As I opened my sleepy eyes I laughed at the look on his face. "Yep, grapefruits *always* grow on trees, grapefruit trees."

Later that afternoon Ray came home from what I thought was a sightseeing trip with Aunt Esther. To my surprise he had a job.

"Hey, Baby, I did it. I got a square's job and a place for us to live at Sky Harbor."

"What? Sky Harbor?"

"It's out on Just Island. I got us a house right on the North Miami River."

I was trying to take in what he'd just said while he kept talking.

"Baby, do you remember the night in Montréal? We were sitting under the tree in the park with that beautiful moon."

"How could I forget?"

"What did you call that moon?"

"Do you mean gibbous?"

"Yea, gibbous! Well, from our bedroom window you'll close your eyes at night with a gibbous moon streaming through the palm trees. The first thing you'll see in the morning will be…" He paused and wrapped his arms around me. Those sensuous arms were covered with the finest strawberry blond hairs, which softened the muscle definition in his forearms. He laced his fingers together and pulled my buttocks toward him. "We'll make love with the wind coming in off the river. I'll make love to you for hours and hours…until you beg me to stop."

As usual, my knees buckled; there was such mischief in his eyes. But I had a sick feeling in my stomach at the same time.

"Ray. Where did all the money come from to do this?"

He stiffened and pulled away from me. The look on his face changed. It was as if I had been talking to Dr. Jekyll and now, just a moment later, the diabolical Mr. Hyde.

"From this point forward, Baby, you are *never* to ask another question about my business."

His expression, his eyes, scared me. I took a deep breath.

"My life outside of our house," he continued, "is none of your business or anyone else's. When we're around Esther—or anyone—you are never to ask me questions about my business or my money."

***

I did as I was told. I never again asked Ray how he'd managed to get us a house. I guess I was relieved in a way that we had a place of our own where we could start our life together. And when we drove out to see it the first time, I knew we could make it a home. It was a big, rambling antebellum structure with sagging wraparound porches and a rusty metal roof. It had both Spanish and French architectural influence, by way of the Caribbean, all lending to a distinct character. It was shaded by giant hardwood trees.

Everything needed to be painted inside and out. I found the darkened rooms a refreshing retreat from the blistering Florida sun. One upstairs bedroom had a little porch of its own, and we decided to use that one for ourselves. A smaller bedroom, right across the hall, would be the nursery.

The house came furnished with old overstuffed chairs and sofas and heavy oak tables and dressers. I thought some new curtains and house plants would brighten things up. There was a formal dining room and a huge kitchen whose linoleum floor had long ago lost its shine. All the other rooms had hardwood floors, which creaked as we explored every inch of the place.

After four or five shopping trips to buy pots and pans, dishes, silverware and linens, Ray and I moved in.

"Call me as soon as you're ready for me to come for a visit." Aunt Esther said, as we pulled away from her house.

"I will." I said, tears welling in my eyes. "I'll invite you for dinner—well, that is, if I can learn to cook really fast!"

"If I know you, dear, you'll be throwing dinner parties in no time."

Aunt Esther had confidence in me that I didn't have myself. Once we were settled in, Ray started his disappearing acts. It reminded me of our life back in Canada; only his mother wasn't here to talk to. At first, I was still working at the boutique and I stayed busy in the evenings decorating the nursery. But Ray soon insisted that I quit working. He said that I was now a housewife and he wanted me home whenever he needed me. I was afraid to stand up to him; things were going smoothly and I didn't want to risk triggering one of his blowups.

Once neighbors heard there was a new young couple on the island, they started coming by to introduce themselves. They brought homemade bread, muffins, Key lime pie, and other goodies. Many of them were "live-a-boards"; people who lived on their boats. I made some wonderful friends, and whenever I got lonely I would have someone over to drink sweet iced tea on the front porch and visit, or I'd call Aunt Esther.

I was happy for those first few months, but as my belly grew and my due-date got closer, I guess I panicked. How can I be a mother? I asked myself. I'm a teenager! I don't know the first thing about babies. What have I done? Then the crying spells started. Maybe it was hormones; maybe I was frightened about the "unknowns" ahead of me. Whatever the reason, Ray wasn't there to soothe me. The moment I began to cry, he left the house, sometimes for a few hours and sometimes for days.

***

Ray and I went downtown one Saturday to do some last minute shopping for the baby. All of a sudden I felt light-headed. "Gee, honey, my stomach hurts and I feel kind of dizzy."

"Well, Baby, for the last two weeks—every time you've had those pains—we've taken you to the hospital. And every time they sent us home 'cause you weren't in labor."

"Yeah, I guess I should just ignore it."

There were new slippers and baby doll pajamas in the cart for me to wear in the hospital. In Florida, it would be too hot for much more.

"Okay, let's just get this stuff and head home." I said. I took a few more steps toward the checkout counter and stopped. "Ray, I don't care what you want to call this but I'm about to pass out!" I doubled over in the middle of the aisle, grabbing Ray's arm. It was quite some time before I could stand up straight again.

Trying to catch my breath and get air back into my lungs, I moaned, "This is labor; it's time!"

"Okay Baby, okay, don't worry. I'm gonna go call Bob. You wait right here."

As he turned to run and find a phone, I squealed, "Wait, what about me?"

There was a store clerk walking toward him. He put both hands on the poor, unsuspecting woman's shoulders and announced. "That's my wife. We're having a baby right now!"

With a startled look on her face she said, "What do you want me to do? I don't even work in this department. It's my break time."

"Well you're not taking a break." Ray said. In a demanding voice he issued an order. "You take her to the most comfortable chair now, and don't leave her!"

All the blood drained from her face, but she complied. "Yes, sir, yes sir, I won't leave her. We'll be right here." she said.

The clerk kept telling me to breathe as she paced back and forth in front of me.

Finally I looked up and saw Ray with his friend Bob in tow. Bob lumbered down the aisle wearing his big heavy Harley boots. I adored "Indian Bob". He wasn't an Indian, but he and Ray had Indian motorcycles, and the nickname had popped out of my mouth not long after Ray and I met him.

Bob weighed at least three hundred pounds and was six feet, three inches tall. His hair was long and greasy with unruly curls pointing in all directions atop his head. He looked rough and scary, but he was the gentlest of souls and I was so glad to see him.

He approached me and knelt down on one knee. "It's okay, Gabbi. I'm here now. Everything is going to be fine, no need to worry." It sounded to me like he was trying to convince himself. "Alright, don't worry; I'm going to drive us to the hospital. Shall I carry you? That's it! I'll carry you; that's what I'm gonna do."

"Oh no, Bob, I'm alright, I can walk."

"If that baby comes out now and hits this concrete floor, he'll break his skull! You just sit right there. I'm gonna scoop you up and carry you to the Karmann Ghia."

"Oh no! The Karmann Ghia?" I said as I looked up into Bob's face. "My tummy will be against the dashboard."

"Don't worry, the seat goes back."

"If you move the seat back, there won't be room for my knees." whined Ray.

"You be quiet Ray, I'll get us all there." Bob said, patting Ray's shoulder and rolling his eyes.

I started to panic. After all, Indian Bob would be driving and he didn't seem to know one thing about speed limits!

Bob lowered me into the front seat of the car and gingerly closed the door. I sat back, took a deep breath, and prepared to be bounced around in Bob's little tuna fish can on four wheels. At first, he was driving so slowly it seemed like it took fifteen minutes to go one block. This was not what I had expected, and in the middle of a contraction I turned and screamed, "Will you drive this damned car! I'm having a baby!"

His huge, meaty hands were gripped, white knuckled, around the steering wheel. I looked at the speedometer and it read twenty-eight miles per hour.

Then I had the contraction from hell. The devil had seized me, the demon that lies dormant in every woman, waiting to be released during the excruciating pain of labor. I screamed through gritted teeth, "Do you want me to have this baby in your front seat? Right now, right here?"

I guess that image worked. The speedometer jumped from twenty-eight to sixty-two miles per hour. As I brushed the hair out of my face, I eased the two little red horns back down into my skull.

At the emergency room an orderly came out with a wheel chair accompanied by a nurse. She directed that I be taken to the maternity ward. I was in that room for twenty-seven hours, experiencing the worst pain of labor. No woman should have to endure that. I was acting like the girl in the Exorcist, but Ray told me to pull myself together. "Don't you dare embarrass me," he warned. "here, take this." he handed me a rolled up terrycloth towel. "Bite down on this. Scream into the towel."

"Like this?" I said, as I tried to push the dry terry towel into my cotton dry mouth. I prayed the towel would absorb the screams of labor. Bringing shame on Ray just would not do. And then he left the room.

Many, many hours later, he came back and sat down on the bed next to me. He put his head in his hands and started to cry.

"What's the matter, Ray? What's wrong?"

"You're gonna die." he moaned into his hands.

"What? I'm going to die? Why am I going to die? I've been in this bed and in pain for over twenty-seven hours. I'm not dead yet."

In a slow and deliberate manner he said, "Gabbi, the doctors have decided to do a cesarean section."

"Is there something wrong with the baby?"

"No," he said. "The baby is perfect. It's you that isn't perfect; it's your fault. Your pelvis is too small and not flexible enough for you to deliver the baby."

After a minute or two passed I began to laugh. It started out as a low quiet chuckle and reached a crescendo of a loud riotous laugh.

"What's so damn funny at a time like this?" he asked.

"Didn't you just say they were going to do a cesarean section?"

"Yes."

"That's an operation, right?"

"Yes." He looked devastated. "And everyone who has an operation dies. It never fails. They go in healthy and they leave dead. Everyone I've ever loved who's gone to the hospital has died."

"But, Ray, they'll give me something for the pain. They'll put me to sleep and—"

"That's the problem. They'll put you to sleep and you'll die. I even had to sign a piece of paper releasing them from responsibility if you die."

I didn't have the energy to keep laughing, but the smile on my face said it all. They would take me to paradise; ahhh, drugs! At least, that's how I'd seen it happen in the movies.

Just then, two transporters came in, put me on a gurney and wheeled me down a long hallway and into the Operating Room. As they were moving me around the room and transferring me to the operating table, I felt like I was in a movie theater or amphitheater. Above, on a balcony, were many men and women. Some wore white, some wore green. It was obvious to me that these were medical people. If I hadn't been so tired, so physically spent I might have been concerned to see all of those strangers in a room where all I was supposed to do was have a baby. They were talking amongst themselves. They had pads and paper and were taking notes.

Dr. Bossette came over and took my arm. He held it close to his chest and said, "You're going to be alright very soon."

"But Dr. Bossett, am I in the right room? What are all those people doing here? This must not be the right room to have a baby in."

He bent over and explained, "This is a wonderful opportunity for the medical students to see a Cesarean section done between contractions."

"Oh Doctor, don't tell me anymore, I'm gonna vomit. Isn't somebody just going to come and put me to sleep?"

"Yes dear right now. You are going to sleep and when you wake up you will have the most beautiful baby."

"Thank you Dr. Bossett. Now put me to sleep, please."

The anesthesiologist came over. He covered my nose and mouth with a mask. He told me that I might remember counting to three.

I didn't! I think my will to go to sleep was as strong as anything they were giving me.

***

I had a beautiful baby boy. Thank you God for hearing my prayers.

I was in Intensive Care for seven days after Caleb was born by emergency Cesarean Section. I had been three weeks overdue. I always knew my first born son would be named Caleb. I'd read the story in the bible and was touched by it.

By the time our little family came home to Sky Harbor on Just Island, Ray had the nursery all set up. He'd purchased the most beautiful black kid glove leather recliner.

"Alright Baby I'm going to sit you in this chair and lay this bed pillow across your lap."

"Why?"

"My mother nursed all twelve of her babies and we're all very healthy. Now I'm going to teach you how to nurse our baby."

Next, he placed the baby on top of the pillow and said, "Always remember equal time on each breast otherwise you'll be in a lot of pain."

**

My friends on Just Island flocked to our home, like a never ending parade. They'd come to cast their eyes on the most beautiful baby boy any of them had ever seen. I beamed with pride. One visitor said he looked like a magnificent gardenia, with his pure white skin and his snow-white hair.

Another said that his powder blue eyes reminded her of the robin's eggs in the tree just outside her kitchen window.

Another said, "His skin is so white and translucent. It's as smooth as the fine porcelain used to make a Dresden Doll."

Yet another said, "I can just imagine kissing the rolls between his chubby thighs. I could just melt into those fluffy rolls."

The last one added, "And his smile is Angelic!"

Ray was a fanatic about germs. He would meet friends at the door with a can of Lysol spray. They had to wear a surgical mask, go into the bathroom and wash their hands, and dry them on clean towels. Only after passing Ray's inspection could they go into the nursery and "look" at our baby. No touching; just looking.

***

One night Caleb began to cry. He cried for hours and hours. All I could do was hold and rock him. Each scream caused a stabbing pain in my heart. Mothers should have the power to comfort and make good all that is bad in their child's life. As I cradled him close to my breast I was powerless. Finally I'd lay him in his crib and escape the constant screams by going out onto the porch outside my bedroom. It overlooked the tops of palm trees and houseboats with their live-aboard owners. As I sat on the little wooden deck, peering through the palms, I gazed up at the moon and prayed that when I got up and went back into my bedroom and my baby, I'd find that it had all been a horrible nightmare.

The dock master, Felix, had come over to discuss something with Ray. I carried the baby down to the living room where they were talking. "Felix, you have children don't you?" I asked.

"Yes ma'am, I have four."

"Well, Callie's been crying for hours and hasn't stopped. I've tried nursing him, rocking him…everything I can think of…but he doesn't stop."

"I recall the wife telling me that's how babies exercise their lungs." He said as he took the pipe out of his mouth and tamped down the tobacco. It wasn't lit. He'd never come into our home with a lit pipe. He kept it with him, kind of like a pacifier.

"Oh, okay…but four hours?"

"Well, that does sound a might long, ma'am."

I looked at Ray. "I'm going upstairs to get dressed. I want you to take us to the hospital…now."

As I dressed, Caleb had stopped crying. He was so still. Ray came in and looked at him. "You're right; let's head for the hospital."

***

The doctor in the ER at Jackson Memorial was a young woman from Germany. She examined Caleb and asked us questions. Finally, she said in a very impersonal manner, "This baby is hungry." It was as though she was telling me that my car needed an oil change. "He's not getting enough to eat. I want you to go to the store and buy baby bottles and formula with iron." She said this in a stern voice, as if we were children.

We stopped at a drugstore on the way home and Ray stocked up on everything he thought we would need. At home, he started immediately boiling water in the kitchen. After sterilizing everything, he prepared the bottles and instructed me how to feed Callie. Being one of twelve children, he knew everything there was to know about diapering, feeding and burping.

***

I had a good understanding of what I was to do, but Caleb didn't respond. His mouth never opened enough to take in the nipple on the bottle. As I sat in my rocker cooing at him, I sang little songs. I pleaded with him to take what was in the bottle. He wanted nothing to do with it. When Ray came home that second night, after we'd started the formula, I was beside myself. "Ray, where have you been?"

"I had business to take care of. What's the matter? When I left this morning, you had enough bottles for the day. All you had to do was give them to him, burp him, and change him." he spewed.

"I don't know what the matter is, but I want to go back to that ER and I want to do it *now!*" Then I told him that when I looked into Caleb's eyes, they were vacant. I didn't feel like he was still there.

Ray ran down the broad wooden steps of our front porch. "Where are you going?" I called after him.

"I'm going to get Indian Bob, I'll be right back." he yelled.

I guess Ray needed Bob for moral support.

We all got into Bob's car—he now had a big Cadillac—and rushed to the hospital. For the first time, I saw a degree of anguish in Ray's expression, which scared me even more. Over the years I've looked for signs and actions to validate falling in love with and being devoted to such an evil man. Like day and night, good and bad, there were such occasions and this was one. This time in the ER, Ray did the talking. He told the doctor we weren't leaving until someone told us what was happening. He told them about the first visit when we'd seen the German doctor.

As he listened, the young doctor placed Caleb on an examining table. He raised both his arms above his head and brought them slamming down on the table just above the baby's head. I was startled and Ray jumped; Caleb didn't flinch. We just stood there and stared. "What the hell did you do man?" Ray shouted. "What does this mean?"

"I want the two of you to sit down in those chairs and be quiet!" the doctor ordered. He grabbed the phone on the wall and after a quick conversation, another doctor joined us in the room. They spoke to each other as though Ray and I weren't even present.

The second young man looked at Ray and said, "We're going to send this baby for some tests. We need you to go sit in the waiting room. We'll call you when we know something."

We were dismissed from the room just like that, as though our being there was incidental. After more than an hour, a nurse came out and led us back into the examining room. This time there were three doctors.

"Mr. and Mrs. Fortier, my name is Dr. Schultzgarten. I'm a pediatric neurologist. We've just done a spinal tap on your son and I've never seen a tap with so much blood. I believe he has a ruptured cerebral aneurysm."

He explained that an aneurysm is an abnormal ballooning of a portion of a blood vessel. A cerebral aneurysm refers to a blood vessel within the brain that weakens over time. As it weakens, it begins to bulge out like a balloon. The larger the balloon becomes, the greater the risk it may burst. It would then bleed into the brain.

"In infants," he said, "the ballooning can obstruct the flow of cerebrospinal fluid and cause hydrocephalus."

I had the urge to vomit. My knees got very weak; I fell into a chair.

"Well, what does this mean?" Ray asked.

"I won't be able to answer any of your questions right now. We'll have to do more tests. He's being admitted to the hospital as we speak. Once he's in a room, someone will come and get you."

There were tests and more tests on my baby. We were told very little; only that Caleb would be undergoing brain surgery the following day. We couldn't take him home. He was in critical condition. I didn't sleep or eat that night, and sobbed until my eyes were swollen shut. Ray was silent, angry and brooding.

Chapter Six

The day of Caleb's first brain surgery, Ray's mood was fairly even. I needed him to be nice, caring, and supportive of me.

Raging nausea had replaced the normal joys of delightful subtropical meals that I was learning to cook. For weeks now I couldn't even look at food without that rage savaging my senses. As I looked in the mirror I witnessed my collarbones protruding; my body was starting to look skeletal. The image reflected back to me registered in my subconscious mind, *what the hell was happening to my body?* My conscious mind had neither the time nor energy to address that question.

The image of Ray coming up behind me caused the reflection of an almost emaciated young girl to go dormant. Yet again, I was forced to allow the reality at hand to take center stage.

"Hey Baby, your clothes are starting to fit you perfectly, I hope you don't gain any more weight. Remember you have that modeling gig for Helena Rubenstein in a couple of months."

I had modeled with John Robert Powers, all through high school, so Ray thought that this modeling gig would be a good distraction and a way to earn big bucks.

"I was looking in a magazine to see what this Island of Mykonos was all about. I want you tan and thin for that gig." he commanded. "After all they chose you as their Mykonos Girl because of your shiny, wheat colored blonde hair, your pretty face and sparkling blue eyes. If you show up fat, you'll be replaced."

As he turned to walk away, he said in French,

"Vous Etes si Beaux!"

("You are so beautiful!")

How can he say I'm beautiful, after speaking to me like that?

Most cosmetic houses did yearly promotions to draw attention to their lines. The "look" chosen for that year by the heads of Helena Rubenstein was to be the blonde haired, sun-washed face of a typical Greek beauty, from the Isle of Mykonos. Modeling agencies from all over the state of Florida had been contacted to send talent meeting those prerequisites. I had been fortunate enough to be chosen as The Mykonos Girl!

As I looked back in the mirror those words rolled through my mind, *if you show up fat,* like a forty-five rpm record, with the needle stuck in one grove, going around and around and around, replaying the same line. How could I look fat? I only weighed a hundred and thirteen pounds!

As a young girl of thirteen, living in Cherry Hill,

New Jersey, just across the river from Philadelphia, my mother had gotten me involved in modeling for the John Robert Powers Agency. I'd always been told that I had a pretty smile, beautiful hair, and captivating aqua blue eyes. One day after a modeling job my mother sat me down on my vanity bench and told me to look into the mirror. "What do you see?" She asked me.

I told her I saw a girl with blond hair and blue eyes.

"Gabbi," she said, "in your life now as a young model you are constantly being told how special you are. Everyone makes a big fuss about you. I want you to close your eyes. Imagine that you've been in a terrible automobile wreck. Okay, now open your eyes. What if you had to live the rest of your life with a scarred face? You need to understand that you are a beautiful young woman on the outside, and you should thank God for that. You must also grow into a beautiful woman on the inside as well."

"What do you mean mommy?"

"Gabbi, it's important that you learn humility, compassion and empathy. These qualities will help you to become an asset to society. That's what I mean honey."

I smiled at my mother. She was, I thought, a very wise woman. She was just trying to give me tools for making a success in life; she wasn't the pushy stage mother type at all. As for Ray, I believe he was

interested in how my "outer" self could benefit him—
much more than what was inside of me.

***

When we arrived at Jackson Memorial Hospital,
I forced myself to smile; that's what Ray expected from
me, regardless of the circumstances. But I was terrified.
Jackson Memorial was a teaching hospital, which meant
that Caleb would get the best care available; we were in
the best place possible to save his life. Nevertheless, the
idea of surgeons cutting into my baby's perfect little
head was unthinkable.

As I walked down the long dreary hallways
looking for the waiting room I had a sudden urge to
vomit. I choked it back. There'd be no time to deal
with my emotions. I needed to be the strongest I could
be and I knew I couldn't depend on Ray. I never knew
from one day to the next when he went to get a loaf of
bread if he'd really be gone for days or weeks. There
seemed to be a pattern. Stresses and pressures of life
were triggers that would set off his need to run away
and escape real life. It was by the glory of God that I
had the strength. Many mothers going through this
would fall apart and expect their husbands and families
to be supportive and protect them from this pain. *That*
was never an option in my life. Ever! My Father God
always gave me the strength to carry on, to provide for,
to protect, as best I could, my little family. Someday,
Atlas Would Shrug.

The long passages with their dull green painted

walls seemed to have a demonic life of their own. They were closing in on me; sucking the oxygen from my lungs. The final goal of these walls and hallways was gifting the traveler with a sense of doom; that was a gift I simply would not accept.

Crossing the threshold into yet another drab dull green space, the waiting room had in it two small sofas and several upholstered chairs. They were strategically placed to simulate a cozy area where most families and friends would sit and comfort one another. In one corner of the room was a secretary desk and ladder-back chair; there for the use of those waiting for time to pass, to hear news of their loved one or friend. There was a telephone, donated magazines, a Gideon's bible and a carafe of coffee, that hours ago had been piping hot.

And there was an odor. I thought how odd that in a hospital where everything presumably was sterile, this room smelled musty and old. I guessed that years of witnessing the raw emotions of grief and pain had left something behind that could not be sterilized away. I allowed the corner section of a sofa to provide for me what I would never get from Ray; security and support.

Ray began pacing the room and within a few minutes said, "Okay, Baby, you stay here. I'm gonna run downstairs to the cafeteria and get something for us to eat. What should I bring you?"

Translation: "Hey, I can't take this; I'm outta here."

On one hand I was relieved to have him with me, but on the other I was acutely aware that at any moment something could tick him off and he'd erupt. The next hours dragged by, with Ray coming in and out, giving a variety of excuses for abandoning me.

I prayed and prayed for Caleb. There was one sign of life in the room—a huge aquarium with an assortment of freshwater fish. One angel fish seemed to be watching me, and I imagined that it was God sending me a sign.

It was November, right after Thanksgiving. The temperature outside was forty-nine degrees; a major cold front for subtropical Florida.

I was wearing my Jackie Kennedy inspired coat. The fabric was red and black herringbone constructed with princess seams.

Seeing the pattern of that coat, a thought flashed across my mind. My mother was making me in the image of Grace Kelly; blond hair, blue eyes, coquettish smile; a John Robert Powers model in Philadelphia. I was a work in progress. It breaks my heart now as an adult. I realize the pain and angst I must have caused my mother, at a very early age. Her future as a vivacious, stunning blonde debutante was dashed with the surprise growing in her teenage belly. She hoped to play out her missed years as a free spirited bon vi vante in the persona of her cherub daughter. History had indeed repeated itself, destroying my mother's dreams and goals for me. Forgive me dear Mother. I love you now as I always have. It's in the years of lessons not learned in college classes that I now understand why you cut me out emotionally from your fragile inner self. Oh, the world sees you as a pillar of strength. People all over the world respect your knowledge in animal behavior. You are a brilliant woman, albeit frail and vulnerable under that tough weathered hide.

I wore my black leather mid-calf boots with three-inch heels. That morning I sat on the side of my bed contemplating what shoes to wear. Something inside my head said, "Wear the boots, you'll need the support they'll give you."

After several hours of tormented waiting a nurse appeared in the doorway and asked if we were Mr. and Mrs. Fortier. I bounded up from the chair, my legs feeling stronger than ever. I quickly walked over to the door. The adrenalin caused by this anticipation must be our body's way of keeping us strong.

"Yes I'm Mrs. Fortier and this is Caleb's Daddy. Is our baby okay?"

"But my dear, you don't look old enough to be a mother." She might as well have said do you have picture I.D. to buy this bottle of wine?

It was all I could do to hold back my tears. I wanted to scream "For God sake, are you here to tell me about my baby?" Instead, I took a deep breath and calmly said,

"Yes, I'm Mrs. Fortier and I want to know about my baby, now please!"

"Alright, just follow me." she said with a little pfttt!

I followed her down a hall unaware of my surroundings; oddly unaware of whether Ray was even with us. All I could think was...just get me to him...fast...please!

She took us through two large glass doors and told us to wait as she went through another set of doors. Shortly, two men wearing green surgical scrubs and shower caps approached me. The shorter Asian one introduced himself as Dr. Fujmoto. Standing next to him was Dr. Schultzgarten. To me, both looked too young to be saving lives.

Dr. Schultzgarten took one step forward and said, "Well the surgery is over. Your baby is alive. But the entire left side of his brain is completely destroyed." He didn't stop to take a breath or touch my hand or console me. He forged ahead. "Your baby will never walk, talk, or see."

***

Just as the bright shining ball of fire, the sun is interrupted by an eclipse, so too would our lives be interrupted by a great shadow. It would shake the strongest of all of us. It would obliterate our joy, our laughter and smiles. Worst of all, our dreams and hopes. Six weeks after our sweet Caleb's magnificent entrance into this world, a cloud darker than night would put an end to the joy of his bright light.

The room swirled around me. The black boots I'd worn for support couldn't hold me up. I collapsed into a red and black puddle. Ray must have picked me up and carried me back to the waiting room; when I started to come to, a nurse I'd never seen before told me to take a whiff of the ammonia stick that she was passing under my nose. I was still pretty groggy, but noticed movement to my left. At first I didn't recognize the man standing in front of the aquarium was Ray. When I was able to focus, I saw that the two doctors were talking to Ray and he was highly agitated.

I wanted to get up to calm him down, but I couldn't stand. In a split second, I watched him draw back his arm and fist. As he went to punch one of the doctors, a security guard came up from behind him. He spun Ray like a quarterback being sacked, deflecting his fist from the doctor to the huge tank. Prevalent now to my senses was the sound of shattering glass. My eyes fixed on the old worn terrazzo floor. I watched the frantic fish starving for air thrashing about the floor amidst the pools of water and broken glass.

I guess I fainted again, because I woke up in a stiff vinyl reclining chair in a hospital room. Somehow I had been taken into Caleb's recovery room. The crib he was lying in was made of metal with tall bars on all four sides. It was cold, stark and inhumane. That wasn't right. Why wasn't he in something soft? He deserved to be in my arms, not a metal cage.

They had tubes and lines coming out all over him. His whole head was wrapped up in white gauze. The bleeding in his brain had caused his cranium to expand abnormally. The heavy gauze wrapping exaggerated the light-bulb shape of his head. His skin was gray; he looked dead. Yet he was the most beautiful baby I'd ever seen in my life. Even if his brain was destroyed, there was no love on earth stronger than what I had for him. I made my way over to the crib, dragging a little chair to sit on. I sat there sobbing uncontrollably; the strong smell of iodine attached itself inside my nostrils. I could still smell it days after leaving Caleb. The room was silent except for a high-pitched humming. It seemed to be in my head; the strike of fear and terror attacking every sense of my being. I was terrified, disoriented, and alone.

As I sat there, fighting to control the need to escape this hell, I reached in through those cold metal bars to stroke his cheeks melding his flesh to mine, that being the greater need. What I was looking at took on a life of its own. The easy way out was going with the fear which when finally elevated would take me to that safe place in the form of a faint.

The mother instinct pulled me back like the helium balloon tethered to a little child's finger at a birthday party. If only I could be that balloon. One little pull on the slipknot, I could escape and float away, not having to deal. No! My job, my duty, my instinctive calling was to tend to Caleb.

I was touching him, stroking him. I was telling him how much I loved him, oblivious to everything else around me.

A nurse tapped me on the shoulder. "He can't hear you! He doesn't understand a thing you're saying." She said in a matter of fact way. She didn't put her arm around me or try to console me. "We have work to do here, you will have to leave."

It broke my heart to walk out of that room, but I didn't dare challenge the authority of that nurse.

Well, Ray had managed to do it again! He found a way to escape reality. Apparently busting up that fish tank had done a lot of damage to his hand and arm. Doctors and nurses were comforting Ray and stitching him up. *He* was being consoled. They were taking care of him! *I* had been kicked out of my baby's room. My support would have to come from those drab, dreary green painted walls.

Ray was patched up and ready to go home. We were told that Caleb would be staying in the hospital for about four weeks. My job now would be to minister to Ray between trips back to the hospital to be with my baby.

***

Ray had a compulsive need to gamble, especially at times of high stress. I'd witnessed this compulsion cost him businesses, pink slips to cars and thousands of dollars in cash.

"Come on, Baby, we're going to the dogs!"

I did as I was directed. Keeping the peace meant keeping me safe. I found some small comfort in knowing that Caleb was being cared for by the Doctors and Nurses at Jackson Memorial. And, the Doctors had put a limit on the number of hours I was allowed to stay at his crib-side. I had been staying with Caleb all day and all night, barely leaving his side and certainly not thinking of food. It was obvious to everyone, except me, that I just could not keep that up.

We drove over to the Flagler racetrack. At the door Ray bought every racing form available, took me to a seat, and told me to stay put. I knew what he was doing. He would leave me sitting there, go to a quiet place on the floor with the pari-mutuel windows and study the forms. He'd choose a dog and tally how many starts, how many wins, how many places, and how many shows. In each box, he'd mark the dog's weight and time. After he was sure of his calculations, he'd go to the window and buy his tickets; some quinellas, some perfectas, some exactas, some straight-to-wins.

I sat alone during the races; Ray always stood at the track-side railing. I guess he thought the sound of his voice yelling would insure his win. "That's it, Bingo...bring it home, Bingo...you can do it!" He'd beat the rolled up racing forms against the rail. You could see the veins in his face and neck bulging, he'd be so excited. I was sure he'd have a stroke, trying to *will* his dog across the finish line first.

On this day, I thought about an incident at the Hialeah Dog Track, when all hell broke loose. I had been sitting by myself for three races, and I was getting scared. All kinds of men were watching me sitting there alone. I wondered if Ray had forgotten me and gone home.

I decided to leave my seat, even though I'd been told to "Stay there!" by Ray.

I made my way through the other people sitting in my row with no real problems; only a little heckle here and there, which I ignored. But as I climbed the concrete risers up to the main floor, where I hoped to find Ray, someone grabbed the inside of my thigh.

I looked down at a nasty-looking man with his hand just above the top of my boot, holding onto my leg. Before I could think, I screamed "Help!" with all the breath I could muster. People began to see what the lecher was doing and a crowd was gathering. "Raaaaaaymond!" I screamed.

In the midst of the chaos someone was pulling me back by my shoulders, away from two men where were now fighting. I shook myself loose from the man who'd pulled me out of harm's way and realized what was happening on the steps. Apparently, Ray had come down the steps, saw the man accost me, and then punched him in the face. There was blood everywhere.

Ray continued to beat the pervert, who was choking and squirming, trying to break loose of Ray's grip. His battered head looked ready to explode. Trickles of spattered blood ran down Ray's cheeks. Just as I was getting my wits about me and looking around for help, Ray grabbed the man's hand, put it in his mouth and then spit out a finger. It landed on the filthy concrete step right in from of my feet. The man was moaning and crying out for help.

"Now, grab her leg again!" Ray growled.

Police suddenly appeared and Ray was tackled and thrown to the ground. He fought like a mad man as three officers dragged him away. An ambulance had been called for my attacker; his finger was retrieved, packed in ice in a paper cup that previously contained beer, and was carried away by the paramedics. Fortunately I had a key to Ray's car. I drove to the police station, bailed him out, and took him straight to the hospital. Because Ray was defending my honor, nothing more came of this disgusting incident.

***

My sweet Caleb came home to Just Island about four weeks after his brain surgery.

We were given basic instructions. At that point, once the surgical incisions had healed, we were quite capable of taking care of him. And of course, Jackson Memorial was just a few minutes away.

During the next few months, our lives at Sky Harbor Marina were filled with turmoil. There was the constant fear of Ray becoming overwhelmed with Caleb's health issues. There were the times he'd leave to get the loaf of bread and be gone for one, two, three days or more, leaving me alone and scared to death. He'd bought me my own Cadillac. If the need arose I could drive Caleb to the emergency room. And so he felt he was free to just leave.

We didn't go out and leave Caleb frequently but when we did it was to dinner or the store close by. Living on one of the houseboats was a girl, two years my junior. Noreen and I shared many things. We had much in common; music, makeup, clothes, silly, giggly girly stuff. On the rare occasions that Ray did take me somewhere Noreen stayed with Caleb.

One evening I was sitting in the rocker on the front porch with Caleb nestled in my lap. It was just before sunset. The island took on an eerie, haunting fascination to me at this time of day. Being surrounded by water, there was always a brisk breeze. It would move the long flowing palm fronds back and forth. Many nights I sat in that rocker and allowed, in my imagination, that the palm fronds were doing the dance from the Disney movie Fantasia. In the shadows of twilight the palm fronds would dance around and around and around almost to the point of spinning and dancing in and out of the trees. This would entertain me. It was as if the breeze and palms knew that I needed to be carried away from the heavy responsibility nestled in my lap.

"Hi Gabbi!"

I looked across the yard and saw Noreen skipping toward me, her long blonde ponytail swinging side to side. Her body like mine was bronzed from the Florida sun. She was bare foot as usual.

"Hey Gabbi do you know who's gonna be in concert at the Dinner Key Auditorium?"

"No. Who?" I could feel the excitement as she anticipated my guess. "I have no idea. I've been too busy to pay attention to concerts. Who is it?"

Bounding the steps, taking them on the balls of her feet so as not to wake the baby, she sort of resembled a frog. I could see the excitement and energy oozing from her while she tried desperately to land on the porch and not allow her bare feet to come down on the rickety porch boards, making cracking sounds that would startle the baby. Still on the balls of her feet she knelt down close in front of me to look me in the eye and in one long whisper, said,

"It's Jimmy Morrison and The Doors. You know, 'Come on Baby light my fire'." as she sang off key. "Didn't you tell me that you know him personally?" She whispered, at the top of her lungs.

During my time working at the Hotel Marquise, I'd been introduced to and met movie stars and actors, songwriters and singers, story tellers and book writers. Arlo Guthrie, Buffy St. Marie and Gordon Lightfoot were some of the folk singers I'd met. And that was where I met Jimmy Morrison of The Doors and his friend Robert Palmer. They were young, up and coming rock and roll singers. We had in common the love for music; we believed it fed our souls.

Now Noreen's eyes were as big as the double white hibiscus bloom to the right of the porch. She had to continue to whisper so as not to awaken the baby but the veins in her neck were protruding and it was all she could do to not jump up and down like a three year old at a first sighting of Santa.

"Oh my God, Noreen, The Doors?" Not wanting to startle the baby I yelled it from under my breath.

"Yes, can you imagine? He's coming right here to the Dinner Key Auditorium, can you go?"

"You mean with you? How can I go with you? You're my babysitter!"

As she scrunched up her face with wishful thinking, she said, "Maybe we can convince Ray to stay home with Caleb so we can go. After all he is kind of old. You don't think he'd want to see them do you?"

She was trying not to offend me about the age difference.

Noreen went on with great excitement, "Well what do you think? What do you think? Should we ask him? Come on it will be wonderful. It will be wonderful for you to get out. You're with the baby twenty-four, seven. You're still a kid; you know you love The Doors."

"Alright Noreen, I'll tell you what. He's in the kitchen at the table with his racing forms. I'm afraid he'd holler at me, so you go in and ask him. Just don't get him mad at me. You've seen how he can be."

Without saying another word, she bounded straight into the house. In no time at all, she was back and from behind the rocking chair squeezed my shoulders and whispered in my ear. "You're free! You're free! He said we can go and he'll take care of Caleb."

"Alright! Now I will contact Jimmy's girlfriend; we still keep in touch. She'll get tickets to us."

The night of the concert, I drove. We got there early enough to find a parking space and find the seats that matched our ticket stubs. Dinner Key Auditorium sits right on the water in Coconut Grove. The two of us were on a natural high. We both owned all The Doors record albums and knew the words to every one of their songs by heart. Growing up I had been to many rock and roll concerts. But nothing I'd been to in the past could have prepared me for what happened this night.

As the band approached the stage and took their appropriate places, Jimmy was missing. The kids in the audience starting chanting *Jimmy, Jimmy, Jimmy*…until it was almost at a fever pitch. Then all of a sudden out of the wings *he* appeared and walked as though in slow motion. His shiny black leather pants looked like they had been painted on his body, divulging his sensuous anatomy. His white linen shirt with bishop sleeves was tucked in but unbuttoned. And it wasn't long before I could sense that he was drunk or stoned out of his mind or maybe even a combination of both. He took the hand mike and stumbled to his spot at the front of the stage. He began singing Light My Fire. By this time none of the audience was sitting. He was inciting the audience by saying,

"I want you to fuck, I want you to fuck, I want you to fuck until your balls fall off!"

There was chanting and screaming at hysterical levels.

Girls had already jumped onto the stage and were rushing him. The stage was mass chaos with Police rushing it. They were coming from both sides of the stage forcibly removing the girls. Oblivious to all that was going on around him, Jimmy now had the mike stand between his legs, using it as a sensual prop as he swayed and sang. Anticipating that all hell was about to break lose, I grabbed Noreen's hand and yanked her up out of her seat.

"Noreen, follow me, this place is going crazy; it's verging on a riot. We have to get out of here before someone gets hurt."

As we fought and pushed our way through the hot, steamy, already half naked crowd, I looked up at Jimmy and stood frozen for a minute. Someone walked out on the stage with a goat. In the chaos I saw Jimmy open his fly. In a matter of seconds, the police had stormed the stage and grabbed the goat. Jimmy was still singing and fornicating with the mike stand.

At this point I locked Noreen's arm with mine, turned to her and screamed, to be heard over the fever pitch in the auditorium, "We're getting the hell out of here Noreen! Don't stop moving!"

By the time I got to my Caddy, the keys in my hand were rattling loudly. I had to try to calm myself before I could even start the car.

I was urged on by a policeman, waving at us and yelling, "Get moving girls, get moving!"

***

It was many months after the concert that I received a court subpoena to testify on behalf of James Morrison. Since they'd sent me the tickets, they obviously hoped I'd attended and would testify. Jimmy had been arrested for lewd and lascivious behavior in the concert at Dinner Key Auditorium. By the time they had the trial I was pregnant with my second son. It had been arranged that I would be picked up by Jimmy's personal body guard, Babe and taken to the courthouse in Miami to testify. Babe arrived in a black stretch limousine and took Ray and me to the courthouse. Since I was a witness, I was made to sit in the lobby until it was my turn to testify. My hair was in two long pigtails; hanging over the front of my shoulders. I was wearing a soft cotton, yellow halter top dress that fell over my baby "bump".

This was all something new to me; even being in a courthouse was new to me. When it was my turn, I took the oath and sat down in the witness chair. I was questioned by first one attorney and then another. It didn't last very long, but the biggest issue seemed to be, did I see Jimmy expose his penis on the stage during the concert?

I gave a factual answer. "No, I did not see him expose his penis on the stage."

No one bothered to ask me if I wore glasses, because without them, I'm as blind as a bat. At the age of five my first pair of eyeglasses were said to be made out of coca cola bottle bottoms. They were pink and white striped frames.

The last attorney to question me thanked me very much, helped me out of the seat and told me I could go. It was just a few steps until I was standing next to Jimmy. I knew I wasn't allowed to touch him, but I stopped and we made eye contact. I let him know through my gaze how much I adored him; how sorry I was that this was happening to him. I whispered I love you. As I stood next to him, I realized that my Jimmy Morrison, the Jimmy I'd known and partied with wasn't sitting in that chair. This Jimmy had gained weight. His stomach was bloated. He wore his hair and beard like a commercial depiction of Jesus Christ. *My* Jimmy hadn't shown up.

In high school as an editor on the school paper, I learned that in journalism the end of a story is represented by the number thirty. It is sad to say that thirty did not follow the Dinner Key concert. Jimmy's conflicted mind was not finished wreaking havoc.

It wasn't long after that that I found out that Jimmy Morrison had died.

It was always said that his drug of choice was alcohol. I'd never been much of a drinker and other than marijuana never experienced the drugs that he and most of the others did at all the parties. I'd always thought that he lived his life on a path of self-destruction and inevitable suicide. A thread shared by Jimmy and me was our dysfunctional relationships with our fathers. It was something we had in common and talked about often. I always wondered why I didn't end up just like him and many others.

Weeks after the court hearing I received a package in the mail. It was a book that Jimmy had written; a book of poetry. I think it was called The American Dream. What I do remember about the book was the language. The language was so filthy that I didn't understand how it could be called poetry. While my brother was in college, he asked if he could borrow it to show to some of this friends and I never saw it again. It doesn't matter. I'm happier with my memories of partying with Jimmy and the long walks we'd taken on the pure white snow with the pure white light of a full moon above our heads in Québec, the St. Laurentian Mountains. I listened to him talk about all the injustices of the world and so many things that he would like to see changed.

I'd shared many similar walks on those snowy paths with the same illuminating moon with my friends Gordon Lightfoot and Buffy St. Marie. Their philosophies and stories were very different from Jimmy's. I never knew whose was right, but always wanted to hear everything they had to say. Most of my friends were many, many years older than me. At that point I had not lived enough of life to form my own philosophies and judgments and wistful thinking. I was still in my teens.

***

When Caleb was about seven months old he developed a problem called posturing. That meant when I would try to feed him, his body didn't cuddle into the crook of my arm. He became as stiff and hard as a board. The first few times this happened I tried to bend him by pushing on his tummy. After a few tries I stopped for fear that I would break him.

When Ray came home, I said, "Ray put your shoes back on; we have to take Caleb back to Jackson."

The three of us had become familiar faces to the Emergency Room staff. Jackson almost felt like a safe haven. That's where I was getting the answers to keep Caleb safe and prolong his life.

This time the doctors explained to me about posturing. It is because of scar tissue forming in the brain. They also explained that there was nothing we could do for those spells. Not long after the posturing developed, we were called to the hospital to meet with Dr. Fujimoto. I was excited and Ray was upbeat. We thought perhaps something "new" was available to help Caleb.

When we arrived, a nurse led us into a tiny room—no bigger than a broom closet. There were no windows or plants. Dr. Fujimoto came in and sat across the bare table from us. He read from a stack of notes; cold clinical information that made no sense to me. And then he said, "It is time that this child is institutionalized. Neither of you can give him the quality of care in your home that he will require for the rest of his life."

Without taking a breath and without allowing me to exhale, he continued.

"Your son will never walk, talk or see. He will never live to see his fourth birthday."

Was this real? Was this another one of my nightmares? Was I really sitting in this cold, hard, impersonal, stark room with an almost stranger telling me that I would have to give my baby up? And, that he was going to die soon?

Yes, this was real. Yes, this really did just happen. There was no compassion; nothing to soften the edges. The blows came straight, direct and right at the solar plexus. When I finally did exhale, it wasn't silent. For the first time I screamed. It was primal. It didn't sound like a scream. It sounded like the howl of a wounded mother wolf, throwing her head up to the moon, in utter despair. I felt the need to console and be consoled, but I had learned the hard way; no one touched Ray unless he was the initiator. I witnessed a look on his face that the reality had hit him for the first time. So I'd just sit there, feeling and living in real time the horror of the words I'd just heard.

Chapter Seven

"Ray, I don't care about your lifestyle. I don't care how much it costs. I want my baby."

"Look Gabbi, you've known since day one that I am a rounder. Everything you want just makes my life miserable. You and the baby continue to throw a monkey wrench into my life."

Tears were running down my cheeks.

"Alright Gabbi, here's how it's going to be. I'll hire a live-in nurse. You'll have the baby here with you. It will *never* interfere with my lifestyle or my business, period! And when I expect you to be with me looking like a million bucks, you'd better be ready."

He must love me a little bit or he wouldn't be willing to do this much. But if I have to make a choice between Raymond or my son, I'll pack up the diaper bag, and we're outta here!

We would not put our child in an institution. We would keep him with us, at home. We would make it work. Ray would take care of finding us the help we would need.

One of our favorite local haunts in the Miami area was called Bella Napoli. On nights when Ray didn't take us out for fine dining, at a waterfront restaurant, we'd enjoy the best pizza there. Keeping true to his personality, Ray made friends with the old couple that owned the eatery. After Callie was born, Ray would stop there on his way home and order veal scaloppini, chicken Marsala and an antipasto. On one of those nights he announced that he'd hired a nanny to assist me at the house. She was a relative of Mr. and Mrs. Valentino. They called her Zia; she was born in Palermo, Italy. Her children were first generation American, born in Miami. Zia was on duty from six in the morning until ten o'clock at night. Her spirit was warm, nurturing and empathetic. It was clear to me that her calling in life went beyond doing household duties, e.g. cooking, cleaning and caring for the baby and me. In short time we developed a bond more like mother and daughter than employer and employee. She spoke to me in Italian with some English words and lots of pantomime. The speed at which she used her hands to communicate a thought, reminded me of a secretary speed typing.

She told me to call her Zia, which means Aunt in Italian. She was instrumental in teaching me how to cook lamb stew, cannoli from scratch using farmer's cheese, and spaghetti with the best gravy I'd ever had in my life.

"Gabbi!" she called with a thick Italian accent, "Come, you will nurse the baby in thirty minutes. Drink this."

"But Zia, what is it?"

"You don't ask. You just drink. You don't ask. You do what Zia tells you to do."

"Yes Zia." As a child I was raised to answer, "Yes Ma'am". I knew that I'd better respect the woman of the home as she deserves; there was no doubt, Zia was the woman of this home.

The glass was small only six ounces. The first sip I thought I was drinking grape juice and I liked it. Half way through the refreshing beverage, I felt giddy and lightheaded.

"Zia, Zia what kind of grape juice is this?" I exclaimed and giggled.

"You don't ask, you drink." she commanded; her thick lips turned up in a smile. She had a plump face.

By now there was a silly smile on my face.

Later that day I noticed a beautiful bottle sitting on the kitchen counter. It had a woven basket made especially for it.

"*Chhe aanti*! That's what she's feeding me." I said aloud. I ran into the nursery. She was putting a fresh diaper on the baby.

"It's *Chhe aanti* you're feeding me!" I announced.

She laughed and pinched my cheeks and said, "It's *key-aunti*. *Chianti*! In Italy, mamas drink wine or beer with every meal; it helps the bambino to sleep."

Zia had six children of her own and there were several dozen grandchildren.

Ray's wisdom, in hiring Zia, aided me immensely since I had no idea what was abnormal. She knew when to call the doctor. She was the liaison between Ray and the doctors. For the next year and a half she took over all of the responsibilities of a housewife and most of the responsibilities of a mother. She was, after all, caring for a baby who'd had a baby.

***

One afternoon Callie and I were playing on the center of our king sized bed. My girlfriends had come over.

"Gabbi, what is that strange movement that Caleb just made?" asked Gloria

I looked at her and looked back at Callie. He looked fine. But the question jarred something in the back of my mind. Many times when we were playing or I was just cuddling him he would throw his right arm up over his head. Then his head turned from twelve o'clock to nine o'clock, and his body became rigid. These movements were repeated many times within a minute. Gloria's eyes were fixed on the baby. All of a sudden she grabbed my hand. The room fell silent. She was referring to one of Caleb's stretching episodes.

"I don't know, I thought he was stretching or yawning." I said.

The other young mothers in the room looked from one to another and then me.

"Oh Gabbi, our babies never did anything like that." my neighbor Sharon said. "Maybe you need to take Caleb to the Emergency Room."

I got that sick, queasy feeling. I asked Gloria if she would drive us to Jackson Memorial. We were back home a few hours later. The doctors in the emergency room assured me that there was nothing wrong.

When Gloria was leaving I asked if she had a Polaroid camera.

"Yes I do."

"Could I borrow it for a little while?"

"Sure," she said, "but why?"

"I've got to have a way to show the doctors what my baby is doing."

"Oh, what a great idea! I'll go get the camera and be right back."

That night after I bathed the baby and laid him on the changing table; he did one of his special stretch/yawn movements. I documented it immediately. I had set up a small clock, with a second hand, on the nursery dresser. In the space of one minute, he did his special yawn/stretch eighteen times.

The next morning, Ray had to take care of business. Fine I thought. I can't deal with him and his temper. I need to get Caleb to the Emergency Room. I called Gloria and she drove us back to the hospital; my proof in hand--the pictures.

***

Petite Mal seizures. That was the proper medical name for the yawning/stretching movements. They were caused by scar tissue forming around his brain. This time on the way home we had to stop and fill a prescription for Phenobarbital. Twenty-four hours later his seizures had not changed in frequency or severity.

When I called the doctor, he simply said, "Up the dosage." No further instructions.

Didn't they understand? I was a Mommy not a nurse, not a medically qualified caregiver and not a pharmacist. I don't how many times I overdosed him. There but for the Grace of God, I could have killed Caleb with the Phenobarbital.

It was all too much. I'd been thrown into a role that I was not prepared to deal with in my short time on this earth. I'd better learn quickly! But I would need my Father's help.

"*Lord Father.*" I prayed. "*I think you're going too fast. I think you're expecting me to grow up way too soon. After all Lord, I haven't been a Mommy very long.*" I was on my knees. My arms and head were resting on the side of my bed, sobbing to God. Begging God, *"Please make this all stop! Please let me awaken to find this was a horrible nightmare. I want my baby back! I want my magnificent, beautiful, healthy baby back as he was."*

I crawled up onto the bed, curled into a fetal position, grabbed my pillow and hugged it. I prayed; that was my lifeline. And then I sobbed myself to sleep.

***

I didn't have a label for what was happening. Perhaps I was maturing; maybe it was woman's intuition. I was beginning to have the first thoughts that I had made a horrendous mistake falling in love with Ray. Not many of life's experiences come with an owner's manual. Falling in love with Ray, becoming pregnant, giving birth to Caleb and all that had happened in my life, could not be found in a book, unless it was titled "How to Make Bad Decisions." However, as much as I was questioning and doubting the choices I'd made, giving birth to Caleb, holding, smelling, touching and kissing that child was the best thing that had happened in my life, to date. The sicker Caleb got, the more times we were at the hospital, the more my body ached to have his sibling. I knew in my heart that I had to have his brother or sister to love and care for, for the rest of my life. And with that decision, I once again pushed my concerns about Ray to the back of my mind.

We didn't practice birth control, but it took almost a year before the dreaded twenty-four hour "morning sickness" consumed my days. Finally, I got my wish.

With this pregnancy, the doctors continually assured me that this baby would not have the medical problems that Caleb had. They said a brain aneurysm is a fluke; it isn't hereditary. So eight months and two weeks into the pregnancy, I was told to arrive at Jackson Memorial Hospital on a Monday morning at seven a.m. At nine a.m. I would give birth via a planned cesarean section.

It was all so easy: no labor, no pain, no thinking I was going to die. I simply checked in, was put into a hospital gown and walked to the operating room. I was put to sleep. When I opened my eyes, Dr. Bossett, for the second time in my life leaned down and stroked my forehead. "You've just given birth to the second most beautiful baby we've ever seen. Caleb has a new baby brother."

It was a few hours later that Ray strutted into my hospital room and over to my bed.

He threw his shoulders back and said, "That's the ugliest baby I've ever seen. There's no way he could be mine!"

I didn't answer him at first. I searched his face, trying to determine if he was joking. But his body language and tone of voice told me that he was dead serious.

"Ray, don't you understand? Caleb was born three weeks late and had more time to develop and look like an older baby. Sean was born two weeks early. Of course, there's less definition of his face. His hair is so white that it doesn't look like he has a forehead." I broke into tears and said, "Raymond Fortier! You are the most vain, self-centered man I have ever known. Your priest can't give you enough Hail Mary's to make up for what you just said."

***

Zia was a godsend. She tended to Caleb while I nursed Sean and enjoyed watching him grow. She cooked huge Italian feasts for us; and of course the Chianti regimen continued with afternoon meals. For a short time I thought my dream life might be possible after all.

***

"Baby, Baby, where are you, come see who's here!" Ray said as he burst through the door.

I came out into the living room, from the nursery and there stood the most slimy, skanky, slithering, tall, skinny, scary looking creature I'd ever seen. "It" wore a beige trench coat, a brimmed hat cocked, covering his eyes. On his feet, the final touch of this costume, spats! Did he have misguided visions of grandeur too? It was too early for Halloween. But, the most disgusting part of this vulgar looking "man" was the balanced, half chewed, repulsive smelling cigar dangling between his yellow-stained fingers. He was an assault to all of my senses.

I'd never been in doubt that some of Ray's "business associates", had spent stints in prison. Standing before me now was the poster boy of a newly released ex-con.

Are you out of your frigging mind? I wanted to scream, but didn't. *Hi honey, what have you found on the side of the road?* Nope, don't dare say that either. I took a deep breath and sheepishly said, "Hey Ray, who's this?"

"Hammi is one of my business associates from Montréal."

I was expecting to hear a thick French accent.

"Nice to meet ya." he croaked.

"Oh, you're from Montréal, but you don't sound like Ray?"

"That's right! I didn't have to jump the pond like the Frogs did. I'm a proper born Englishman." He said sarcastically.

That took the cake; I thought I'd vomit; proper born Englishman? My arse!

"Where are you staying Hammi?" I dreaded the answer.

Hammi looked at me and then at Ray. Ray looked at Hammi and back at me.

Simultaneously they cheered, "Here!"

"Hammi and I are headed to the track. He has a fantastic system."

System. How many times would I hear about the system? Yea, Ray had a system, it was a ritual. Losing! The only guarantee was, it overrode the role of husband, father and provider.

And then the scenario that I was becoming accustomed to played itself out yet again. He kissed me, squeezed my ass and the two of them walked out the door. As usual I wondered how many *days* it would be before they came back.

As I watched the odd couple drive away in Ray's candy apple red Cadillac convertible, the dam burst and I started wailing. It took me some time to calm myself. I knew this man was bad news. Didn't Ray understand, this is not the type of person to bring into our home? My hope for us to live as "Squares" was dashed. That "life", our lives were in jeopardy. It felt as if the floor would give out under me. I'd run into the bedroom to the security of the one place where life with Raymond was always safe. In our bed under the blankets, curtains closed and one of our favorite LP's playing. I'd cry until Sean needed my attention. I was scared to death. At times like this I wanted to get the baby, get in the car, drive to Chalk Airlines and fly over to our new home on Lyford Cay, in the Bahamas. Maybe it was time for me to find my brave; time to show him that I have a mind of my own; time for him to worry about where *I* was. In the top drawer of my nightstand was a set of shiny new house keys. I remember the night he made that "presentation".

"Close your eyes Baby, don't peek." Ray had whispered into my ear. He held me close after another hectic "business" day.

"What are you talking about?" I heard his exasperated sigh. "Alright, alright, my eyes are closed."

He reached down by my side and took my hand into his, I felt something metal and cold being pressed into my palm.

"What is this? Can I open my eyes now?" I said with great excitement.

As he released his hold on me, he said "Okay, open your eyes."

"Two keys? Two keys, I don't get it. What's going on?" I was feeling a rush of excitement. Life was always exciting with Ray. I think it was one of the reasons I stayed with him.

Ray, get me a glass of sherry and come sit with me. Tell me everything

As he handed me the Harvey's Bristol Cream poured over two ice cubes he said. "Here Baby, just the way you like it. Can I tell you about the keys now?"

"Yes my love." I purred. "Part of your mystique is showering me with extravagant gifts."

He took a deep breath and proceeded to lay out the latest of his adventures.

"Well Baby, see it goes like this. I had to go to the Bahamas today for a couple of hours on business. As Captain Clifford and First Mate Gill were docking the yacht, I saw a house for sale, right on the water. Just like you said you wanted."

My eyes were getting bigger and bigger.

I saw the twinkle in his eyes that told me I was reacting exactly as he hoped.

"Wow! Cool!" I said.

"Well, here's the keys! Don't you get it? Here's the keys; the keys to our new house in the Bahamas!" he held his breath waiting for me to respond.

And when I did, I was like a whirling dervish; spinning, screeching and squealing. "A house in the Bahamas? Right on the water? These are the keys?" As I wove my arms around his neck, I kissed every inch of his face and neck. "I love you Raymond, more than anything in the world. When are we going? When are you taking me there? Now?"

"Calm down Baby. I've hired a team, an entire crew to make it the way you would want it to be. You know, sunny, bright, lots of wicker furniture, Gabbi style. It even has a wraparound porch for your rocking chairs; it's a typical Bahamian house!"

Oh my. Back to reality. That was then, this is now. I don't know who to call to get everything set up; to open the house and have it stocked with needed provisions. No. I'd just stay here and hope he would come home. He never called. Will this be one of the times that he would stay gone for three days?

I was frightened when Ray wasn't at home but there were times when I was just as frightened when he was.

I would never call my mother or Aunt Esther during Ray's disappearing acts. It would have been shameful for me to have to say the truth. I knew that if he really loved me, he wouldn't just disappear for days at a time. That's not what a loving father would do. Then I would tell myself, he does love us; he just had very important business to attend to. When thoughts of leaving him crossed my mind, I'd feel faint and the room would begin to spin. Where would I go? Where could I go? Who would want me and two babies, one of them needing around-the-clock care?

Chapter Eight

One afternoon, when Sean was eight months, Ray came home with a plan.

"Come outside with me, Pet!" he yelled. "I have something to show you."

Life with Raymond was always exciting. But, I was maturing as a mother and realizing that life, as Ray was living it was wrong. He sensed these changes in me. He grabbed my hand and pulled me outside. The mischievous kid inside that dangerous man was beaming.

"Do you love it?" He asked teasingly.

"Love what?" I asked.

"The car!" he yelled. "The car! The canary yellow Lincoln!"

"Yes Ray, it's beautiful but", I hesitated.

"It's yours Baby, it's yours." I stared at him in shock.

He said, "How fast can you get the house packed and the babies ready?"

"Ready for what?"

With his two hands he cupped my face and said, "I know you're not happy. I think you want to leave me. I've found a way to change my life."

With his hands still cupping my face I looked up into his eyes.

"How?" I asked

He threw his arms up in the air and yelled, "I bought a ranch! I bought a ranch in Saratoga, Wyoming!"

"Where the heck is Wyoming?" I exclaimed.

Of course, I'd do what he asked. I still loved him enough to do anything to assure that we'd spend the rest of our lives together. He was making an attempt at a fresh start.

"I'm willing to follow you on this lark. I'm not willing to subject Caleb to a five day trip in an automobile. And it sounds to me like our nearest neighbor will moo."

"You're right Pet, I hadn't thought of that. You make whatever arrangements you want and it's fine with me."

I made an appointment with a twenty-four hour nursing facility in Homestead. The next morning I took Zia and Caleb and toured the facility. I met the staff and explained this was not a permanent placement. My family was leaving the state for a period of time and I didn't feel it would be safe to take him on the trip.

The Sunshine Home was not as depressing as I had imagined. It was set in the midst of an orange grove. There were lots of open windows and fresh air. It had brightly colored walls with age appropriate murals. All of Caleb's doctors were on staff there to care for him. If he needed hospitalization, they'd take him into Miami, to Jackson Memorial.

I sat in a soft rocking chair with Caleb. I sang to him as if he understood every word. I explained what was happening and why. And then I turned my precious son over to the head nurse, Mame. There was something in her eyes that led me to believe that she loved her job, loved her clients and would do all in her power to keep Caleb safe until my return.

Like a woman in control, I walked out to my car with Zia. We didn't speak. Half way down Farm Life Road, I pulled onto a dirt road leading into a grove. As I parked, the suppressed emotions erupted. I sat balling my eyes out; questioning my decision to leave him there.

***

The day we drove out of Miami, my cherished Zia and some of her grandchildren stood in the driveway. As we pulled away, I turned toward them and blew kisses, saying goodbye to my security blankie,

Zia; praying that I wasn't making another horrible mistake.

PART TWO

Chapter Nine

Knowing little about geography, I'd come up with a picture of Wyoming in my mind—tall mountains with snow-capped peaks, dense forests of tall, lush evergreens. When we pulled into the little town of Saratoga, I was shocked. We'd driven through low, rolling hill country and prairie land, and now this? It was like a scene out of *Gunsmoke*.

The "sidewalk" was wooden planks that ran along the length of Main Street, but only on one side. The streets were mostly dry dirt, and dust puffed up from them in a faint breeze.

Nothing was green.

Fortunately there was clear blue sky overhead. "Look at that," Ray said, pointing up.

"Welcome to Big Sky Country, Baby."

"Yeah," I said in a weak voice. How could I get excited about the sky when everything else in this place was brown? Brown, tan, beige…and more brown. My eyes were accustomed to the sharp, brilliant Florida colors: deep shades of turquoise, bright minty greens, and hot pinks.

The ranch Ray bought was just as bad. The long, low ranch house was a muddy brown, with lots of heavy, uncomfortable brown furniture.

I was sick inside but I pretended to be excited. Ray was in high spirits, apparently unconcerned about the bleak landscape around us.

"Oh, look, this little room will be perfect for Sean," I said, as we toured the house. "Can we paint it? Blue, maybe?"

"This place is ours Baby!" Ray boomed. With that, he took my hand and had that special twinkle in his eyes he said, "We can do anything we want to it, follow me."

"Oh Ray, not now, I don't have the energy to make love with you now."

"Shhh! Don't say anything; just follow me. I want to prove to you how much I love you and how hard I've worked to make this move to Wyoming a new beginning." We walked to a door at the end of the hallway. "Close your eyes Baby."

As exhausted as I was I began to feel excitement. I was wondering what was on the other side of that door. Just then he threw open the door and pulled me inside a tropical paradise set right in the middle of dusty brown Wyoming.

"Well what is this? How? What?"

"My father always told me *'if you're going to keep a bird, make sure it loves it's cage.'* Now, stop talking Baby, just take your clothes off for God's sake."

"But the baby."

"Don't you worry about the baby; I'll take care of him and put him down for a nap. Then I'll come back in here to join you."

As I watched him leave and close the door behind him, I was standing in the midst of a subtropical rain forest. The room was made entirely of glass. Every inch of wall space was thick with exotic flora and fauna. As I looked up, there was nothing fracturing the rays of the sun, except glass panels. The flooring was tile, pink of course. At the head of the open space were two teak chaise lounges with extra thick cushions, done in a bird of paradise pattern. In the center of the space was an octagon shaped hot tub. Needing to pinch myself, I realized standing in a corner was a two person sauna. The only thing missing, I thought, was an open air shower. When I turned around I saw in the opposite corner a huge shower head and special panel full of controls. There was a thermostat and climate control on wall. And as only Ray would have it done, he made sure there was room for a two seat bar; complete with stools and a refrigerator.

Oh my, I thought, what's a gal to do? Strip I guess and start enjoying this paradise. I lowered myself into the hot tub and rested my head on the built in pillow. I looked up into the massive blue sky. Under my breath I said, *thank you for this Victor.* If this isn't love, what is? Ray returned; fixed us cold drinks and joined me in the hot tub. As he slid down, he wasted no time finding that special place between my legs that would insure us a passionate first time in this hot tub; followed by dessert on the thin cedar planks of the sauna bench. The evening ended with an erotic shower, using all the positions of that fancy shower head. Obviously I was not too exhausted to make love with him.

"See Baby, even *here* you can stay my little Coppertone girl."

I was starting to understand what my world was really all about. It was dangerous and frightening; *and* exciting. It was filled with exploration. I literally lived waiting to discover what the next excitement would be.

***

The next day Ray took us to town. We went into the bakery, the butcher shop, the pharmacy, and what I guess you'd call a general store. He introduced himself to the managers and store owners as the "new owner of the Arthur Ranch". He seemed to delight at informing them that I was to do my shopping in their stores and sign for the goods; then they were to send him a bill. I'd never heard of such a thing.

The next day he told me I was to go to town and get whatever I'd need to make dinner for us and four guests. Ray seemed to think that when we crossed into Wyoming, I was going to be magically transformed into the perfect wife, chef, and hostess.

You've got to be kidding me! I thought to myself.

Unless I can serve grilled cheese sandwiches, Campbell's tomato soup and a cold pitcher of Tang, I'll never pull this off. And WHERE would I find Tang in Saratoga, Wyoming?

"I suggest you start at Mr. Wyatt's butcher shop. I feel like having pork. Don't forget, all I eat is center cut. And be sure to have a bottle of chilled Mumm's Champagne."

After he left, I put Sean into his stroller. We ventured out into what felt like the wild, wild, west. I mean, where else do you live, drive down the road and have to wait for a herd of what looked like deer, to cross before continuing on. Not Miami Beach! To this beach bunny, I considered that cause enough to stay home and have meals catered.

There was a large metal cowbell hanging above the door to Mr. Wyatt's, it startled me as I pulled the door open. I was trying so very hard to feel grownup. Mr. Wyatt, the butcher, was a *huge* man—huge head, shoulders, and upper body, which was all I could see of him since he was behind the counter. I didn't expect a warm welcome in the Wyatts' store, because I'd heard Aunt Esther say how cold and aloof *Northerners* are (and as far as I was concerned, anyone who lived north of Florida was a Northerner). So I was surprised when Mr. Wyatt actually smiled, revealing two-thirds of his teeth.

I explained to him that my task for today was to gather all the provisions needed to make a dinner consisting of pork, in quantity enough for six. As if there were a statistical formula, I stood silently, allowing Mr. Wyatt to calculate just what was needed.

"Do you want a pork roast, pork chops or pork tenderloin?" he asked.

It had taken all the emotional strength I could muster to walk down that wooden sidewalk. Now I was being asked questions I had no idea how to answer. And for some reason my mind leaped back to the day in Florida when I messed up breakfast. *Typically, Ray cooked breakfast on weekends. One morning I told him to stay in bed, I would cook. I would prepare breakfast for him. I wanted to take the plunge at becoming Betty Crocker. There was bacon in the refrigerator. There was flour and there were eggs; all the fixings for pancakes and bacon. I put flour, eggs and milk in a bowl. I mixed them all together, but somehow or another, when I poured the batter in, it ran all over the pan. It never did make a pancake. Just my luck to have defective flour! Oh well, I was determined to make Ray breakfast. I still had eggs, milk and bread. I remembered my mother made French toast. So, that was it, I made French toast and bacon, orange juice and milk. Running into the bedroom, I grabbed his hand, pulled him and said,*

"Come see what I've done; just come see what I've done."

I was like a little kid dragging their parents in, to see a surprise.

"What's that mess?" he snarled.

"That's your breakfast; that's the surprise I have for you."

As he looked around the kitchen, he saw the mess from my attempt at making pancakes. He turned back to stare at the plate I was holding.

"What is that mess?" he said again.

"That's French toast. This is your surprise. I just made it for you."

"Well where's the coffee?"

"I don't know how to make coffee. But I made you French toast and bacon and juice and milk." I looked up at him and started to cry.

He picked up the plate, simultaneously grabbing my ponytail and slammed my face into the French toast. He didn't realize that I had cooked it in the hot bacon grease.

When I started screaming, "You're burning my face!" he dropped the plate and ran out of the house.

Now, standing in the butcher shop, I knew that I couldn't fail again in the kitchen. Who knew what Ray might do to me this time, far away from anyone I could turn to for help?

As huge as Mr. Wyatt was, he had a smile that whooshed away the turmoil he read on my face.

"Would you like to have leftovers?" he asked.

"You know, Mr. Wyatt, I remember my mother making meals one day and then coming up with the most interesting meals another day from what was left. Is that what you're talking about?"

Mr. Wyatt looked down at me from behind the counter and started to laugh. "Yes, ma'am, that's what I mean by leftovers."

"Well Mr. Wyatt, here's my problem. I never know how many people he will bring home for me to feed. I just don't know how much to get." I tried to smile but tears welled up in my eyes.

"Hey, wait a minute, you don't have to cry. We'll figure this out." His huge Adams apple seemed to disappear, as he gulped and swallowed. He was obviously very uncomfortable with my emotional outburst.

From behind a white curtain hanging over a doorway behind the counter, a little gray-haired woman with a soft and tender look appeared; her butcher's apron just barely tied around her plump body. The Wyatts just looked at each other. Mrs. Wyatt came around the big glass display cabinet.

"I couldn't help but overhear the conversation between you and my husband," she said. She came over to me and put her arm around my shoulders. "If you can come in everyday at about this time with an idea of what your husband wants you to prepare, you and I will work up a menu. We'll write down the directions so that when you get home, you'll know just what to do." She looked over at her husband and winked. "Everything will be perfect...just as your husband expects it to be."

I tried to calm myself. I was so embarrassed. I was raised that you never brought attention to yourself. I especially didn't like revealing my vulnerability to these strangers.

"Thank you." I whispered as she handed me a tissue.

The Wyatts didn't remain strangers for very long. Mrs. Wyatt guided me through the menu for my first dinner party, and then every day thereafter. I would walk that wooden sidewalk to the butcher shop. Mr. Wyatt would always ask the same question.

"Well, Mrs. Fortier, how did it go last night?" He'd look at his wife for a sign that he'd asked me gently enough. She would smile to indicate that he had done just fine. Then I would tell them step by step what had happened the night before, in the kitchen.

For that first dinner party, Mrs. Wyatt had sent me home with a package of meat wrapped in brown butcher paper, and a heavy black wrought iron frying pan. She also gave me a little white kitchen timer. I had baked the potatoes exactly as Mrs. Wyatt had instructed—wrapped in foil and baked in the preheated oven. They were delicious.

I don't remember what else I prepared for that meal. I can remember I had to fight the urge to vomit from the time I left Mrs. Wyatt until I went to bed that night; questioning how in the world I would pull this off? Suffice it to say, I did it!

***

I can't say that all of my cooking expertise came from Mr. and Mrs. Wyatt's butcher shop, because Zia had given me such a great foundation, in *Italian* cooking. The Wyatt's taught me about meat and potato meals; what I called *cowboy* cooking. I learned about meat and how much I needed for how many people. That was one of the problems. I never knew how many people he would bring home, or if he would even come home. I couldn't tell that to Mrs. Wyatt. She had said so many times how lucky I was. I had heard this many times before. *You have such a handsome, adoring, loving husband.* I could never admit that things were not as they seemed. I'd gotten good over the years; pretending my life was one way, when the cold, stark truth was, it was nothing like people thought.

***

One day, as I entered the butcher shop, it was quarter till, not one-thirty. No one was there. Since we had become friends, I headed to the white sheet that covered the door. I pulled the curtain back and took several steps into a big room. I let out a screech and a scream. You would have thought I was being murdered. There, hanging on a huge hook coming down from the ceiling, was *Bambi*; or his mother or his father! Oh no, a familiar feeling; tiny stars danced in front of my eyes. I had no more air left in my lungs. I fainted from the shock of the site, falling into a heap at Bambi's feet. When I came to, Mrs. Wyatt was wiping my forehead with a wet, white cloth.

"Come on now honey, you'll be okay. This *is* a butcher shop. What did you think went on back here?" she said. "Mr. Wyatt was getting ready to dress Mr. Blackhawk's kill for today."

I looked up at Mrs. Wyatt's face. I said, "But Mrs. Wyatt, it looks like Bambi."

"Honey, that's not a deer, it's an antelope. Don't you know what antelope look like?"

"I don't think we had antelope in Miami." I said.

"No, I guess you didn't." She chuckled.

***

When I told Ray about what happened at the butcher shop that day, he just laughed.

"Honey, when they coined the phrase *dumb blonde*, I am convinced that they were thinking of you.

***

Later that week I saw Mr. Blackhawk walking toward me on the street. He bowed his head, slumped his shoulders forward and just kept going. When I told Raymond about it that night, he explained why Mr. Blackhawk didn't make eye contact and avoided me.

"That is a very proud man. He, his wife and their six children are from Hawaii. They moved here because loggers in Hawaii are falling on hard times. Baby, it's like this. Mr. & Mrs. Blackhawk work very hard and still can't make enough money to take care of that huge family. So what you saw in the back of Mr. Wyatt's butcher shop was illegal. It was poaching."

"But Raymond, I didn't see anything illegal. No drugs, no gambling, and no guns. I didn't see anything illegal." I said.

"You have got to stop watching Mannix. There are other things illegal, besides drugs, gambling and guns."

My heart skipped a beat. My mind thought frantically, why does Ray know about other illegal activities?

"Mr. Blackhawk had been poaching." Raymond continued.

"So, do you see now? Mr. Blackhawk was ashamed. He has to poach antelope to feed his family of eight; he can't make enough money. Mr. Wyatt butchers it and Mrs. Blackhawk puts it in her deep freezer. Do you understand how important it is, *not* to talk about this in front of anyone?"

"I get it Raymond", I said, "He was embarrassed, but I would never say anything to him or anyone else about killing Bambi."

I saw the look in his eyes. I knew that look very well. *What he meant was, if I opened my mouth and said anything to anybody, about anything, I'd be punished, I'd be hurt.* I took a deep breath and filed that conversation away, deep down inside my memory. His punishments hurt. His beatings hurt. I'd keep it locked up with all the secrets that were under my pretend lock and key, that was for sure.

***

Mrs. Wyatt had a niece Gillian. She was fifteen years old; just the right age, wanting to earn money by babysitting. Her plump rosy cheeks and freckled nose were veiled by cascades of fire engine red ringlets, leaving no doubt this shy child was a throwback to the *Clan McKearnan*. Those long red, tightly spun curls hung just below shoulder length, giving her the appearance of having no neck! I was never quite sure if her eyes were blue or green, because as she smiled her cheeks forced her eyelids to almost meet, never allowing the viewer to see her eye color clearly. Her body, in the most comical way, resembled Humpty Dumpty. When I would approach the Wyatt's butcher shop, there she sat in the Adirondack chair. Her short plump legs didn't quite reach the sidewalk, under the chair. As she rocked to and fro, I was certain she'd be catapulted out of that chair and break into pieces like Humpty Dumpty. This stirred up memories of my own awkward teenage years. For that reason, I instructed her, "The baby has had everything he needs and is asleep. Unless there is a major catastrophe, you are not to lift the baby out of his crib. There is ice cream and soda in the refrigerator, a bowl of chocolates on the cocktail table and feel free to watch any television show you like."

***

One afternoon Ray told me he'd discovered a magical place and he wanted to take me there.

"Get the babysitter." he said.

It was November and had already gotten frigid cold. The winds whipped down through the hills and swept through the ranch. It was so bleak I couldn't see how we'd make it through the winter and couldn't believe Ray had found anything magical in this wilderness. But, I phoned Gillian. Once Ray decided on something, there was no discussion.

Gillian arrived at the appointed hour. Ray told me that we wouldn't be near a phone, so I told Gillian to call her Aunt if anything came up that she couldn't handle.

Ray fumbled around in the closet and pulled out my long fur coat. It had been in a zipper bag since he'd given it to me in Miami. It would be perfect for tonight.

"Where are we going?" I asked as we drove off the ranch. "There aren't any restaurants or clubs out this way?"

"You'll see." he said, grinning.

***

The "magical" spot turned out to be a mineral springs tucked away in a stone grotto, on the bank of the North Platte River, just outside Saratoga. As we drove closer, the strong smell of sulfur permeated the night air. Ray pulled off the road into a thicket of trees. We got out of the car and he told me to get undressed.

"What? Are you kidding? It's freezing out here!"

"Trust me Baby. Just strip and then put your coat back on." He was already out of his boots and jeans.

As soon as I was ready, Ray guided me down a winding path and then up and over a mound of smooth rocks. At the top I could see a glistening pool of water with steam rising from it. The full moon bathed the whole spring in a golden light.

"Oh," I squealed. "This *is* magical!"

"Buck told me that the Indians call this 'the place of magic waters'."

Ray laughed, delighted that he surprised me like this. He slipped the fur off of me and laid it across the big smooth rock outcropping, then helped me down, after he'd waded in.

We soaked in the soothing water—very warm but not so hot as to be uncomfortable—and he kissed me and held me in the most loving way. He had rarely been tender like this since we first met in Canada. I began thinking that this move to Wyoming might be the best thing that could have happened to us. He was more relaxed than I had ever seen him.

For nearly an hour we lolled in the hot springs and enjoyed each other; our bodies entwined beneath the water. I'd wiggle and squirm and revel in any loving he would give me.

Then suddenly he said, "Baby, you wait right here. Don't move."

"Where are you going? Don't leave me!" I said, terrified of staying there alone.

"I'm going up and over that wall to take a dip in the North Platte."

"Why?"

"It's invigorating; gets the blood circulating."

He ignored my plea and went right on and scaled the stone wall that divided the hot mineral springs from the raging, frigid North Platte. In spite of being immersed in the hot water, I was shivering. *What if he drowns?* I thought. *Who would come and find me? Where are his car keys? If I found them, could I even find my way back to the car?*

I kept my eyes glued to the top of that wall and finally, after what seemed like an eternity, I saw his head. He stood up, then looked down at me and laughed, pounding his chest like Tarzan. I had to smile as he dove into the water just a few feet in front of me.

The swim had invigorated him. He caressed my body, beginning with my breasts. I felt the excitement grow between his legs. He made passionate love to me right there. Like the crescendo in a Tchaikovsky symphony, we would reach a climax that shook our bodies and gave proof to what I knew; Ray was a soft, loving, passionate man. Under the safety of the night sky, I shed tears of joy.

The mineral springs became a regular "escape from reality" for us. My Dr. Jekyll and Mr. Hyde were always predictable on these special nights. No beatings; no harsh treatment. If I died at this special place, my fairytale life would be fulfilled.

***

As a child in New Jersey one of my hobbies besides music was horses. My parents bought me a horse named Susie-Q. She was an all-white Quarter horse. We boarded her at the Parker's ranch, which was within bicycle riding distance from my house. My parents were given a discount on the boarding because on weekends I would spend the days slopping stalls, cleaning water troughs, replacing salt licks, mucking stalls and brushing down the horses as they came in from trail rides. Every second I was there was a magical escape from my adoptive father.

There is no comparison between a casual trail rider and a working rider. I very much wanted to be a part of this ranch; feeling so hopeful recently about this move to Wyoming. Buck, our foreman, agreed to teach me to barrel race my horse Black Magic. I thought it would give me strength and show Ray that I could be more than just his beautiful "trophy" wife; an accessory. Well, Buck knew Ray's schedule better than I did. Whenever we had a couple of hours without Ray at the ranch, Buck would drag barrels out into the paddock behind the house.

I progressed quickly and we had a plan for "showing" Ray. One morning, he was at the ranch, playing with and feeding Sean for the morning. I thought that would be the perfect time to tell him I was going to town to pick up provisions for a couple of days worth of meals.

"Yea, okay. Sean and I are doing fine. Take your time. Oh don't forget to pick up some thick sliced bacon."

Once I knew I was getting close to ready to perform for Ray, I'd stashed a special outfit in the barn; hat, boots and all. Buck would set up the paddock for me. When I was in costume and mounted, Buck would go get Ray to show "boss man" something outback. And then Buck would signal to me and Black Magic.

I was so excited. And it looked like the plan was going to work perfectly. Buck set up the old, rusted, dented barrels and I was in full cowgirl costume. It was show time. Buck went and got Ray, with Sean on his hip to the back fence. Then Buck put his two fingers in his mouth and let out a whistle that would wake the dead! Black Magic and I were off! I galloped down the dirt path from behind the barn. I headed right for Ray, Sean and Buck, horse's hooves pounding. Ray stepped over to the paddock, close to the rail as this mystery rider entered. I pulled on the reins to slow the horse and began weaving and winding him through the barrels. "Magic" was cutting it close and several times I'm sure it looked as if I was about to fall off the horse. By now, Buck started howling and pointing at Ray and then me.

"She took to it like a real rodeo rider!" Buck said, spitting a little jet of tobacco juice into the dust. "Reckon you won't need me 'round here much anymore with a rider like that!"

Ray had been a Canadian Jock's Agent, and was an accomplished rider. When the dust settled and I could see his expression, it was exactly what I wanted!

My new horse and I had won his favor; at least for the moment.

"Baby, get down off that horse. I want to squeeze you and make love to you right here in this paddock; in front of Buck and whoever is watching!" I guess he read the expression on my face, because he quickly added, "Oh, Baby, I'm joking. You are amazing!"

Passionate love making was my reward. Ray was so proud of his "Little Cowgirl".

***

I got to the butcher shop the next day at one-thirty. I wanted to pick up the bacon and more importantly, I wanted Mrs. Wyatt to tell me how to prepare the roast beef feast Ray always raved about. His mother made it with turnips, carrots and potatoes. I had no idea how to prepare such a meal; what was a turnip? Mrs. Wyatt explained many families living in a northern climate utilize *root vegetables* in their meals; such as, but not limited to carrots, potatoes, turnips and onions.

"I'm going to suggest a three pound roast, allowing for half a pound per person. That should do no matter how many guests your husband brings home. Gabbi dear, the preparation for this meal is so easy it should to be against the law." She chuckled. "The best part, Ray and your guests will never know you cooked the entire meal in the black wrought iron skillet and simply made a tent from a piece of aluminum foil. Remember Gabbi, the roast goes in the center of the skillet; the vegetables will be mounded around the meat. Mmm, now for a *little bag of magic.*" Those words were said through her pursed lips, as though she was allowing a well-protected secret to escape. She held up the small bag of aromatic spices; with a mischievous look on her face, she continued, and I could swear that her eyes had turned from pale blue to magical black.

"Sprinkle these over the meat and vegetables, add a quarter cup of water and then the foil tent. As these foods cook the flavors will meld and the aroma will waft throughout your house. The tent keeps the natural juices inside the meat and your guests will think you are a gourmet chef, Gabbi!" She gave me the most reassuring look and said, "Honey, you can do this."

I believed I could! I *was* becoming a woman and a wife! But if Ray ever found out that I was spending my afternoons in the Wyatts' butcher shop, taking cooking lessons, he'd blow up. Ray's words flashed through my mind; *"Remember Gabbi, don't embarrass me; nobody is to know my business!"* I was now reflecting on the reality that if he found out, he'd probably kill me.

***

Around dusk, playing my Santana Abraxas album, I was experiencing such highs. Natural highs of being in love, being a mommy, cooking and preparing a dinner that smelled so good! *And* I was high because

Raymond would soon be here. I'd get butterflies anticipating him coming home after a day without him. Would he scoop me up, throw me down on the bed and start kissing me behind my earlobes? My panties would get wet in anticipation. Those were the times that I was the happiest in this world.

Today I knew by the slamming of the door and the intensity of his footsteps that my sensuous needs would not be addressed. I wished I could stay hidden in my bedroom. I couldn't; I had to go out there.

"Hey Baby, how was your day? I missed you. Give me a big kiss." I cajoled him. He didn't even look at me as he thumbed through some mail on the kitchen counter.

"Where's my clean clothes?"

Oh my God! Oh my God! I thought. His clean clothes? He'd always sent laundry out or had someone come in to do it, or on rare occasions, wash his clothes himself. I even remember times in Miami that we would drive to a store like Jordan Marsh, and buy him clean black socks on the way to a party.

"Yes!" he'd said, "I told you I needed those clothes clean. I need them. Don't be so stupid."

My crying just escalated his agitation. I was terrified. I didn't have the answers.

As I tried to walk away from Ray, he grabbed my arm. He yanked me and spun me back around in front of him.

"Look!" he said. "What kind of a woman are you anyway? I shouldn't have to tell you to cook my meals and clean my clothes. Look at this house, it's a mess."

As I started to answer him, he smacked the side of my head so hard that I went flying across the room. I knew better than to get up, which would put me back into the line of fire and getting hit again. Crouched on the floor, I was afraid to look sideways, or to lift my head; afraid to breathe or to move. I focused on the beautiful roses in the Oriental rug. If I wasn't near him, I wouldn't get hit again, or kicked or smacked. But I was there, not able to escape. He reached down, grabbed the hair on the side of my head and was dragging me. He violently threw me onto the long low sofa across the room; tearing my clothes. He jumped on me and raped me! I didn't know he was raping me, I thought that I deserved what he was doing. I was bad and didn't do his laundry, I deserved this abuse. I kept thinking this hurts. I'm not getting that tingling feeling. He's not kissing me and making me feel special. This was painful. I knew better than to make a sound. He just pounded and pounded and pounded away at me. But I knew him. I knew that very soon he'd reach that point where he would finally be finished. I just had to lay there and be quiet; just melt into the sofa. Eventually he got off of me and went into the bathroom. When I heard the shower running, I'd take *that* chance to run to my bedroom. I'd climb into the bed, get under the covers and curl up. I couldn't let him hear me cry, that might set him off again. Santana had long since finished playing. All I could hear now was the shower. The baby was asleep in another room. There had been times when I had been holding the baby in my arms and *that* didn't stop him. This time I didn't have to think about protecting the baby while taking the blows.

My God, I must escape; but how?

It wasn't until twenty years later that I understood I had been raped; he had violated me. I also discovered that I didn't deserve it.

After what seemed like forever, he came into the bedroom and acted as if nothing had happened. He gathered up the clothes he wanted me to wash.

"Get a shower and get dressed; it time you learn how to do my laundry." he ordered.

What I remember next is learning about the virtues of the laundry booster, Boraxo.

***

The following day, Ray informed me that we were invited to a Gala.

"A gala?" I said puzzled. I couldn't imagine any sort of fancy party or ball in this little town. "Where?"

"Over in Old Baldy, Babe; at the Storeys' Ranch."

Old Baldy was where the real muckety-mucks lived. "But…what will I wear? I don't have a gown and I—"

Ray laughed. "We're not going to the Fontainebleau. This is a big shindig after a roundup. I'll show you what to wear."

As the day progressed, Ray had been dropping names like Vanderbilt, Firestone and Post; names you hear on the news or see in the paper.

He also made a point of warnng me, "Don't forget Gabbi, keep your mouth shut."

"What are you talking about? Keep my mouth shut about what?" I asked.

"You just keep your mouth shut. My business is nobody else's business."

I sort of frowned, turned around and went back to my closet. I prayed—literally—that I wouldn't make a fool of myself. I asked the Lord to please, please put the words in my mouth to get through this without embarrassing Ray.

Ray told me to wear my dingo boots, my hip hugging wrangler jeans, my form-fitting cowgirl snap up shirt and of course, the Stetson hat he had bought me.

"Hey Ray. Why don't I wear my Lucchese Boots?"

"That will be fine; that's a good idea." he said.

I got out my tan, Mad Dog, quill Luccheses'. He'd had them custom made in Italy.

I always wondered how he knew where to have custom clothing, jewelry and leather goods made in Italy. Someday, when I felt brave enough, I would ask that question.

My jeans fit so tight that I had to lie down on the bed and wriggle into them. Ray would have to zip them for me. He ran his eyes over me with that look; I knew we were going to arrive late to the Gala. But it was okay. *This* was real love.

When we were through, he said "Get out of here, you little hussy.", and smacked me on the behind.

I have to admit that I did feel sexy when we drove off to Old Baldy that afternoon. But one thing did terrify me. Ray warned me again as we turned into the Storeys' compound.

"Be careful what you say, Gabrielle. Keep your mouth shut about my business."

I thought to myself, *we are ranchers now, what do we have to hide?* My heart pounded.

As we pulled around the back of the Storeys' enormous house, I scanned the crowd of guests clustered around a table piled high with hors d'oeuvres. There must have been a hundred people. No problem with that; I figured I could disappear into the mob, maybe go unnoticed. Ray never stayed at my side. He always liked to "work the crowd".

What bothered me was that I seemed to be the youngest person there. A handful of the guests looked about thirty or so, like Raymond. But most were a lot older. I felt inadequate, out of place and completely lost. After Ray had a glass of champagne, he went off riding with some of the men. There I stood, not far from a long—very long—picnic table where women my mother's age were seated. They didn't look like Mothers' mahjong crowd though, more like Barbara Stanwyck types. Here I was on the set of Big Valley, the television show, with nothing to say and no script to follow.

I felt so intimidated. Even though they had on prairie skirts and cotton blouses, I could see by the quality of their clothes and jewelry—and the way they spoke—that they were women of influence in the world. I knew we wouldn't spend the afternoon talking about *Boraxo*!

Before Ray abandoned me, he introduced me to our hostess, Celia Storey. She came up to me, took my hand, and led me over to a small group of women clustered around the end of the table. "Gabbi," she said, "please join us. I want you to meet some friends of George and mine." The names she rattled off floored me. I don't recall all of them and probably shouldn't divulge them anyway, but hearing them resulted in my mouth hanging open. I managed some smiles and the occasional, "Hello, so nice to meet you."

As a child, I learned that children were to be seen and not heard. Since I was feeling very much like a child, this seemed an appropriate time to bring that little rule into play.

I sat and listened as they talked about their family businesses, about their charity work and the various boards they sat on.

Mrs. So-and-So said, "Well, circulation is up at two of our newspapers."

The stunning woman beside her smiled. "How wonderful, Emily, we'll run a few extra ads for the bank with you this month. I'll have Ben call Thomas."

Mrs. Storey chimed in. "I really shouldn't be sharing this girls, but George is hinting about a merger with Mountain Air. Can you imagine? Doing business with Howard Hughes would be a nightmare!"

I was mesmerized by Mrs. Storey's necklace and complimented her on it when there was a lull in their conversation. "Oh, thank you, darling." she said. "George bought this for me. It's King Manasseh turquoise. He got it at Boyer's."

"Boyer's?"

"Oh, my dear, don't you know about Boyer's?" Before I could respond, she went on, excited. "Well, we will just have to go on a hunt! We'll make a day of it. We'll do lunch with Dick and Skippy Boyer at one of the old Jackson Hole hotels. I'll have them put some pieces aside for you—something appropriate for your age. Turquoise will be perfect for you; lovely with your eyes."

Before we could go any further with plans, one of the women raised her hand and pointed off in the distance and said, "The boys are coming." They came riding in on horseback, in a cloud of dust.

Soon the head cook, fittingly called Cookie, rang the triangle and we all gathered around the cook fire. He had the biggest iron skillet I'd ever seen and he was frying up a mound of "chicken livers". Everyone oohed and aahed, but me; I never really cared for liver of any kind.

"Honey, I hope I don't have to eat much of that liver." I whispered to Ray. He looked down at me with a loving smile. It was a smile I didn't get to see much anymore, so I held on to it.

"That's not liver, Gabbi. Those are prairie oysters."

"But I don't eat oysters." I whined . "That's the one seafood I don't like."

He grabbed me, held me tight and looked down at me. I knew he wasn't going to hit me; I could see the love in his eyes.

"Baby," he said, "they're prairie oysters, not seafood. The whole purpose of this party is to castrate all the little male calves and cook up their testicles. Out here this is considered quite the delicacy."

As much as I wanted to please Ray, I knew I couldn't eat calf testicles and I guess my face said that. I began to stammer.

Ray cut me off, chuckling. "Don't worry, Pet, you're not expected to eat the oysters. How about if I get you some cold lobster salad?"

"Oh, would you? Please?"

I had begun enjoying listening to the women, so I sat back down at the picnic table. I noticed that they all had one oyster each on their plate. I could see that sometime in my future, I would have to be a bit more adventurous with my culinary explorations.

There was entertainment provided by a cowboy band, but Raymond came over and excused us. He took my hand, we mounted horses and I followed him. I was absolutely surprised and delighted when we arrived at a huge bonfire with lots of people, more my age. Yee haw we are gonna have some fun now! There were cowboys and their wives or girlfriends. Some were playing guitars, tambourines, harmonicas, banjos and even kazoos. We all laughed and sang old cowboy songs, just like Roy Rogers, Dale Evans and Gene Autry.

As the embers crackled, popped and exploded, I look up and watched them travel to meet the twinkling stars in the broad expanse of a Wyoming night sky.

Despite the blackened teeth and the spitting of chaw, despite the strong body odor of these hard working cowboys, this night would remain one of my favorite Wyoming adventures.

At about eleven p.m., the cowboys started talking about how early they had to get up in the morning for their cowboy chores. Just like that, the party was over. We rode back to the main house and thanked our hosts and drove off.

I couldn't help wondering about Ray. Will he be my passionate lover? Or will something happen before we get home and he'll transform into the monster. Would I say that one thing that will make him so angry that he would kill me?

***

The lines of communication were still open in those days with my mother. We talked frequently by phone.

"Gabbi, are you and Raymond married?" My mother would probe.

Why couldn't she just rejoice in hearing from me? This probing question always led to silence on the line. Shouldn't the most important questions be how are the babies? How is your health? Are you happy?

"Gabbi for God sake, spare us the shame and answer this question. This one time please say 'Yes Mother, we are married'."

It signaled that our telephone visit was over. It signaled to me that this woman that I loved more than anything else in the world, until I became a Mommy, really only cared about how her friends and the world perceived her daughter; her precious, beautiful, intelligent daughter. I was the daughter who should have married the family friend's son; now a famous surgeon. The daughter who modeled, who sang, in whom they felt such great pride and who had painfully broken their hearts. Until Raymond, we were as close as if the umbilical cord had never been severed.

"I love you Mommy, gotta go. Tell Dad I said hi. I'll call you again when I can. Bye Mom." I said.

I'd hang up the phone with the painful emotions of knowing I was no longer connected as I had once been. In every phone call I was reminded what they thought. I was unmarried; a slut; and my children were bastards. *They called my sons bastards.*

***

Ray came from a staunch catholic upbringing;
he believed repentance was his ticket to heaven. After
one of his "dirty deeds", he would bring some
extravagant gift, like a chinchilla coat, or a piece of
exquisite jewelry.

I guess I was learning how to use his need for
repentance to my advantage.

"Ray, my brother is to be married in a week.
You said we could talk about me going home for the
wedding."

Mr. Hyde had been around much more often
lately. I was becoming far too familiar with him. A trip
back east could be my way out, at least for a while.

"Gabbi," he said brusquely. "Here are your
tickets to New Jersey. A change of scenery will do you
good."

"You don't need me here then?"

"I'll eat out in the bunkhouse with the boys."

"You hate that fried stuff Sammy makes."

He rolled his eyes and answered me like I was a
pain-in-the-ass child. "Pack warm clothes, it'll be
snowing in Jersey."

For a brief second I thought he had morphed into a dragon, smoke coming from his nostrils. I sensed he was exerting great control by not "flaming" me.

***

My parents were immediately smitten with Sean. There was a brand new toy box filled with stuffed animals and toys, the cupboards filled with enough baby food to last a month.

I could sense the tension between my parents and me. I wondered if they'd risk ruining this opportunity to love their grandbaby and babysit with him by asking the dreaded question.

Gabbi, are you married?

I called my best friend from high school, Nadine, to come over so we could go out together and shop for wedding outfits. The glee in my mother's eyes was obvious, at the prospect of being alone with her grandbaby.

***

Nadine and I grew up together. On weekends, in our pajamas, we'd toddle over to one or the others houses before the rest of the family was awake. We'd gather up shoe boxes full of our paper dolls and immerse ourselves in our fantasy grown-up world; a mama doll, daddy doll and baby dolls; the perfect family.

I can remember vividly and miss so much our teen years, just entering puberty. We were no longer entertained by our paper dolls. We replaced hurrying over to each other's homes in the early morning with lengthy visits on the telephone. We'd whisper and giggle about the handsome boys in school who were now playing with us in their attempt to act out the hormonal urges, new to them. There was always lots of giggling and blushing and much speculation about who might kiss us first and would that mean that we'd lost our virginity. Oh, to be that naive again.

"I feel so *free!*" I yelled over the wind as we headed out in Nadine's new Pontiac convertible. "It's great to see you, Nadine. I don't have one girlfriend in Saratoga."

"How come, Gabbi?" she asked.

"We live out in the middle of nowhere, Nadine, and Ray…well it's just hard to meet people in a little one-horse town like that." I wished I could tell her that as long as I was with Ray, I would never have friends of my own, or a life of my own.

***

"Mother, I really need some girl time with Nadine." I told her of our plans to go to the Poconos for a few nights. Regardless of the relationship between my parents and me, there would be nothing I would do to keep them from their grandchildren.

"Perfect!" she exclaimed. "After the wedding you girls go have some fun and I'll have some quality time with my grandson."

"Oh mother…" I said as I hugged her neck. "I really need this. I love you."

As we stood looking into each other's eyes, I sensed *that* lingering question. And I think she sensed that I needed to avoid it.

"But Mother remember," I said with a warning tone, "if Ray calls, do not tell him where I am."

"What do you mean? Why should I lie?"

I placed my pointer finger gently over her lips with a shhhhh. "Mother just don't ask. Please do as I say." I instructed.

"Gabbi, I don't like to lie." she said as she let out a sigh "This whole thing doesn't make sense to me. Okay, you go with Nadine and I'll keep the baby safe."

***

Nadine and I arrived in the Poconos and rented a nice room at Strickland's Mountain Inn. My heart was racing; this was my first time away from Ray. I felt confused. Was I a young woman on a singles vacation with a friend, looking to meet people and party, or a wife and mother just getting some much needed time away from my responsibilities?

"The idea is to have fun, Gabbi," Nadine said. "That's all we have to do for the next few days. Don't over analyze it."

We dressed up and put on pancake makeup for our first night on the town. I had mentioned to the bell captain that I was an entertainer and asked where we could catch the best shows.

"Mountain Air Lodge." he said, without hesitation. "The Crystal Room. I don't know who's headlining tonight, but the house band is excellent! Two pretty girls like you will have a ball. The music's great and you can dance all night."

"That sounds perfect!" I said excitedly.

"If you'd like, I will call ahead and tell my maître d' friend to get you a great table. Heck, he'll probably introduce you to the fellas in the band."

"Oh, wow!" Nadine said.

***

The hairs on the back of my neck stood up while waiting for a cab. I had this eerie feeling that Raymond was having us watched. *"Shake it off; I'm here to have a good time. I deserve this."*

We took the cab the short distance up the mountain to the huge resort. As we walked down a long hallway, adrenaline raced through me. I hadn't realized how much I missed this life—the sounds of live music, the chatter of the crowd, bustling waiters anxious to please their customers.

As we entered the huge ballroom, complete with crystal chandeliers, opulent carpets and wallpaper, the maître d' approached us.

"Hello, I'm Gabbi."

"Oh…uh, Joe didn't tell me to expect two young *beauties!*" He beamed and extended his arm in a follow me gesture. He led us to an empty table. "Your waiter will be right here to take your drink order."

"Great!" I said. I now turned my attention to the bandstand. There were seven men in the group. The sax man was singing and if I closed my eyes, I'd have thought Billy Eckstine was onstage. "Who is that singing?" I asked the maître d."

"That's Wayne Reynolds. He's a brilliant sax man; plays baritone, tenor and soprano. What do you think of his voice?"

I was too entranced with the bearded crooner to answer. And I was feeling guilty, I guess, because I was not thinking—or feeling—the way a married woman should.

Nadine was watching me, giggling. I think there was a sparkle in my eyes that she recognized from the old days. Oh, how could I ever explain to her what it was like for me tonight? I had been living in terror, like a caged bird, so this night wasn't just a night out for me. I was like a woman in prison, getting a life-saving pardon.

When their first set was finished, the guys made their way to the table, stopping to shake hands with guests along the way. Finally, here he was. I wasn't paying attention to the others; as I was introduced, I politely shook hands, but I barely took my eyes off of Wayne.

He pulled the chair out next to me, sat down, and asked what I wanted to drink. I ordered an apricot sour; he ordered a 7 & 7 for himself, a double.

Unlike most front men, Wayne didn't seem all caught up in himself. He wanted to learn about me. Where did I live? Was I gigging now? How long would I be staying? I was so flattered. I hadn't had this kind of attention in…well, it felt like forever.

I told him I was living in a tiny town in Wyoming, was not happy and not singing anywhere. "We're just here for a few days." I said.

Talking was difficult as the headliner was performing and his backup band had amped up the volume.

"Would you like to go for a walk and see a little more of Mt. Airy?" Wayne asked.

I guess he could read my hesitation; he turned to Nadine, who was engrossed in a conversation with Gary, another band member. "Hey, Gary, let's take the girls and show them around. We don't go back on for fifty minutes."

Before we left the smoke-filled ballroom, Wayne ordered another double to take along.

***

It was a crisp, cool evening in the mountains. Wayne took us to a small intimate lounge to escape the boisterous crowd. Except for a few other couples, the main attraction in this room was a roaring fire in a rustic old stone fireplace. There was also a cozy crescent shaped, upholstered sofa with tufted back and two small tables. As we slid in, Nadine cozied up to Gary, and Wayne guided me so that we were sitting shoulder to shoulder.

The fellas told us they had a log cabin in Mt. Pocono, very nearby. They had been with The King's Band for nearly ten years. They loved the life up here. Wayne's younger brother owned and operated a hardware store in Phillipsburg, which he called "P-burg".

Soon it was time for them to do their next set and this magical time came to an end.

***

"Nadine, oh my goodness, Wayne is so nice; he seems so easygoing and caring. What about Gary?"

"Did you see his eyes? Dark blue. It seemed like they were undressing me as we sat talking!" She turned red, as she often did when having such thoughts.

"Gabbi, Gary wants us to stay with them. He said they have a big guest room with its own bath. I told him we don't even know them. But, he said they're well-known around here and would never pull anything. He promised they'd be gentlemen."

"Gosh, I don't know Nadine. I--"

"They want to show us around, and it'd save us a lot of money."

Hmm, I thought, that's something to think about. Plus, I had unloaded all my woes on Wayne. I was surprised that I so easily confided in a perfect stranger.

I hemmed and hawed and then said I'd stay— but only if I could call my mother and make sure Sean was all right and she wouldn't mind if we stayed a few extra days. I also wanted to see if Ray had called. The idea of him crashing in on our lively getaway gave me chills; I knew what he'd do to Wayne and Gary if he found us with them.

Gary and Wayne planned each day for us. They slept till around 11 a.m., giving us time to sleep in and then do our primping before they woke up. Gary cooked dinner for us several nights, as Wayne played and sang at our request. I remember at one point taking in a deep breath, sighing and thinking: This is what my life should feel like—safe.

As the week progressed, I shared with Wayne more about my life with Ray, how I felt in danger most of the time and had no way out.

"Gabbi," he said, looking straight into my eyes, "here's our phone number. Keep this piece of paper; don't lose it. I want to help you. I'm sure you can get a job singing up here. You and the baby can live with Gary and me until you get on your feet. I've already spoken to Gary, he rushed on with the plan in such a way as to prevent me having time to say no, and he agrees with me; you need to get out of there!"

"But you don't understand. He doesn't give me money of my own. I can never leave him!" I started to cry softly, and he tenderly took my hand in his.

"Gabbi," he said, "all you have to do is call me; day or night. I'll get you here."

***

Chapter Ten

On the flight home from New Jersey, my mind was swimming. My Pollyanna-self believed that when we moved to Wyoming, the skeletons in his closet would stay behind. The move to Wyoming had a purpose; that's what he told me. No tracks; none of his gambling friends or, to me, the deviants that he went with on disappearing junkets. A fresh start, just the three of us; I knew that once we got settled in Wyoming, he would let me bring Caleb out to us. But so far he's said no every time I broached the subject.

The mere thought of a fresh start and I got excited. Such a deep love for him still ran through my veins. Maybe it was possible to save our little family! Oh, was it all a fantasy?

With Wayne, it was so different, such a new experience. Truthfully with Wayne I didn't experience the tingles of excitement I always felt around Ray. On the other hand, there was no fear factor with Wayne. I felt totally safe with him.

Just the thought of seeing Ray at the airport in Wyoming caused mixed feelings within me; fear, because I didn't know what kind of mood he would be in and excitement about being in his arms again. I was in such conflict.

Looking back on it, I was pathetic. The moment I saw Raymond at the gate my heart leaped. He looked so handsome in his tight jeans and cowboy shirt. And he seemed absolutely overjoyed to see me— and Sean. He grabbed Sean from me and lifted him high in the air. The baby drooled right onto Ray's face. Ray was disgusted by this and quickly handed the baby back to me.

"Come on Baby, let's get your bag and head on home. I've got some surprises for you." he said while wiping baby spit from his face.

On the drive home, I could tell he was just busting to show me all he'd done while I was gone. We gave the baby a bottle and put him to bed.

Turning to me Ray said, "Come on Baby, I've been to Cheyenne." He picked me up in his arms, threw open the bedroom door and whispered in my ear, "Merry Christmas Baby, I sure missed you."

He laid me down on the chaise; spun around and said "I've been doing a little shopping while you were gone." There were boxes upon boxes. I recognized the names of the very expensive boutiques where he had bought me a whole new wardrobe. I burst into tears. I'd thought he had packed me off to my parents to get rid of me. But now, I could see he really loved me and had missed me.

"What's wrong?" he asked, impatient.

"Nothing Honey! Nothing's wrong. These are happy tears! I love everything you picked out."

With that he grabbed my arm pulled me up off the chaise and threw me on the bed amidst the jumble of clothes and bags and wrapping paper. We made love until the sun went down.

"Are you hungry Baby? Do you want to get up and shower and have something to eat?" he whispered to me.

"No, I'm too high on love to be hungry for anything; except more of you." I said as I pulled him back on top of me.

***

The next morning the Wyoming sky couldn't have been a more unique shade. As I sat sipping my coffee, I gazed up into the Lapis Lazuli deep blue. Persian legend says that the heavens owed their blue color to a massive slab of Lapis upon which the earth rested. Lapis Lazuli was believed to be a sacred stone, buried with the dead to protect and guide them in the afterlife.

Ray had been up early, made the coffee and gone out. He left me a note on the kitchen table. *Baby, I'm having 8 men in tonight for dinner. Not entertaining, just a meeting. See Mrs. Wyatt for what you need. Love you.*

Oh my God! Here we go. I know I can do this dinner party, but I sure would have appreciated a little more notice. Yep. I'd be in the afterlife if I didn't get it together, go to Mrs. Wyatt and make this night a spectacular one for Ray and his buddies.

The dinner party was a huge success. I would take a dozen roses to Mrs. Wyatt, the butcher's wife, tomorrow. She deserved the accolades.

"Delicious dinner Mrs. Fortier." chanted several of the guests.

"Ray, you've got a real keeper here!" sneered another.

I smiled and blushed.

"Gabbi, we'll take coffee out on the veranda." Ray said, as his dinner guests filed out of the formal dining room.

"I'll get the Courvoisier and demitasse glasses, you get the coffee." He turned and gave me a yummy wink!

Pitter-patter went my heart!

"Oh, bring out the humidor as well, Baby."

Ray had arranged for some of the cowboys' wives to serve and take care of the kitchen chores; I couldn't have been more relieved. I decided to take the baby for a stroll on the lawn. It was getting dark; I'd have to use the mosquito netting around his carriage. Wyoming mosquitoes seemed as large as hummingbirds. I slathered us with fragrant body oil that worked fine as a repellant. We headed out for some fresh air before Sean's bedtime.

"Listen man, I don't want any mess ups on this one." The sounds of a male voice wafted over to where we were sitting in the yard, hidden by a stand of evergreens.

"I mean it now! Last time I had a lot of cleaning up and explaining to do with the authorities. We hadn't filed a flight plan and they were not happy about that night flight. You're all lucky I think fast on my feet. What if they had wanted to inspect the Cessna and found those bricks? I'm not doing time alone; I'll guarantee that!"

The next voice, I recognized. "Look, Mac, calm down. It's nothing! Everything is cool. Nothing came down on you. I'll personally see that the next trip is flawless." *That* was Ray.

What now? What night flight? Who's plane? Where did it come from; where did it go? Bricks? I knew what bricks were, and they weren't the type used in house building. I broke into a shivering sweat. Somehow I managed to move on, push Sean, who was now fast asleep, around the back of the house and out to the barn. I stood there shaking, listening to the soft whinnies of the horses in their stalls. The scent of the hay, sawdust and sweetness of molasses covered oats kept me in the moment. I was looking at the black dome of sky overhead—just filled with thick bushy clouds that I wished could blanket me for protection. There were no stars tonight.

Thank you Jesus for knowing which prayers to answer; I am beginning to understand why Caleb isn't here with me.

I waited until all the men pulled out in the trucks and limos. Once I was sure they were gone, I put Sean to bed and headed to my tropical paradise, Nirvana. I *had* to get away from the realities of drugs and mysterious plane trips.

***

Ray was on a high that night after the dinner; he praised the job I'd done on the meal. In bed, I froze when he pulled my nightgown up, began kissing my neck and pressing himself against me. Instead of melting as I usually did whenever he touched me, I held my breath. I could feel every muscle in my body tensing. I lay there and gritted my teeth, waiting for him to rolled off of me. I just wanted it over. I wanted to lie there and sort out my thoughts, planning what to do.

Confronting him about what I'd overheard would only make him furious, and I didn't want to be beaten. I thought about calling Aunt Esther. I thought about calling my mother. How pathetic. How could they help me sort out the mess I'd made of my life? I was so ashamed. I was disgusted with myself. I'd never felt so alone in my life. Never!

At some point in the middle of the night, after praying and praying for answers, I suddenly saw everything clearly. Ray and I came from totally different worlds. He wanted to make lots of money. He wanted to live the high life; doing it any way he could, legal or illegal.

He expected too much from me. He expected a gourmet cook, a model mother, a sex kitten, a trophy wife. My expectation for our future was a life modeled after the Ozzie and Harriet TV show. How could I ever have believed harmony could exist between those two worlds? I had my moment of clarity.

As the sun came up, I felt that God had given me a plan. Wayne!

***

The population of Saratoga, Wyoming, was three hundred and twenty six. There was a chance someone would spot me on the pay phone. I pictured someone calling Ray. "I saw your wife on the pay phone down at Nichols' Drugs. Is your phone out of order?"

I had an answer ready for Ray if such a thing did happen. "I wanted to call my mother and our party-line was busy all day."

From the pay phone, I gave Wayne a fast, sketchy explanation of what was going on. He said if I could get to the airport in Denver, the closest commercial airport to me, he'd have a ticket to Pennsylvania waiting. I really don't remember hanging up the phone. As I leaned against the glass wall of the phone booth, I was in a full blown state of panic; sweating, shaking, heart racing, mind spinning.

I took a deep breath and walked into the kitchen, Ray was having his coffee and reading the local Cheyenne paper.

"Mother's visiting an old friend in Denver and wants me to bring Sean for a few days," I said leaning down to kiss him. "I told her there was no way."

"Why?" Ray said, not even looking up from the paper. "Why would you tell her that?"

"Well, you're busy with the ranch, and—"

"You just tell me when you want to go and I'll have Al fly you over in his Cessna."

As he folded up his newspaper and set it next to the coffee cup, he looked at me, his expression remained the same. I looked at him, trying to read his mind through his icy cold blue eyes. But that would never happen. His mercurial ways never offered a hint of what was coming.

"Could Al take me tomorrow? Mother is dying to show Sean off to her friend."

***

For the next twenty-four hours, I felt like I was in the Twilight Zone, a kind of surreal dream world. I packed a diaper bag and shoulder bag with enough clothes for a few days. If I took more, Ray might get suspicious.

Again, I was awake most of the night praying. Please let the ticket be waiting for me in Denver. Please let me touch down at the Allentown, Bethlehem, Easton airport and find Wayne waiting for me.

If Wayne wasn't there to meet me, I wouldn't know what to do. I would have no money either, unless Ray was feeling generous and sent me off with some shopping money.

***

Everything went off without a hitch. Ray drove me to a small private airport south of Saratoga to meet Al. Al deposited me in Denver and apologized for not being able to wait and see if I connected with my mother. "If there is any problem, just call and I'll have someone back here with another plane." he said.

My ticket *was* waiting for me and the plane took off on time.

Sean was excited as they pinned "wings" on his shirt. We were seated at a bulkhead so we'd have lots of room. I wanted to sit there and cry with relief as we lifted off. "Goodbye Wyoming." I said under my breath, with mixed emotions.

I couldn't breathe freely yet. Not until I was safe…safe in Pennsylvania with a new job, a new place to live, maybe even a new identity. And free! Free from the prison I'd been living in since the day I met Raymond Reginald Fortier.

Chapter Eleven

The Pocono Mountains of Pennsylvania were beautiful and the people friendly and helpful. I was in my early twenties, on a journey that demanded I reinvent, not only my life, but who I was.

Wayne's parting words when I left him were, "If you ever need me, all you have to do is call."

And, I did.

***

Wayne *was* there at two o'clock in the morning. He wasn't a big man; about five foot ten inches and maybe 170 pounds. He was well dressed and wore tortoise shell glasses, which complimented his salt and pepper colored hair and goatee. When I got off the airplane, he had tears in his eyes and roses in his arms; ready to rescue us. I told Wayne that one of the first things I had to do was figure out how to let my mother know that I was safe *and* not in Wyoming. He immediately suggested that I call mother once a week; and get a post office box in Stroudsburg for correspondence. Mother had to understand that for her safety, Sean's and mine, this is how it would have to be.

We pulled up to his cabin and there on the front porch was Wayne's band mate, roommate and friend, Gary. Wayne handed him the baby, as we unloaded the car. As I entered the cabin, it was warm and welcoming. There was a fire in the fireplace and candles burning.

Gary asked, "Does the baby need a bottle?"

I was so tired and bewildered that what he said to me didn't register. He took a bottle from the backpack and warmed it on the stove; then he took Sean over by the fireplace and cuddled and fed him.

I'd been in the cabin for about twenty minutes when Wayne said, "Gabbi, come here for a minute."

I followed him down a hallway. "Wayne, if you have a big dresser drawer we could pull it out and put a blanket in it for Sean and put it by my bed."

Wayne didn't answer; he just opened a door at the end of the hall.

It took my eyes a few seconds to adjust. The little room was aglow with candle light. To my right, along one wall was a baby crib with bumpers and a circus mobile. To my left were a rocking chair, a low bookcase with a radio playing soft music and a twin bed for me. I couldn't believe it. Wayne had not only rescued us but looked ahead to the needs of a young mother with no money and nowhere else to turn. Here I was surrounded by people with warm hearts and caring souls, ready to provide for our every need.

I ran over to him and hugged him. "It's beautiful! It's perfect!" I cried.

***

Wayne and Gary were very protective of Sean and me. I told them that it was very important to me to find a job and a place of my own, as soon as possible. They helped me in every way imaginable. During the day, they took me to job interviews and auditioning with bands.

Because they were with the most popular band in the Pocono's in those days, Wayne and Gary had to work most nights, so they slept late in the morning. Wayne provided me a set of keys to his car. It was a Swiss-made Volvo, burgundy—not brand new, but in tiptop condition and with all the bells and whistles. The first time I got in it, I shyly told Wayne that my bum was getting warm. He laughed and said the seats are heated, "very necessary in these cold mountains".

In the early morning hours, while the guys were sleeping, Sean and I would slip out and explore. We'd drive along those mountain roads, taking our time. Sometimes we got lost, but some friendly local person always turned up at just the right time to give us directions to town. More angels watching over me, I figured.

I often stopped in the little country stores, and we made friends with the owners and people behind the counters right away. Having Sean was a great icebreaker. Everyone wanted to pat his little blond head and give him a toy, a cookie or some other goodie.

One day we stumbled upon a great little diner that made the best grilled ham and cheese sandwiches I'd ever tasted, and they had a highchair for Sean. The next time we went into the diner, the waitress brought him crayons and a coloring book as well. We quickly became friends with the owners, Flo and Eddie. They had moved from Chicago twenty years earlier with their life savings and bought the diner.

Owning a diner was their lifelong dream. They did all the ordering, cooking, cleaning and bookkeeping. They even waited tables to help their only waitress, Margie. I had never experienced a public establishment before where people wanted to know their customers' names, what they did, and how their families were doing.

"How you feelin' today?"

"How are the kids?"

"Did you fix that snowplow, George?"

This was so different to me coming from busy cities where no one cared who you were. Growing up and going out to eat with my parents you just ordered, ate, paid and left. Here, the customers were like family.

I soon learned that Flo and Eddie had been unable to have children; that explained why they were so warm to Sean. In the few weeks I stayed with Wayne and Gary, Flo became Sean's fairy Godmother; especially when she kept him overnight, so I could sleep in. The minute she saw us driving into the parking lot, she'd start whipping up little silver dollar-size pancakes. Sean loved that he could pick them up with his fingers and eat them.

"Flo, you're going to make him fat!" I teased.

"Fat is happy, honey." she said. She was a bit on the chubby side. She wore her curly gray hair pulled back and held in place with a hair net. Her little Ben Franklin glasses teetered on the edge of her nose and that made me nervous. It looked like they were ready to slide off and into someone's food. But when she looked at her customers, it was obvious that feeding people was her passion.

In the afternoons, Gary and Wayne took me to job interviews. They were so cute pacing around outside while Sean toddled around picking up sticks and rocks. After ten appointments in a five-day period, I was running out of options. I'd gone through almost everything in the want ads. I felt sick at heart—and terrified. If I couldn't get a job, I might crumble and go back to Ray.

"Look, Wayne," I said after being turned down for a clerk-typist position at an insurance company. "This may be my only option." I pointed to an ad for a hostess at Strickland's Mountain Inn.

"Stricklands!" Gary said. "Why didn't I think of that? Ann Davis is a doll. She's the owner. She'll have an idea."

"Yea," Wayne chimed in. "She knows everybody in town and everything that's going on."

The following Monday, during my interview with Ann, she said the boys had told her, I was a singer. "Gabbi, we have a house band, 'Frankie and his swing band'. Their singer has left the band due to pregnancy. How would you like the opportunity to audition?"

It was all I could do to stay seated and not jump up and down, squealing. "You're kidding! I'll do it." Instead, in the magic of the moment, I looked up and gave a little wink to my guardian angel and calmly answered, "Yes, Ann, I'd be delighted."

Ann explained, my audition would be the next day at two o'clock. If all went well, she'd have a six month contract ready for me to sign. Ann's demeanor was all business; I sensed that she was actually a very warm woman. I hoped I was right; I really needed this job. The audition went better than I could have hoped for. I got the gig!

I was so relieved that I would soon have a regular paycheck coming in and would be able to pay Wayne back for all that he'd provided. He insisted it was not necessary.

***

After landing the job, I was excited about finding an apartment or cottage for Sean and me. I was ready for my own little nest. This made Wayne and Gary sad. They tried so hard to convince me to stay with them. Wayne reminded me that I didn't have a car, didn't have money yet, and didn't know my way around the mountains. Gary said I was way too young to live alone.

One Sunday morning, when I knew that Wayne and Gary didn't have a gig that night, I presented them with a newspaper. I had circled places for rent. Gary got Sean all bundled up in his snowsuit. He'd proudly bought it at the big department store in Stroudsburg.

Bundled up and loaded into the Volvo, newspaper in hand, we all headed out. Excitement was raging in my veins; freedom in my mind and hope in my heart. Neither Wayne nor Gary could find a smile. This outing to them meant they were losing us.

The first place that I had circled in the paper said, Cordial Cottages! Seven private cottages located on 20 acres in Swiftwater, Penn., Hwy. 611.

That was where I wanted to go first. After reading the description, Wayne said he had a pretty good idea where it was. He said he'd passed it a while back on the way to a ski lodge gig out on Shawnee Mountain.

"There it is!" I shouted out excitedly, waking Sean. I'd seen the rough-hewn wooden sign that said "Welcome to Cordial Cottages". Wayne made a right turn onto the only road that led in or out; it went straight down! Calling it a road was an exaggeration. It was a dirt path, with deep holes from years of abuse by snow, ice and heavy automobiles. It really seemed more appropriate for deer and bears and mountain lions. The cottages were spread far enough apart that one could not be seen from the other. The dense woods gave each cottage the feeling that it stood alone in the midst of a wooded glen.

We passed one cottage and another and another. It felt like I had been magically inserted into the childhood fairytale Hansel and Gretel. I even thought it would be a good idea to sprinkle stones or crusts of bread as I traveled deeper into these woods, so as to find my way back out again.

And then to justify my fantasy as real, we came upon the most delicious looking cottage of all. It looked just like the gingerbread house I'd made for the baby at Christmas. The chimney was red brick and even though the exterior of the building was made of logs with cream colored mortar, that isn't how I saw it. I saw graham cracker walls, studded with jewel colored gum drops. Their crystalline sugar coatings sparkling brilliantly as the sun caught them.

The front door was a split Dutch door, but I saw it as a solid chocolate door with a red candied apple for a door knob. And no one would be able to convince me that I wasn't seeing exactly that! The windows were huge. They were set in with cozy green colored shutters that were old and worn.

"Gabbi, come on dear the realtor is waiting for you in here."

Oh, don't do this to me; don't make me leave this fantasy. It feels so familiar. I thought. But I shook it off and entered back into reality and stepped up onto the front porch. Gary stayed in the car with Sean. Wayne and I went in for the tour.

As I crossed the threshold into the cottage I noticed the floors throughout were hardwood, a light oak. I stood long enough to look at the boards and got the sense that there had been other young mothers, perhaps making their journey into life on these same floors. In some areas the patina had darkened over time. Yet in the high traffic areas the wood was worn smooth. I imagined young children with their toys running in and out of their bedrooms and back into the living room. That's what I wanted for my son and me, memories. So far the aura in this candy crusted cottage was nurturing and welcoming. On the right was a small but efficient kitchen, with a three-burner stove and little bitty oven. There was a split door Frigidaire with just enough room for ice cream. After all, what mommy wouldn't have ice cream in the freezer? There were two metal ice trays with that pull up handle to release the ice cubes. It struck me that these could become my very own ice trays. Mine! They belonged to me! It would be up to me to fill them and use them and fill them again, *or not!* There would be no one to holler at me,

"Gabbi did you fill those ice trays?"

The drop-leaf chrome kitchen table was a two-seater. The Frigidaire was pink and matched the vinyl top of the table and chairs. Opposite the kitchen was the living room. The realtor pointed down the hall, saying the first door on the right was one bedroom and the other room down the hall was the master bedroom. He stayed there as I proceeded to the first bedroom. I stood in the room that was to be Sean's and held back the tears. I wanted to cry and scream out loud, *this* is mine! *This* will be my baby's room.

I can decorate it with Little Black Sambo, Br'er Rabbit and Br'er Fox. I can surround him with the stories that so nurtured me as a little girl at Aunt Esther's.

The cottage had one bathroom. There was a front and back porch.

"Can I have it right now? Can we move in today?" I asked the realtor.

Wayne looked at the realtor with concern and said to me, "But Gabbi, you have six other places circled to look at."

"Oh no, I don't have to look at anything else, this is going to be our home." I said.

The realtor handed me the key, after I signed the lease. I turned to the boys and said, "I want to move in this Wednesday."

"But Gabbi?" Wayne said.

"I know, it's fast. But I want to be settled before I start my new gig on Friday. And, I have to shop for at least one gown, to hold me over until I get my first paycheck."

Wayne and Gary had already said they would take care of the realtor. I'd pay them back, as I could. I hugged Wayne, kissed his cheek and we went back to start packing.

"I even love the furniture." I babbled on the way back to Wayne's. "In my whole life I've never seen furniture like that. It's not Florida or Wyoming furniture, I guess it's Pennsylvania furniture!"

Wayne interrupted my excited chattering, "It's called Pennsylvania Dutch."

There were two huge upholstered overstuffed chairs in a needlepoint tapestry fabric. Their well-worn cushions sunk down two or three inches; as though saying *you will be so comfortable here*. There were two wooden ottomans and a long green sofa. The fabric was so rough I would have to cover it with a soft blanket. An old oval braided rug covered the hardwood; perfect for Sean and his Lincoln Logs. The most exciting element in the room was a wood burning fireplace. Nothing in this room matched; not the textures, the colors, or the fabrics. In my mind, it was all brilliant and perfect. The huge bay window would let in the warmth of the sun and keep out the cold and the snow. It was going to be mine. I'd found home. It was Kismet!

***

My little cottage, on moving day, was like a train station. People were coming and going; bringing food, homemade breads, jams and jellies. Gary brought his bass guitar. Soon the trumpet player, the drummer and guitar player, who were all now my neighbors, started to jam, right there in my living room!

I couldn't help wondering if this was what my life was going to be. *This* would be the paradise.

Harry, the trumpet player was a portly fellow with thinning brown hair; calm and peaceful by nature. He was tall enough that I had to stand on tip toes to hug his neck.

Daniel, the guitar player was a shy fellow. I remember him sitting on the edge of the ottoman, strumming his ax; that's what musicians called guitars. I was so impressed with his acoustic Martin, one of the finest handmade guitars.

Shane, the drummer, was sitting at the kitchen table, doing paradiddles with his hickory Vic Firth sticks.

Each of the players had brought his girlfriend or wife and they were playing with Sean; he was always happy with the attention.

In one corner of the living room, resting on a stand was Wayne's baritone sax. When had he brought that over? It struck me as odd. This was my place. He wasn't moving in. Oh, I guess he knew everyone would bring their instruments and have a jam. I picked it up, handed it to him and beamed with pride while waiting for him to strap it onto his lariat, moisten his reed and join the jam. Before long it sounded like I had Billy Eckstine and his band singing and playing *Blues in the Night*, right here, in *my* living room.

As things were winding down, Wayne went out the front door, and returned with two packages. I could see one was a bottle of champagne. Someone headed to the kitchen and gathered as many glasses as they could fine. Wayne popped open the bottle and poured as glass for everyone.

"Toast! Toast!" they all chanted, extending their glasses.

After the toast, I set my glass down; Wayne handed me the second package.

"Open it, open it Gabbi," one of the girls said.

"See what it is."

I took the gift from Wayne and held it close to my chest; I wanted to savor this moment.

I ripped the wrapping off. It was a wooden plaque about a foot long. Hand-carved on it were the words "Gabbi's Gingerbread House."

"Oh, Wayne, this is wonderful!" I said, my voice cracking with emotion. I went over and hugged his neck and turned to the others in the room. "Okay, I'm going to hang this right away, but then I'm gonna buy one more sign to put up next to it. That one will say 'Welcome, Friends'." Everybody cheered at that and clinked glasses again.

Joy such as this would weave in and out of my life. Permanency on any level would never be commonplace for me. To date, my life had been one train wreck after another; around which bend might this journey derail? I fought hard, wanting to see life through rose colored glasses. It was *that* credo that fired up the engines that kept this train rolling.

These new friends welcomed me into a very close and closed group. There was jamming, eating and laughing. I had little experience with this type of partying, but I noticed Wayne was consuming large quantities of alcohol and it wasn't even one o'clock in the afternoon. It did register in the back of my mind, *this* is not normal behavior.

Those were the days of sand candles and I had an abundance of them; all rainbow colors, strung from their jute hangers. As the first layer of colors were burning off and the hour getting late, this group of talented, caring, loving and protective new friends, started to leave and return to their own cottages. As the last person left and I closed the door, I was feeling a sense of family, togetherness, safety and brotherhood.

***

The gingerbread house was eerily quiet. I was in the middle of a forest with no phone and no car. I realized that I was totally alone for the first time in years. *I* was the adult.

The moon beamed off the crystalline snow outside my window and every moving shadow on the wall set off my imagination. The symphony coming from outside was that of every wild beast I could conjure up. I lay in my bed shivering, more from terror than cold. What kind of terrifying creatures were lurking out there? Whatever they were, I was sure that a big, furry, four legged monster would crash through the window and devour me.

Tossing and turning in time with my pounding heart, I finally threw off the comforter, got up and headed down the hall to Sean's cozy little room. I scooped him up and hurried back to my bed. It amazed me how often over the years, holding my sweet baby, provided me with a sense of courage.

As I lay there, watching the moon, I did what always brought me comfort and peace. I prayed; speaking softly to God, until I finally drifted off to sleep.

***

"Gabbi? Gabbi? It's Ann. Are you there?"

Unlocking the door--all three locks!—I remembered making plans with Ann the night before to go shopping for a car. "Ann! I'm so embarrassed, I overslept…I'm a mess…this place is a mess…I don't know what—"

"Yep. It is a mess!" she said laughing. She scanned the room for a second and then headed toward the kitchen. "I'll make the coffee," she called out. "Why don't you hop in the shower?" Ann was always dressed as if it were a day for shopping and fine dining, and this early morning hour was no exception.

As I enjoyed the soothing warm water and smelled the coffee, I breathed a sigh of relief. Ann was a tiny woman. She kept her hair cropped very short. Her delicate glasses rested on her aquiline nose. She reminded me of a frail, fragile little bird. But don't be fooled, for inside was a soaring eagle with the skills to master any business situation. Her focus and direction was exactly what I needed this morning.

With Ann's help I managed to clean up the wreckage of the day before, get the baby ready to take to the baby sitter and we were off.

Our mission was to find a good used car for me. This would be the first car I ever bought. I would choose it, test drive it, negotiate the price and I would drive it off the lot. I wanted to be frugal with the money Wayne loaned me; I was determined to pay him back every dime.

By the end of the day, I had a new best friend and big sister. *And* I drove home in my used, but new to me, Chevy Impala. It was a rich deep blue, with powder-blue cloth seats. I felt like I'd just been given the keys to a Rolls-Royce.

***

I made it safely up the mountain roads to my precious gingerbread house, in my "new" ride.

The next morning Ann called. In her usual perky manner she said, "Hey! Can you get Flo to take the baby for today and tonight?"

"Well", I stuttered, "I bet I can. Why?"

"All right, you be ready in two hours. I'll pick you up and we'll drop Sean off at Flo's and then we'll have a girl's day out."

"What? Why? What are...?"

"Just hang up and I'll be there in two hours. By the way, be dressed up!" and click, she was gone.

I had to scramble a bit, but I was ready.

Punctual as always, Ann arrived in her silver Mercedes. Sean and I climbed into the front seat and we were off.

"I must say, you clean up well." Ann chuckled.

"Thank you." I said, "I guess that means I pass inspection for our mystery day."

I kissed Sean goodbye, handed him to Flo and jumped back in the car; off we went.

"Ann, do you have kids? Are you married? Tell me about your life."

"We have a two hour drive into the city, so I'll tell you my story. Just remember that today, my dear, is all about you."

Ann shared her life with me. She was the mother of twin daughters, thirteen years old and one son, sixteen. They were typical rebellious teenagers.

"I keep all three of them busy working at the inn." she said. "That's about all I know to do. Keep a tight rein on 'em; wear 'em out."

She had divorced Michael Davis.

"When the kids leave the nest, I will go back to Strickland."

"Oh, so your maiden name is Strickland?"

"Yes, my dad bought the inn when I was a baby. It's all I've ever known."

"Did your father retire?"

"No honey, he died a few years ago. I was torn up over it, but I had to hang in there and run the business...which was a blessing in a way. Strickland's is the second largest honeymoon resort in the United States. It's a huge responsibility and I thrive on it. By the way, one day next week we will have another girl's day out, in the mountains closer to home."

I looked at her quizzically.

She added, "I'm going to take you out to one of our loveliest tea rooms for lunch. After that, you my friend, will start giving back."

"Giving back?" I wrinkled my brow; feeling absolutely confused.

She explained, "Blessings Gabbi. You are being blessed right now with help in all facets of your new life. One life lesson my father taught me at a young age, giving back! I volunteer at our local Women's Clinic. We need all the help we can get. A young mother like you can relate on a special level with the young gals that come in."

My heart was skipping beats, as she spoke. I had more friends now than I'd ever had in Wyoming. I was receiving help in ways I'd never imagined possible. How exciting, someone thought that I could make a difference in others' lives. I sat quietly trying to digest so many blessings. *See mother, I'm not the failure you think I am.*

Watching this petite and brilliant woman weave in and out of the Manhattan traffic, I decided I would aspire to be more like her. I was sitting next to a life mentor; *my* life mentor. I'd learn from Ann how to be a productive and independent single mother.

***

I'd been to Manhattan many times with my parents and brother. Ice skating in Rockefeller Center was a holiday must for our family.

"Okay now Gabbi." Ann said while winding up the public parking garage, looking for an open space, bringing me back from the then to the now. "We'll park here."

"Dare I ask where we're going?" We interlocked arms and like two school girls headed for the subway.

"First Gabbi, I'm taking you to one of the most exclusive, vintage women's clothing shops in the East Village. You'll need at least four gowns; a change for every set. With your body type, we want to get gowns that accentuate your tiny waist and 'those'." She said looking from my abundance to her flatness. "Oh well, such is life." she quirked.

After a subway ride and short walk, we stepped over the threshold into a showroom packed full of the most gorgeous vintage gowns I could ever have imagined. As I tried on gowns, I oohed and aahed. Choices were made, Ann paid, and informed the shop keeper that "we will be back to pick up the days finds after the matinee of Evita."

Out on the sidewalk and out of view of the shopkeeper, I took Ann's petite hands into mine, threw our arms up into the air and screamed "I feel like a movie star!"

"Well my dear, that's as it should be when performing at Strickland's."

She then added on in a lighter note, with a wink of her eye "Marilyn Monroe, that's all I can say. You look like a young Marilyn Monroe."

We'd worked up quite an appetite and slipped into a yellow cab for our next stop; Mama Leone's. We had one hour before the show. I ordered the Braciola and Ann had the Italian Wedding Soup followed by an espresso each and one cannoli, which we split. Having been spoiled by Zia's authentic Italian cooking I still gave high marks to our eating experience at the Manhattan landmark.

***

Much had been accomplished in the whirlwind of the past two weeks. Now, sitting in my cozy living room, I knew it was time to make two very important phone calls.

First, Miami to check on Caleb. Mame, his nurse and I had become very close. I explained to her that for reasons I could not share, I had left Ray and would be calling her on a weekly basis to check-in.

"I've started a new life with Sean. I've found a job and a house...I'm going to figure out how to get Caleb with us if it's the last thing I do."

She asked where I was living. "I can't tell you Mame. I don't want Ray to know where I am and I don't want you to have to lie if he starts asking you questions. I hope you understand."

"I'm not really sure I do, but all that matters is I know how much you love your son."

When the call ended, I just sobbed. I ached to hold him. I wanted him with me; he belonged with me and his brother.

After I composed myself, I called my mother. I dreaded talking with her, but I needed to find out if Ray was searching for us. In my mind, having him show up here would be far worse than any wild animal I conjured up during my night terrors.

Chapter Twelve

The frightening sounds at night never diminished, even if they were only in my imagination. After the phone was finally installed, it became a habit to call Wayne after he'd gotten home from a long nights playing at Mt. Airy. I'd ask him to come and stay with us. In the beginning of my needy calls, I was grateful that he came and cuddled in the bed next to me and kept me safe until morning. One night our relationship crossed over, from plutonic into the romantic.

I'd been a virgin when I met Ray; Wayne was only my second sexual relationship.

Talk about fireworks and the earth moving! Talk about the best sex I'd ever had! Wayne rocked my world. I was amazed that a man of such slight stature would make such a *huge* impression in bed. Oh, that's what they mean by "don't judge a book by its cover".

Was I confusing great sex, romance and attention for love? I wondered.

There came a point when I no longer needed or wanted Wayne to be my rescuer in the night. But I'd set a precedent that I would pay dearly for later. Over the next six months I became acutely aware that Wayne was a full-blown alcoholic. He drank from morning, through the afternoons and the waitresses at Mt. Airy were instructed to keep his place at the band table seven deep all night. I also sensed that Wayne was falling deeply in love with me. It was a love that I could not reciprocate. I loved him as a friend, my hero and my rescuer. He saved my life, of that I am absolutely sure.

***

As I'd come and go, day or night, I was aware that Harry and his girlfriend could see me pass their cabin on that pothole filled "trail" that wound past each cabin.

"Gabbi, just so you know, we are very familiar with your routine. Please don't feel that we're spying on you. But if we don't see you come home one night, we will send out the FBI, CIA and even The Canadian Mounties, to see if you've driven off the snowy mountain road." Harry chuckled.

Wow! I thought. I like that.

***

I never stood up to Raymond, but now I was developing a mind of my own and one night I shocked myself when Wayne showed up at my cottage—drunk and uninvited. I told him that it was over. I didn't want to see him anymore. I tried to be gentle, but he cried. He said he couldn't live without me, and then he left. To me he looked and sounded like a wounded animal.

I got up the next morning and left the cottage to do my normal daily errands. Later, I took Sean to Flo's and went to do my nighttime gig. At 2:00 a.m., with three feet of snow on the ground, I picked Sean up and headed home. There were no lights on our dirt road. I was living in the wilderness. The only illumination came from the headlights of my car. I'd been warned not to put the trash out early as that would attract animals. There were always raccoons and many times I swore I saw a bear!

I would drive up to the front door and proceed with a ritual that played out every night at 2:30 a.m. Without the help of a full moon or streetlights, I'd leave the headlights on, ease out of the car and into the deep snow. I'd make my way to the front door, prop it open, turn on the inside lights. Then I'd make my way back to the car, scoop Sean up, and repeat my journey through the snow, back to the front porch, then inside and down the hall to his bedroom. After he was tucked into his crib, I would go back outside, back through the snow, turn off the headlights and make my way back to the cottage in the pitch black dark. Now, inside, I yearned for a long hot bath to thaw out my frozen fingers and toes.

Lately, when I unlocked the door shivers ran up my spine. Was I really alone? I felt like I was being watched. Was it my imagination? Was there a watcher? Did it have four legs or two?

What if Ray had followed me? What if he paid some body to follow me? What if the shadows weren't my imagination? What if the shadows were really the spies and it would be just a matter of time before Sean and I would be snatched up and taken back to him and *that* life. Or what if their mission was just to find me and kill me. *If I can't have you, no one can!* I'd heard that enough times.

And what about Sean? If Ray had me killed, and had the shooter take Sean back to him in Wyoming, would he make him into a clone of himself? Oh, my God! Stop it Gabbi! I thought, pull yourself together. I've tripled bolted the door. Now, a hot bubble bath; that will be the fix!

After a nice thaw in the tub, I put on my down filled robe and headed to Sean's room. I bent over and scooped him up, holding him close to my breast as I often did. I carried him to my room and placed him under the comforter in the middle of my bed. I checked that all the doors and windows were locked. Then I climbed into the bed and snuggled with this blessed baby and fought the boogieman until the sunrise, which would wash away, for another twelve hours, the thoughts and fears that haunted me nightly about Ray.

For several days after Wayne left my cottage in a huff, it was eerily quiet. I had thought Wayne would come by to apologize, maybe bring flowers as he often did. But he didn't come and he didn't call. I knew he was hurt and I figured he was pulling back from me for a while. In a way, I needed a break from him anyway; honestly, I was enjoying the freedom. I would come home after work, tuck Sean in and then just do my thing—light my sand candles and listen to some *Jessica*, cranking up the Allman brothers. As much as I loved singing the old standards, I was a rocker at heart.

One night I had just come out of the bathroom from washing my face; my long blond hair in a ponytail, as usual. I had to take off the pancake makeup and heavy mascara that I wore on stage with my trusty Pond's cold cream.

Suddenly there was banging on the front door. I knew that this banging wasn't one of my imaginary, four legged demons. It had to be Wayne. I put on my robe and tiptoed into the hall and then out to the front room. The pounding continued. "Who is it?" I said in the boldest voice I could muster. There was no answer but the pounding stopped. I walked over to the front window and peeked out through the drapes. Wayne's car was in the driveway. It was running, I could see the exhaust was coming from the tailpipe.

"Wayne," I called. "I'm really tired. Why don't you come back tomorrow and we'll talk."

Nothing.

"Why don't you come over for breakfast?" I said, grasping at straws.

Again, there was no response. Now I was shaking. He was obviously drunk and might keep this up all night, waking up Sean and frightening him too.

"I'm exhausted, Wayne. I'm going to bed now." I said, trying to control the situation.

With that, I clicked off the one little lamp, and started down the hall toward my bedroom.

I've never known where my strength came from in a time of crisis, other than my strong belief and my fervent love for God. I guess the usual protective angels were on other duties that night. As I stood shaking, I heard the sound of shattering glass.

The door splintered, there was wood and glass flying everywhere—it happened so fast. It was like a scene from a movie, playing out in slow motion. It seemed to be happening to someone else not me. The man who came through the door wasn't the slight, soft-spoken sax player I knew.

He grabbed me by the hair and started beating me. He would beat me, stop and cry, beg forgiveness, and then start again. I could see the torment in his eyes. I was terrified. I lay in a heap on the floor, he continued to kick me. I prayed he wouldn't wake Sean. I have often wondered why I didn't get up and run. I was frozen in fear. He started up again, grabbed my ponytail and dragged me down the hall. He threw me on the bed.

I can't say what happened next; it was all a blur. One of the few things I do remember was him using my head as a battering ram to shatter the mirror that hung over my dresser. He flung me back onto the bed, where I rolled myself into the tightest ball I could; my head throbbing. Then he passed out on the bed next to me, while I went in and out of consciousness. I was terrified, afraid to breathe or talk or cry; afraid I might wake him up and he would come at me again.

Once the morning light began to filter into the room, I eased off the bed, walked through the sea of broken glass in my bare feet, and made my way to the telephone. I called Ann.

Ann called the police. She also called Flo to come and take Sean.

I heard the sound of tires crunching on the snow-packed gravel driveway. The nightmare continued; the home I adored, my first place of independence and safety, was filled with State Troopers. Ann was there, Harry and his girlfriend were there, and soon Gary showed up. In a surreal way, the scene shocked me back to my moving-in day—all the same people here to welcome me, make me feel safe and secure in my new home. But it was real; there was the sign, the placard lying in the middle of all the rubble. Don't these uniformed strangers know the importance of the piece of wood they are walking over? "Gabbi's Gingerbread House".

I was taken to the hospital. The ER doctor said it was a miracle that *all* I had was two black eyes, three cracked ribs and bruising up and down my body. I had some pretty deep cuts on the bottom of my feet from walking in the shards of glass, but no broken bones in my face.

The town of Mt. Pocono had a Justice of the Peace. Wayne was arrested. Due to his stature in the community, he was released, so he could entertain two thousand people in The Crystal Room each night, as he had done for so many years. All he had to do was pay a fine! He also had to agree "in writing" that he was to never come on my property again. If he did, all of the appropriate charges would be put in place and he would be arrested and face a trial.

Ann and Flo decided it would be best and safest if Flo kept the baby for a time. Ann had arranged to have the cabin repaired, cleaned up and put back to together again. She kept me at her house for a week trying to accomplish the same with my mind, body and spirit. I healed quickly. With the help of pancake makeup and an elegant oriental hand fan, I returned to the stage four days later. To those who didn't know me, it was as if nothing had happened.

***

Ann and I were volunteers at a Women's Clinic. That gave me access to many doctors and counselors. They were more than ready to help me through this new life crisis. They offered to be available to me, emotionally, twenty-four hours a day.

The blush was off the rose. A week later the cottage looked as beautiful as before, but the charm and ambience were gone.

***

Sean was asleep and I was looking forward to climbing into bed and delving into my book "The Hobbit" by Tolkien.

I enjoyed this time of night. The hippy in me loved pretending that I was one of Bilbo Baggins friends. I allowed myself to escape in the antics of Frodo and the others. Their fairy tale adventures transported me into a mystical, fantasy world.

Suddenly there was pounding on the door; I froze for a moment. I hoped it was Harry or his girlfriend June checking on me. Only musicians would be up and about at 3:00 a.m.

As I walked out to the living room and peeked through the drapes to see whose car was there, I had a feeling of *deja vu*. This was exactly what had happened the night Wayne crashed through my front door. And *there* was his car! It was idling, which was obvious from the exhaust spiraling up in the frigid air.

I sprinted down the hall, grabbed Sean and headed barefoot out the back door. I jumped into

Wayne's car, threw it into gear and spun out of the driveway. At Harry's house, I laid on the horn until he came running out. This night the angels were not busy with others; they had guided us to safety.

"Get the baby out of the car!" I screamed. "Wayne's at my place!"

He kicked into high gear; pulled Sean out of the car, and called over his shoulder to me, "Get the car keys, lock it and get in here!"

They called the police.

***

Wayne was arrested and kept in jail overnight. We stayed with Harry and June. In the morning Ann picked me up. Since there was no judge in Mt. Pocono, I had to appear before the Justice of the Peace at 10 a.m.

"Well, young lady," the Justice said to me, "seems we have a problem here."

"Yes sir," I said. I was afraid to look at Wayne. Even though he had beaten me to within an inch of my life, and raped me—I found myself feeling guilty. He had been arrested because of me. Was this my fault? Was I the cause of all this? I wasn't sure. Later, my friend Abbey, one of the counselors from the clinic told me that women, who are sexually abused as young girls, as I was, often think that every bad thing that happens to them is their fault.

The Justice said, "The officers and I have had a very long talk with Wayne and Henry. Henry tells us that Wayne has been permanently fired from The King's Band. He is no longer welcome at Mt. Airy Lodge."

I looked at Henry and could see the pain in his face and tears in his eyes, further deepening my feelings of guilt. He looked like he was at a funeral for someone he loved very much.

The Justice said, "Wayne and I would like to tell you about a plan."

I said, "Yes sir."

"I've just gotten off the telephone with Mrs. Evans. Mrs. Evans is Wayne's former mother-in-law. She lives in Virginia Beach, Virginia."

"Yes sir?" I said. I had no idea what they were talking about. *Virginia Beach, Virginia? His ex-mother-in-law? What was going on? What did all that have to do with Mt. Airy?* By now, the Justice could see the blank look in my eyes.

He explained, "Mrs. Evans tells me that she has always had very strong fondness for Wayne and is willing to take him into her home—after he receives treatment. He has agreed that he will leave here before five this afternoon with all his personal belongings, for his ex-mother-in-law's home in Virginia Beach. Once he arrives there, he is to check into a program for alcoholics. The administrator of the facility is to call me as soon as Wayne checks in."

He paused for a few seconds and then said, "Now young lady, you have a big decision to make. What this man did to you was criminal. You were beaten and raped and held against your will. He could go to prison for a very long time."

I finally spoke up. "I don't understand. Why are we all here? Is this how it all works?"

"I will explain in a moment, my dear, but I believe Wayne has something to say to you."

Making eye contact with Wayne for the first time since the beating, was extremely uncomfortable.

"Gabbi, I love you," he said. "I..." I saw the words choking him. "I love you with all my heart and what I did to you shouldn't be done to an animal. I really don't remember doing it. We were taught, in the Navy, not to make excuses, to take responsibility for our actions. In ten years of Navy life, I received medals and commendations for being an upstanding member of the naval band. I was a leader and proud person. I saw the cuts and bruises on your body. I want you to know that I'm an alcoholic. I now understand that I'm sick, but that's not an excuse."

"You're the best thing that's happened to me in twenty years. When you told me you didn't love me the way I love you, when you wouldn't let me inside the house, terror overtook me. Terror because I knew you meant what you said; you weren't mine and would never be mine. I can't trust that this won't happen again, unless I get help for..."

As he took a breath and tried to compose himself, I looked around the room; there wasn't a dry eye. Even the Justice was touched by the emotions displayed by this man.

"What I propose, Gabbi," said the Justice "is that we give Wayne the opportunity to get his life in order. But the decision falls upon your shoulders."

Ann put her arm around me and cupped my chin. "Gabbi," she whispered, "what they're trying to tell you is, you have a decision to make today. I wouldn't want to be in your position. By every right, this man should be in prison for a very long time, but because of who he is in this small community, the Justice is asking you to give your permission to let him leave here."

The words *leave here* resonated in my head. This was the man who saved me, took me out of hell. He helped me learn to take responsibility and live on my own. He made me feel safe. He had treated Sean like he was his own son. He saw to all our needs, even ones I hadn't anticipated.

I stood and walked over to Wayne. He stood too and we fell into each other's arms and sobbed.

Finally, the Justice said, "Does this mean that Wayne's moving today?"

I took a deep breath. "Yes, sir. I don't want him to go to prison."

I was excused from the room. Ann held my shoulders and helped me out into the reality of the daylight. I looked up. In the puffy clouds and blue sky, I knew that my Father God was somehow going to show me the way. I let out a deep sigh and I never looked back.

Chapter Thirteen

A month after Wayne left, I was offered a job at Mt. Airy Lodge.

"Ann, Mt. Airy has offered me a job at double the pay I am making now, and top billing. But I don't want to desert you!" I explained.

"I've never told you this before, but I am having such difficulty financially maintaining my son Caleb in the facility in Florida. I'm not even sure if the Mt. Airy offer will be enough."

Ann was an amazing friend in so many ways, and insisted that I accept the offer.

"Just don't get a big head over this Gabbi."

"Oh, Ann, I can't—"

"I'm serious. If they're giving you all of that and probably a wardrobe fit for a queen, you must take it!"

***

My next action was to call my mother and brag. I'd really disappointed her and now I guess I wanted to deliver a little message. *Your daughter is not as big a loser as you'd thought, huh?*

Of course I didn't tell her because I still couldn't let her know where I was. But I could at least let her know that I was making it just fine on my own.

"Oh my heavens, Gabrielle. Where have you been? I've been out of my mind with worry."

"I've been busy Mother. I'm sorry I--"

"Did you get my letter?"

"What letter?"

"I wrote you at that post office box you gave me...weeks ago!"

"What's wrong Mother?" I said.

"Someone's been following me...and watching the house."

My heart raced. Ray's face flashed in my mind. "Are you sure?"

With that she started to cry. "Your father's seen him too. He sits and watches the house!"

"Have you called the police?"

"Twice. But both times they've come out, he's just left—minutes before. It's so frustrating. Oh Gabrielle, I'm frightened. Do you think Raymond's behind this?"

"I don't know Mother. And I don't know what I can do about it from here in…"

I stopped myself.

"Is Sean all right? Are you all right?"

I felt sure Ray *was* behind the man at my parents' home, but I had no idea what to do. I wanted to hang up. I was furious that she hadn't asked about Caleb. She *never* did; she wanted to pretend he didn't exist. Having a "defective" grandchild was something she chose not deal with.

"I've got to hang up Mother. I need to get ready for work." I sighed. I could hear her sniffling and blowing her nose.

"Well, what should I do with this other letter, Gabbi?"

"Other letter?"

"Just a minute." I could hear her heels clicking as she left the phone, then came back. "It's from Florida, Sunshine House."

My heart stopped. "Open it! Read it to me."

I could hear her ripping the envelope open. "Oh my…"

"Read it, for God's sake Mother."

The letter was from James Kane, the administrator of Sunshine House. They felt Caleb would need another brain surgery in the near future. I was to call Dr. Armitage, a pediatric neurologist at Jackson Memorial. And I was to call the business office at Sunshine House right away. Raymond had stopped sending money for Caleb's care.

***

I was numb. How I got through singing four sets at Strickland's that night, I don't know I couldn't process the devastating news from Florida. But I couldn't call Ann and say I wasn't coming to work. It was my last week at Strickland's before starting my new job.

The next morning I called Dr. Armitage and talked with him about Caleb. Then I went straight to Strickland's to talk to Ann. Maybe she could help me; I couldn't help myself. I was terrified and didn't know where else to turn; there was no way I was calling Ray.

"Does the surgery need to be done right away?" she asked.

"No, it can wait for a little while, but the doctor said the sooner the better."

"So the big thing now is to find somewhere Caleb can go that won't be as expensive. Is that right; a state-run or county-run facility?"

"I hadn't thought of that…he's in such a wonderful place now…everyone knows him."

"Gabbi, you've been wanting so badly to get him near you. I know that's your dream. Maybe we can get the whole crowd at the clinic to hop on this and see if we can get him moved somewhere up here."

I began to cry, my face in my hands.

"Gabbi? Honey, what is it?" Ann asked. She got up and walked over to me; put her hand on my shoulder.

"I thought of that, but the doctor said no way." I lifted my head long enough to answer her. "He said Callie needs to be in a facility with a highly trained staff…all the latest equipment… neurosurgeons a few minutes away. There's nothing like that around here!"

"Oh, honey. Maybe there is! Allentown? Philly? Calm down for a day or so, let your Mama Ann look into this a little deeper."

Ann was never one to give up on anything. I agreed to let her do some research, but I was shattered. Basically, Dr. Armitage had told me that Caleb would never be able to live under the same roof with Sean and me. I was heartbroken.

Chapter Fourteen

It was at this point that my financial responsibilities for Sean and me, under one roof, Caleb under another became overwhelming. Ray stopped paying for Caleb's care; I knew he was trying to manipulate me to return to him. I contacted the Social Services Department at Jackson Memorial Hospital, looking for validation that I had in fact put my blessed son in the best possible care facility in Florida. I got that validation. It was simply a fact of life; Caleb is my son; he needs special care. I would move heaven and earth to provide him with the best.

One evening after I finished working at Mountain Airy and the other band members had gone home, I was sitting alone at one of the round eight-tops. I sat drinking a Coca Cola and tried to unwind before leaving the comfort of inside to deal with the elements outside.

"Ciao Bella", said Francesco in a singsong manner. I was so deep in thought that his greeting startled me.

"Oh hi. Haven't you gone home yet?"

Francesco had a New York accent. The owners and quite a few employees at Mountain Airy were of Italian descent. He had olive skin, striking dark brown eyes; almost black. His hair was thick, wavy and raven-colored. I always felt his smile could turn a frigid heart into mush. He was a fine example of a young Italian stud; such a handsome young man. He treated me like a kid sister.

Until that night, I'd interpreted his smile as a sign of friendship.

"Look Gabbi, this can't be easy for you," he said, sitting down beside me. "What are you going to do about your son?"

I was exhausted and rested my forehead in my hands. I'd spent the day caring for Sean, and cleaning up our little house. Now at three o'clock in the morning I had finally completed my second job, as singer.

"I don't have that answer, Francesco. But I do have a financial responsibility for both of my sons."

Mout Airy was owned by the Martenz family. Frank Martenz was the hands-on man. Francesco and most of the senior staff considered the band and band members to be part of their extended professional family. There were always golf tournaments, some for charity, some set up privately for visiting guests. The band was always asked to participate in them. One of the perks of being the front "man" for a large band was all the extra-curricular activities I was invited to attend. In retrospect, it's clear to me that I was a commodity; part of a promotional package.

I was described as having a voluptuous hourglass figure, luscious long blonde hair, sparkling blue eyes and a smile that reflected youth, energy, and naiveté.

I didn't know at the time that those so-called assets weren't perceived by others as wholesome gifts. Instead, men read into them flirtation and invitation. The women thought Jezebel had just walked in offering herself up to their husbands, in her tightly cinched corseted gown, with her breasts, round and plump barely nestled into the bustier. All of this was, of course, a figment of their imaginations.

It was true that most of my wardrobe was customized to accentuate my breasts and tiny waist. *That* was show business. It never dawned on me that people would perceive me off stage the same way. If they had ever seen me in my street clothes, I doubt I would have gotten a second glance.

My real life was so very different from my stage life--changing diapers, running errands, building fortresses with wooden blocks on the floor with the baby. I would typically be wearing a cozy pair of sweatpants, and an oversized sweatshirt. My hair was always pulled back into a long ponytail. I wore no makeup and there was nothing to define my body as being male or female.

***

Francesco had become my confidante. He knew about my desperate need to keep Caleb in the private nursing facility.

"Listen Gabbi," he said that night—rather early morning. "I may have the answer for you."

I raised my head, those words pushing the *sleepy* temporarily out of my mind.

"You're kidding? Is there another band looking for someone to front them? Tell me!"

"Gabbi, you know this hotel books conferences all week with business men from all over the country."

"I know, it's a very busy place!"

"Well, when these men are traveling and are away from home they get very lonely. They go to their meetings during the day and after a night of partying and listening to the band, they go back to empty, lonely hotel rooms."

"So?" I said, my eyes wide open. "What does that have to do with *my* situation? What are you talking about?"

"Remember Gabbi, it's only because I feel so sorry for you. It's only because I know how much you love your children that I would even talk like this to you."

"Francesco man, where are you going with this?"

I had a sickening feeling in my gut that Francesco's smile for me was *illicit.*

"Well Gabbi, as Maître d' of this resort, it's my responsibility to see to *all* of the guests needs."

"I know, you book their dinners and get them tables in the lounges. You make sure their room service is taken care of and probably set up their tee times."

"Right." he said. "Right!" There was a smile on his face now that I perceived as evil.

"Well, another one of my responsibilities is to see that they are not lonely."

"Look Francesco, I'm not sure what you're trying to say to me, but I'm starting to get a sick feeling about it."

"All right, listen girl." His tone had changed. His demeanor looked unfamiliar. "I'm going to give it to you straight up. You need money, big money. The way I see it, you need more money than the average man can earn in a year. I've never asked about the father of your children and frankly, it's none of my business. I have great respect for what you're trying to do—running one household here and taking care of a very sick kid down in Florida. But you need to consider alternative forms of income. You can double what you're making now, you know, by keeping some of these lonely old guys company in their rooms at night."

"I can't believe that you're saying this to me!" I snapped. "This conversation is making me physically ill. I thought that you were my friend Francesco."

Surrounded by such opulence. At this moment, I found it offensive. My Coke had been served in a Baccarat Crystal, high-ball glass. The hanging Waterford chandelier in *this* room, dubbed "The Crystal Room", could pay for Caleb's brain surgery. The plush carpet beneath my feet, the red and gold flocked wallpaper—all suddenly revolted me.

I wanted to scream. *Is this fair? My son is a living, breathing human being with huge needs. My son and I need help! This room is filled every night with two thousand people spending huge sums of money.*

There weren't enough hours in the day for me to earn what we need. The pain was indescribable. My tears could fill rivers.

The carpet under my feet could fund his treatment, maybe for years. I was ashamed by that thought. I sat amidst that splendor in absolute despair. A little voice in my head said, *How dare you resent them and their carpet.*

How dare I? Because I'm a mother! A mother will do anything to keep her child alive! And yet I didn't have the money to do what was necessary. I didn't know where the money was going to come from.

As I got up to leave, Francesco stood up; trying diligently to maintain his professional and mannerly facade.

"Don't bother Francesco. Your gallantry is as phony as your concern for my well-being. You are not the man I thought you were." I hissed, through clenched teeth. "What you are asking is for me to sell my soul to the devil. Has anyone ever climbed back out of that hell, as a sane, whole woman?" I slammed my chair against the table, locking my eyes onto his and walked away.

***

Spring finally came to the Pocono's. There was plenty of mud when all of the snow melted, but that didn't bother me. Everything was turning bright green and lush.

"Look Sean, I swear there must be more than two hundred shades of green in those woods." My ponderings did not impede the building of his Lincoln Log fort.

Trees were in bud, but it was too early for flowers. The afternoons were warm enough for Sean and me to do nature walks. I'd point out the different birds and their nests and delight that after such a dull cold winter, new life was becoming abundant in our very own backyard.

At his age he tired quickly of our little outing. We climbed back up onto our porch and pulled off our muddy boots. Next, it was lunch and naptime.

***

Gabbi, I said to myself, it's been less than a year since you left Ray. Whatever made you think that you were grown enough or smart enough to make good life decisions? I've gone from being Gabbi the school girl to Ray's "wife", my sons' mother and headliner at a major honeymoon resort. Dear God in heaven, is call girl the next vocation?

***

I looked up at the kitchen clock and was startled to see that it was time for my weekly call to Mame.

"Oh Mrs. Fortier! I'm so glad you called. They had a special meeting about Caleb last Friday."

"Why? What's wrong?" My heart was in my throat.

"Your husband hasn't paid in months and they're taking legal action against him. But that's not why I needed to talk with you."

"What is it Mame?" I urged.

"They're talking about transferring Callie to another facility…one where I know he won't get the attention he gets here."

"What facility?"

"I don't want to tell you…you'd be so upset. He'll just lie there all day. They're understaffed. They don't have—"

"I'm calling the administrator right now."

"Oh, Mrs. Fortier, please don't let him know how you found out."

I called Mr. Kane. I promised him that I would send money within the week. *That* sealed my fate.

Chapter Fifteen

I called my special friends at the Women's Clinic. I had developed friendships with the doctors, nurses and other volunteers like myself. Occasionally on my one night off, we'd all meet at Donegal's Pub. We were a diverse group. There was Abbey the nurse/counselor, Doctor Truman (Tru to me), Scott the retired lawyer and Bev. Bev was our glue. She was our scheduler and all around office person. Last but not least Professor Dunning; he was at least six feet tall, with a strong physical resemblance to Santa Claus. That made it very easy for any girl in trouble to pour her heart out to him. Initially we had banded together to sip cappuccinos or exotic hot teas, except Ann who in keeping with her personality never varied from her Grenadine and club soda.

Blanketed by the dimly lit coziness of Donegal's, we'd relax and feel safe to talk about anything and everything. Typically these kind hearted intellects would brainstorm for our clients far above and beyond the one hour visit at the clinic. Things like how to get college financial aid, how to find low cost housing, with our goal being the client would be able to enjoy a future life of quality, comfort and security.

On my way to meet the group, I dropped Sean off at Flo's and Eddie's. Tonight unbeknownst to all, they would have a new young woman in the throes of a life crisis. They'd be faced with an issue that none of them could have possibly been prepared to hear.

"Hi guys!" I walked around and hugged everybody's neck. I rubbed the top of Tru's smooth baldhead and picked up his white, intricately carved, ivory pipe. I took a deep puff, being careful not to inhale the cherry blend tobacco.

"Hey girl, what are you doing here?" Ann said. "I thought you'd be at home curled up by the fire place using that lush Chinchilla coat your husband bought you as a lap blanket and starting that new book I gave you. You didn't finish that bottle of Harvey's already did you?"

I looked at Ann and smiled a smile that said, *Oh Ann, if you only knew.* This group had grown very close; we weren't complete until everyone was present. Again, I just knew that my Father had hand-picked all of these souls because He knew they would have to save me, or at least try.

"I had to be here tonight with you all."

Professor Dunning stood up and pulled a chair out for me. It was a sturdy, wooden armed captain's chair. After I sat he slid it back in, securing me at the head of the table; the booth sat six and we were seven.

"What's up young girl? I can see by the look on your face that something has gone wrong." said the professor.

I watched as one by one they'd look from my face to each other, as if saying, *steady now group, steady; this is going to be big.*

When I was sure that I had everyone's attention, I began my story.

"It's about Caleb." I said.

"Caleb! What's wrong with him?" said Bev, with a heightened level of concern. I reached out to squeeze Bev's hand in a reassuring fashion.

"Caleb is okay at the moment."

"We can see you're suffering; just come out with it." said Tru.

The pipe dangling from his lips had been mine. It was a leftover from my coffee house singing days. It was hip then to smoke cherry blend tobacco and sip Grenadines and club soda from tall glasses. I remember the day I came across it in my drawer. I'd wrapped it and gifted it to my wonderful friend Tru.

He was puffing and puffing, as though pacifying his angst about what was coming.

"I'm not sure if I can go on." I paused. "Every one of you has shown me a love and friendship like I have never known in my life."

"Well of course we love you!" Abbey exclaimed. "And don't you ever doubt it girl. Now, Tru over there is about ready to swallow his pipe. Tru! Put the pipe down and let it rest in the ashtray. Gabbi you're going to cause somebody at this table to have a heart attack. Don't pretty it up for our sakes. Just spit it out!"

The tension was thick. As in any melodrama, this intimate cast of characters each played a specific role, as I shared my new career with them.

"I have just accepted a position as…" I could see each of them holding their breath, "…call girl at Mountain Air Lodge." I blurted.

It was like an out of body experience. The words escaped me; replaced by the sensation of white-hot burning embers laid upon my chest. There, I'd said it! It was out. With weighted-relief, I slumped deeper into the captain's chair. I didn't have what it took to sit tall. To sit tall took pride. Rather, I took a position of shame. The first reaction that I noticed was tears rolling down Tru's face. Initially I perceived shock, anger and contempt in the sea of faces.

"Gabbi," Ann said in a gentle, questioning way, "What dear, are you talking about?"

I proceeded to share what had taken place in The Crystal Room between Francesco and me. I didn't cry. In fact, I don't remember showing any emotion as I shared my new "Job Opportunity" with my friends.

A cloud of emotion descended upon the group.

I heard Bev say, "This is the most outlandish thing I've ever heard. It just isn't going to happen."

Abbey wanted to know if this was a pretend story to shake everyone up.

"I'll have that son of a bitch arrested right now." spouted Scott. "It's scandalous that he dares talk to you that way. Give me his name Gabbi, right now. Give me his full name." as he spoke, his face became redder and the veins on the sides of his neck were starting to pop out.

The professor looked at Scott, scowled and said, "Scott! Now is not the time for lawyer speak." he said, trying to bring calm to the table.

Finally, the group was emotionally spent. I witnessed their bodies melding into the back slats of the booth desperate for the support they couldn't muster. Trying to collect his emotional self, my dear sweet Tru, reached over and took both of my hands into his.

"Gabbi my dear, I know that I'm speaking for the group. We will not allow this to happen to you.

Whatever your needs are dear, you put them on a piece of paper and we will see that they are taken care of." He said through moist eyes. If anything could make me cry, it was the fact that I believed that this man not only cared for me, but really loved me. *Why couldn't he have been my daddy?*

Ann said "Gabbi you are very good at keeping your suffering to yourself. Please allow us to help. What can we do?"

"Each of you has your own lives and your own worries. I never have and pray I never will, put my responsibilities for my son, Caleb, off on any other living soul. In the past, you have asked why I'm alone. The truth is simple. There is no man who deserves to take on this burden, except the father of these children; who runs away, like a coward, from all responsibilities. So, it's my trip. It's my journey. It's just me, my children and Father God."

All I wanted to do now was go home and crawl under the comforter, squeeze my pillow and maybe even cry for a little while in the silence and privacy of my bedroom.

No one knew what to say to make this shock and pain go away. Professor Dunning slid out from the end of the bench. As he walked around behind me, he gave me a big squeeze and whispered in my ear, "Please don't do this, let's talk about it more. For the love of God, please don't do anything. Promise?"

I turned toward him and reached up to kiss his cheek before the tears that I had been holding back escaped my stoic façade. I grabbed my coat and quickly left.

***

The next morning I was caring for Sean, cleaning the cottage and listening to Greg Allman's Jessica. I had the Hi-Fi playing loudly enough to keep at bay my thoughts of yesterday and last night; not so loud as to hurt the baby's ears. My hair was pulled up into a ponytail. I was wearing one of Wayne's old flannel shirts and loose fitting sweat pants. This was my typical morning uniform. During the second riff of Jessica, there was a knock on the door. That could easily send me into a panic; but at this time each morning, one of the band members usually came to check on us before going to do their daily errands.

As I opened the door my eyes focused on a mass of yellow roses, two feet wide with human heads peeking through.

"What the—"

It wasn't a band member. As they lowered the roses, I saw my loyal friends from the night before.

"You sillies! Get in here right now where it's warm.", I said, as I took Ann's arm and pulled her forward. One by one, they crossed the threshold. Sean came running in, squealing with joy; he loved company.

"What are these for?" I asked Ann as she handed me the flowers. "It's not my birthday. What's going on?"

"Well," Dr. Truman said in his most business-like voice, "aren't you going to ask us to sit down?"

I knew he was teasing, but I also sensed high tension in my friends.

Ann said, "All of you sit down, I'll make some coffee."

Throwing my hands up into the air, I conceded.

Tru took my hand, as if I were a Dresden doll, highly fragile and breakable; he escorted me over to the sofa and motioned for me to sit down. He sat on a wooden ottoman, directly in front of me.

"Gabbi, please don't be upset that we're here. We brought the roses as a sign of our friendship. More importantly, we have things we want to say to you."

I took a deep breath.

"Please dear child, don't say anything until you hear us out." he continued.

I sat back preparing myself. I wasn't sitting in the safety of a dark, candle lit tavern. It was morning and the intense rays of the sun were reflecting off of what was left of the crystalline snowdrifts outside my huge bay window. In the blanket of darkness at the pub, I had a pseudo sense of strength that was missing now in the daylight. I felt naked; exposed. Here, at this time of day, there'd be no hiding, no faked bravado.

Ann came in with the coffee and stood by the fireplace. "Gabbi, honey, we're here because we love you. There's not one of us in this group who hasn't come to know you as a brave and honorable young woman. We'd be proud to say you were our daughter. We believe that you have made up your mind and will go through with the *Francesco proposition*. It breaks our hearts."

"We are here to support you in any way we can." said Bev.

Professor Dunning stood up, hidden beneath his Argyle sweater vest, he removed a white envelope from his shirt pocket. "Gabbi my dear, in this envelope is a certified check for you. Before coming here this morning, each of us went to our banks and withdrew sums of money. We know it's not much. We understand that your son's needs cannot be met with what's in this envelope. But *please*, take it for now and give us some time to come up with ideas to resolve your situation."

I opened my mouth to protest, but Ann shushed me. "My God girl, we help strangers every day. *You* are anything but a stranger."

I opened the envelope and pulled out the check. Twelve thousand dollars! I began to cry.

Not a dry eye in the room, there was now a box of tissues being passed around.

I knew with clarity that these people loved me unconditionally. *That* was a first in my life. But I wouldn't take their money and I wouldn't take their help. I'd do all in my power to lessen their burden of feeling helpless to help me.

"Listen," I said. "Caleb is *my* son. I don't know how to explain this...but I'll try. If I accepted your help, I'd feel like I was relinquishing *my* responsibility as *his* mother. To accept anyone's help with this child would diminish my definition of being his mother and I can't do that. It's odd, I know. You've given me little gifts for Sean. Every one of you has helped me with him in one way or another: babysitting, bringing over an occasional package of diapers. I acknowledge that I need that help. I even want that help. But the relationship I have with Sean and Caleb is like night and day, black and white. It's just not the same, even a little bit. I love them equally, but in a totally different way. Maybe when I'm sixty and I've learned more about life...and faith...and parenting, maybe then I can put into words what I can't right now. But I just can't take your money. I love all of you so much, and I appreciate your trying to help me with Caleb. I've got to figure this out on my own...for once in my life."

"As I look into the eyes of everyone you, I feel responsible for your pain." I'd do all in my power to lessen their burden. "You're here to support me. Then listen carefully because this is what I need. At two o'clock this afternoon I have my first client."

I purposely did not use the word *john*. I intentionally chose the word client. Saying the word *john* would hasten the reality I had, so far, glossed over. Whether it was to protect my friends or to convince myself, the word *client* seemed to soften the edges.

"At four o'clock this afternoon I want each of you to be at the gift shop at Strickland's. Be sitting at the soda fountain keeping a barstool available for me. When I arrive, I want you to buy me the biggest hot fudge sundae they can make!"

Chapter Sixteen

St. Augustine said "faith is knowledge within the heart, beyond the reach of proof."

***

My first john was very non-descript. There was nothing that would make him stand out in a crowd. He was neither handsome nor ugly; not fat or thin; neither short nor tall; the word marshmallow comes to mind.

His face was round and puffy; probably swollen from a night of hard drinking in The Crystal Room with the other "good ol' boys." His head and face looked like a blob, sitting on top of shoulders. As we stood facing one another in his room at Mountain Air Lodge, he first removed my turtleneck, awkwardly pulling it up over my head; this popped the elastic band that held my hair in place. As my hair cascaded down about my shoulders and breasts, I heard him gasp.

His beady eyes locked on my breasts for a minute; then he dropped my sweater and frantically started unbuttoning his shirt. He began to perspire, sending out a scent. He smelled like musk oil, further making my time with him that much more repugnant.

I stood frozen. Much like when I'd been raped, I was afraid to swallow or breathe for fear of drawing attention to me.

I pretended I was a stone statue; I would not "feel" anything. As he was unbuttoning his shirt, I felt a wave of nausea surge through my body.

His hair and eyebrows were a dull, pale yellow. His skin color looked as though it hadn't been exposed to the sun in years. Sallow, I would call him; a pale greenish-yellow. I did experience a fleeting second of amusement as I gazed upon this sorry-looking specimen. I had actually seen many of his type lying on towels on the Florida beaches. They were typically businessmen taking their family for a week of sun and relaxation on Miami Beach. Nadine and I would pass their beached-whale bodies and giggle, saying "Ewww, gross!"

And yet here I am, standing face to face with this abomination waiting for me to pleasure him.

His breasts were full, like a young girl at the time of life when she requires a training bra. His stomach pooched out from just under his "breast line" and down over his belt. Thankfully, he didn't have a lot of body hair; I think that would have repulsed me even more.

Finally, as if I were having an out of body experience, I heard myself say, "Tell me what you would like me to do."

As if I were an actor in a movie with script in hand, I brought him the perverted joy that he so handsomely paid for. If my life depended on it I couldn't tell another thing that happened in that room until it was time for me to leave. The mind is awesome. It can save us from insanity, as I'm sure mine had done for me during that first forty-five minute visit to hell. When his time was up, I laid the imaginary script on top of the dresser, picked up the agreed upon two hundred dollars. I stood proud with my shoulders back, dressed myself and walked out of his room. I don't know when the actress was gone and Gabbi was back, maybe never. I learned to survive. But I learned that in order to survive, I would have to play it like a bad script. And maybe my life was going to be one bad script after another, after another, after another.

I'd made the decision to sell my body. It was all I had left to make the money required to take care of my Caleb; my son, my flesh and blood. Deep in my heart, I knew I was not walking this life alone. *He* was with me, every step of every day. It was the spirit of my *Father God* that made my life liquid, providing protection from the flames I would pass into and out of on this journey.

***

As I walked into the gift shop and approached the soda fountain area, I stood tall, smile on my face, shoulders back. It was important to me that these blessed souls, that cared so much about me, see me strong, unharmed and intact. At the time I didn't realize I could only show them the flesh intact. The damage to the spirit and soul wasn't apparent. It would be years later when I'd realize the depth of devastation prostituting myself had taken.

***

Not all of my clients were marshmallows. Not in looks or how they treated me. Just as they were all sizes and shapes, they had varied scripts they wanted played out in the bedroom. Though I never asked, I felt certain that most of them were married.

On every face I read the same line. *Make my dreams come true. Do for me here what I can't get at home.* Some were passive, others aggressive.

Script number one was titled "I'm a Bad Boy; Punish Me.", Script number two was called "You're a Bad Girl; You Need To Be Disciplined."

Unlike most sessions where my outer self showed no evidence of the agony I suffered when using Script One, that wasn't always the case with the second script.

Before leaving for the "jobs", I would pack my "Pros Bag". In it I carried large, round, very dark sunglasses; pancake makeup, scarves and hats.

Money was never an issue for these perverts. Many times I'd leave my job with ten one hundred dollar bills. But God help me if I said no; I'd take a beating or be forced to perform in spite of my protests. When it was over, I'd scoop up my money, dig into my bag and pull out the prop best needed to camouflage my blackened eyes and swollen lips. I'd stash the money in my bag and leave.

I always stayed in character until I reached my cottage and closed the door. A pity party on the way home might prevent me from getting there. Typically I prearranged with the babysitter on the nights or days that I had to "work". I taught myself to not cry, no emotions, until I made it home. Once there, I had a ritual. First a long shower, using mostly hot water. The only sounds to be heard were of a wounded child, wailing in the darkness of the bathroom. It was safe, living deep in the woods of Cordial Cottages, to let out as much pain as I could. Next, I'd take a hot soaking bath. Every candle I owned was lit. Finally, Frank Sinatra would lull me into a sense of wellbeing and comfort, while I curled up like a little girl in the middle of my feather bed.

I desperately needed to be held and soothed. It was the feather bed mattress that would cradle me and meet that need. Certainly it would not be a man!

***

I sometimes believe that you have to suffer terribly in order to have the ability to squeeze every ounce of joy from a rainbow, from a rosebud, from your baby son with spaghetti sauce all over his face and in his blonde hair.

I got down on my knees and prayed to God.

"Please Lord, guide me and help me meet the needs of my special children. Doing this even one more day will damage me beyond any survival skills. It is over Lord. No more *johns*." I crumbled onto the bedroom floor and sobbed myself to sleep.

***

To retain my sanity, quitting this hellacious life *had* to happen. The money earned carried us for quite a while. My dear son Caleb got the much needed equipment and care.

***

"Hello, is anybody home?"

I froze. It was a man's voice. Not a familiar one. Hearing it caused cold chills to run up my spine, in spite of the heat of the day. I turned the radio down and made my way to the front door.

"Hi. Are you Gabbi?"

"I'm sorry; I don't know who you are? What do you want?"

"I didn't mean to startle you. Forgive me. My name is James Grant. I'm a private detective. You don't have to open the door. May I just talk to you for a minute?"

Mr. Grant was a tall, well-built man, probably in his fifties. He had a thick, snow-white head of hair. He held up an I.D. with his picture on it.

"Who sent you?" I asked him.

"I was hired by your husband." He continued to talk quickly when he saw the terror on my face. "Ray sent me with a letter for you. He's been looking for you and his son for a long time."

I released the hook-and-eye latch and invited him in. As we sat at my little kitchen table I read the letter; there was no way to hold back the tears; a flooding wave of emotions. Ray said he loved me. He was sorry. He missed Sean and he wanted us back

. I was to trust the man carrying this letter. He would make the arrangements to get us back to Wyoming. I'd have nothing to worry about. The letter closed with these words. "Please Baby, give me another chance. I love you."

I continued to cry, looking down at my lap. I couldn't speak. It was another instance that I was thankful that Flo had decided to keep Sean overnight.

"Gabbi," Mr. Grant said. "Take tonight and tomorrow to think this over. I'll be back tomorrow evening at the same time, and we'll discuss the directions your husband has given me." He placed his business card on the table, said goodnight and left.

***

I lay on my bed for hours, at first in a daze. Then I began to think about everything that had happened to me since leaving Ray. It had been almost a year.

Deciding whether to go back to him or not, had nothing to do with money. My work as a call girl had been very lucrative. The driving force that could lead me to make the decision to leave the Poconos and go back to Ray was like a mathematical equation. Returning to him was the known. Staying on my own was the unknown. I knew what it was like with Raymond. I knew how bad it could be; I figured I'd endured the worst. What I didn't know was how bad it could get *here*. One of the *johns* could have snapped one night and murdered me. Having Sean and Caleb become motherless children was not what I wanted. And hadn't I prayed and prayed to God—begged him—to provide guidance?

***

The next morning, I made one phone call. At twelve noon, I walked into the snack bar at Strickland's. There, perched atop six barstools sat six friends, the blessed souls who had shown me more unconditional love than I had ever known. I approached them one at a time—Ann, then Tru, then Abbey, Scott and Bev. I had asked Ann to make sure that Flo would be there as well.

As I handed each one an envelope and hugged their necks, I asked that they not break the seal until they saw me drive away. The night before I burned sealing wax to secure the envelopes; I left the imprint of my peace sign medallion. I knew that when they read the letters and understood I was leaving—and where I was going—they'd do everything in their power to convince me not to go.

Each letter was addressed to the person by name. Each said the same thing, but also included one intimate aspect of our relationship.

The body of the letter said:

I've learned so much in these months, just shy of a year, sharing my life with all of you in these glorious mountains. But there is a bottom line. I've made more bad choices than good. I've learned that I cannot trust my decision making. Raymond is the father of my sons. He has communicated to me that he wants to change and will do everything in his power to make our lives together right.

We all counsel the young women at the clinic to be independent. We teach them life strategies with the hopes of finding success and happiness. I failed in each area. You can't save every young girl, so please let me go. You did your best.

I'm leaving a huge piece of my heart in the stamp of sealing wax on this letter for you. I pray you will treasure it and pray for me. I don't have to stay at the bottom and I promise to

strive to find my way to the top. I love you so very much, Your
Gabbi.

I'd arranged with Mr. Grant to meet me at the snack bar. I would leave immediately after the meeting, rather than wait till evening. When I stepped outside, he was waiting in a black limousine, having already pick Sean up, ready to drive us to the airport. I wasn't wearing my rose-colored glasses. Instead, I needed the cover of my dark Christian Dior's to hide my true feelings about leaving the Pocono Mountains.

PART THREE

Chapter Seventeen

Ray was either a great actor or had changed a lot while Sean and I were gone. When we walked into the house he behaved as though we'd just been away for the weekend. No anger. No threats or long lectures about what a bad, bad girl I'd been.

"Hey, Baby! You look great," he said, stepping forward to hug me and kiss the top of my head. I was stiff in his arms, and I know he felt it but chose to ignore it. "Look at you, big guy," he said, bending down to lift Sean and swoop him up high over his head. Sean squealed in delight. I wondered if my little boy would ever have an ongoing relationship with this man that he called DaDa; my stomach clenched. Deep down, my woman's intuition screamed, beware!

But *I* had definitely changed. I was going back to Ray for two reasons: Caleb's welfare first and Sean's second. This had nothing to do with me. I'd sewn rolls of bills from my last two "jobs" at Mountain Airy into the lining of my train case. If Ray hadn't started paying for Caleb's care again, I would leave in the blink of an eye. I wouldn't go back to Mount Pocono; I would head back to Aunt Esther's and start all over again, go back in time and begin a new life; one that Raymond Fortier would have no role in.

***

As he had always done in the past after abusing me, Ray, of course, showered me with gifts. But this time he was obviously taken aback by my reaction.

"I can't accept these things, Ray," I said, steadying myself, expecting him to hit me. "Not when Caleb is suffering in Florida without the things he needs. They can't keep him at Sunshine House and he may—"

"Get on the phone, Gabbi."

"What are you—?"

"Get on the phone and call down there. Go ahead." His face was relaxed and flat, but I could see his hands clenching into fists. "Talk to accounting. Call your little friend Mame if you want to. Whatever. Caleb's bill is paid in full."

Was he bluffing? I didn't think so, but I wanted to show him the new Gabbi. I walked to the phone on the kitchen wall and called Sunshine House. I knew the number by heart. Ray had a puzzled look. Hmm, he must have been thinking, this isn't the way the script usually reads.

Forget accounting. I asked to be connected to Mr. Kane, the administrator. Not only was Caleb's bill paid, his care was covered for the next three months and the surgery he needed had been scheduled. Huh, I'll know if this is real in three months. My heart soared as I thanked him and hung up. But I didn't gush and throw myself into Ray's arms like the old me. I just turned from the phone and asked him what he'd like for lunch.

***

One morning while Ray showered, Sean and I played out our morning ritual. He was cutting new teeth and a bagel with honey seemed to soothe his gums. Sean was almost as wide as he was long. I loved to kiss him on the insides of his thighs. His fresh, sweet smelling skin was as soft as silk. I'd blow kisses into his fat little rolls and he would squeal. I'd lick my lips and blow bubbles on his tummy, starting another round of squeals and laughter. We could play forever. That was real. I'd never have to doubt that love.

I was finishing my coffee wondering what to do with the day. It seemed odd not having a schedule, no work to rush to—when Ray came in buttoning his shirt. He leaned down and pecked me on the cheek and patted Sean on the head. It was a real Ozzie and Harriet moment. But I still didn't trust it.

***

"Today Baby is a big golfing day. All of the men are going up to Old Baldy to do eighteen holes. Get the baby and yourself ready."

"But honey, what we supposed to do all day; why can't you just leave us here?" I questioned.

"Because you're mine and because I said that you and the baby will be spending the day with the other wives at the ranch. You'll love it! You'll have fun!"

I wondered to myself, I'll have fun? Most of those women are old enough to be my grandmother. How will I have fun? I don't even know how to talk to them.

As if he could read my thoughts, Raymond said, "I'm warning you, when I'm finished golfing I don't want to find out that anything you or the baby did will embarrass me."

"What do you want me to wear then?" I asked with a sigh of resignation. Raymond walked over the closet. He laid out my soft pink, form fitting cashmere pullover, and a pair of hip hugger bell-bottom jeans.

"Can I wear my Dingo boots today?"

"Yes you can wear your Dingo's. Today is casual, those will be fine."

"And what do you want the baby to wear?" Then I said, "I know, he can wear his new little leather cowboy boots too?"

Raymond smiled at me. It was one of those "I love you Baby smiles".

That made my tummy do a little flip; my heart fluttered. Clearly, the man still had an effect on me. As before, we made love frequently in the early morning hours since I came back. Now there was the chance that he would scoop me up in his arms and we'd fall back onto the bed and make some sweet, passionate morning love.

"Gabbi, it's getting late, don't look at me that way, we don't have time for that. There will be lots of time for us tonight. You look beautiful Baby!" exclaimed Raymond.

"Do we really have to go?" I asked and pleaded.

"Yes." he said as he took the baby and rested him on his hip. I followed him.

We got into the car and drove out of town, up towards Old Baldy. On the drive up the mountain, we had to wait while an old farmer herded his flock of sheep across the only road. Being a city girl I was surprised that he seemed oblivious to the fact that we were waiting to drive on. Oh well, that was life in the wild west. As the last sheep meandered across the road, Ray in his impatience gunned the gas pedal and sped off.

As we drove along, I couldn't help but be impressed by the splendor of the trees. The mountains off in the distance were snowcapped. I was amazed by the brilliantly colored, delicate flowers nestled in a pure white bed of snow. The winter pansies were in all shades of purples, blues, yellows and pinks. Even though this was July, in the high altitude, the snow never went away.

All of a sudden, Raymond pounded his fist on the steering wheel, which startled me back into real time.

"What's the matter Ray, what happened?" I asked. "Why is the car stopping? Are we out of gas?"

"No, we have plenty of gas."

"Well, what are we going to do; we're so far away from anything or anybody."

"Don't worry, I'll fix it." he said.

After steering the lurching car far off to the side of the road, he got out, opened the trunk and found an empty soda bottle.

"Well, what are you gonna do now?" I asked.

Ray stopped, turned to look at me and said in a highly agitated tone, "If you don't shut the hell up…" he stopped for a few seconds sucking up the last few words, "Just sit there and shut up, I've got everything under control."

I sat there, watching him as he walked a few feet off the road and knelt down. I had no idea what he was doing but when he came back to the car, I saw the bottle was filled with crystal clear water he had gotten from a stream.

"Whoa Ray, look at that old Volkswagen that just passed us by and we're sitting here in a new

Lincoln." I knew I was pushing my luck, so I just looked out the window. But I was thinking "naah nah na boo boo!"

He popped the hood of the car and poured the water somewhere. In just a minute, he got back in, turned the key and it cranked right up.

"Well aren't you gonna tell me what was wrong?" I whined.

He answered through gritted teeth, "This car is not set up for high altitude! It's just a vapor lock! For Pete's sake Gabbi, you're being a real pain in the arse, now shut up; I've got it under control!"

With that, he stomped on the gas pedal and we were off like a bat out of hell. And that was certainly a signal for me to keep my mouth shut for the rest of the ride. Oh yesss.

***

When we got to the ranch I was first greeted by Caroline, the wife of the pilot who flew George Storey's private plane. She greeted me as if we were old friends. It was obvious she'd had years of experience being a hostess at fine affairs. She put her arm around my shoulders and guided me over to a huge open tent filled with women. In my peripheral vision, I could see four musicians. Next to them was a long reception table. It was set with sterling, crystal, candelabras, and floral arrangements, the likes of which I'd never seen.

At the end of the table were two Chefs, dressed in white. One wore a full size chef's hat, the other, less distinguished, wore one about a quarter the size. I learned later the full size was the chef, the other the pastry chef.

As I turned to look back at Caroline, I noticed a grin on her face.

"Ray didn't tell me we were coming to a party. What's the occasion?" I asked with puzzlement.

She took my shoulders and pivoted me toward the musicians who started playing "Happy Birthday". It was like a scene from a movie with *me* being the star. They were all singing to *me*. And, here, I thought Raymond had forgotten. I wanted to melt away. I was emotionally ill-equipped to handle such attention from a tent full of strangers.

Bottles of champagne were being popped. I was standing, with the baby on my hip, in front of this group. The pastry chef presented me with a cupcake; it was on a china plate, with a sterling fork and linen napkin. The cupcake was a miniature version of the large cake that graced the head of the table. It was decorated with an Annie Oakley theme. It seems that there had been a comment made during the round up festivities that I reminded them of a young Annie Oakley. As I turned to thank the musicians, I saw the baby reach out. He plunged his little fist straight down through the icing and grabbed the cupcake. All I saw next was the fist with cupcake and icing oozing through his fingers, as he was forcing it into his little chubby face. There was cupcake everywhere. For one fleeting second I didn't know if I should apologize, laugh or cry.

Caroline, with her fine-tuned graciousness, looked at the crowd and said, "Hooray for the baby! Look everyone, the baby loves the cake!"

The tension was broken. Everyone laughed and cheered. I started to feel more at home with this group of strangers. Waiters were coming around with trays of champagne. When they got to me, Caroline said, "Come on Gabbi, take one; it's your twenty-first birthday! You're legal now!"

Later I opened my gifts and got to make requests of the band. I asked for popular tunes of the day like "Strawberry Alarm Clock", "MacArthur Park", and "Here comes the Sun", etc. The orchestra was expecting to play music that was more classical, with their cello, upright bass, and several violins; much more appropriate for a baroque session. I saw Caroline give the orchestra leader a wink, as if to say, *Do the best you can with the Beatles.*

While the crowd was busily passing Sean around, wiping his face and cleaning his little hands, Caroline took my hands into hers, moved in close and whispered, "They'll be here for you in about thirty minutes."

Frantic, I looked her in the eyes and said "Who? Why?" My heart was skipping beats.

"To head to the Bahamas. Didn't Ray tell you?"

Just when I'm starting to feel safe, believing that life is coming close to being normal, someone pulls the rug out from under me. No, not *someone*! It was Ray again! Keeping to his nefarious character, he knew I wouldn't want to go. By bringing me here, I'd have no say. I have no power over my life, over Sean's life. Once again, I was the wicked magician's puppet.

I turned and walked over to one of the beautifully decorated party chairs and sat down defiantly. With my body language alone, I made it clear, *I ain't moving!*

"Caroline, you don't understand. We were living in Miami and Raymond told me to pack up the baby and a suitcase. We were moving to Wyoming. I didn't ask questions of him then Caroline. I had nothing but love, passion and desire for a life with Raymond, whatever that would be. What's this all about? I've got to have answers."

It was Caroline's turn, "Don't you know who you married? Don't you know the world you married into? No need to answer; I can see by the look in your eyes, you don't have a clue." she said.

"No Caroline, I don't! Call me clueless. Somebody needs to fill me in."

"You are aware that some of these women's husbands own big businesses? Take for example Mrs. White. Just because her husband owns one of the largest newspapers in the country, do you think that means that he goes to the office every day and deals with proof-readers, copywriters and editors?"

"Yes, as a matter of fact I do."

"Do you think that because George owns an airline and broadcasting corporation that he goes to an office every day to oversee businesses?"

"Yes." I said again. Now I'm starting to feel that she thinks I'm stupid.

"Our husbands are entrepreneurs by every definition of the word. But what you're about to learn, is the broader scope of that definition, as it pertains to our husbands. Have you ever been present during any of Raymond's business meetings?"

"No."

"Have you noticed that anytime there's a business meeting on any of their yachts, none of the wives are there?"

"Yes."

Now she looked at me as if I was supposed to complete the thought that she started. Much to her frustration, that wasn't happening. There was still a dull, dense look in my eyes.

"For your safety and for your baby's safety, you must never share this conversation with anybody." she warned. "Especially Raymond." and she emphasized that.

In every organization there are ranks. My husband owns a flying business for example. In our business he's at the top. He calls the shots. Without frightening you too much, I'll try to explain where your husband fits in the organization. Without us knowing details and having knowledge that could put us in jeopardy, it's enough to know that the men we sleep with are 'delegators'. I once overheard a conversation that included Ray. He was referred to as 'the custodian'. Gabbi, I don't know exactly what that means, but I can guarantee you, it relates to danger. Aspects of these businesses must be kept from us to assure our safety. As much as you love this man, be aware, you are sleeping with danger."

"Caroline, there have been many clues, but I need you to be specific. Lay it out for me please."

My heart was racing and for what would not be the last time in my life, I was paralyzed with fear.

"What seems like business deals to most people, are only the surface of what our husbands do on a daily basis; they're *dealmakers*. The difference between perceived deals and the dark, quiet, secretive offshore deals are…"

Just then the driver came up from behind and tapped my shoulder,

"Ma'am, the pilot has filed his flight plans; I have to get you to the plane." As I followed him out of the party tent, I looked over my shoulder, wishing that Caroline had finished her sentence.

The young woman that arose from that cream colored, satin covered, gala party chair and followed the driver, left behind the naïve little girl. I *would* never be her again. I *could* never be her again. I walked out of that big party tent, knowing who I'd left behind in that chair. This now twenty one year old mother was embarking on a new passage of life, with no clue as to where it was headed or what dangers lie in wait. For one split second, I wanted to turn around and extend my hand, palm up, pleading, don't stay behind. I'm not ready for this new journey.

I walked out of the tent alone and on my own. And maybe, just maybe a tiny bit stronger. Yes, I had made the bed and *we* would lie in it. I knew from that moment on that Caroline's chilling words would dictate the speed at which I learned to be a protective mother and a very clever woman. The thought flashed through my mind, Oh my God, my life in the Poconos was one mistake after another. I came back to Ray because I didn't trust my own decision making. It's becoming clear to me now that there's no one to trust but me. Behind the rose colored glasses would be a bright, intelligent, worldly young woman. I looked up into the big Wyoming sky. With God's help, we'd come out of this alive.

When the driver arrived, he had done as Raymond had instructed. He'd packed all the essentials and anything else that was needed would be purchase later.

"Thank you for taking care of the preparations." And then with my strengthening backbone I said, "We'll be going *home* tonight. We will leave *tomorrow*." He started to talk and hearing the emphasis on tomorrow, decided he would be better off with "yes ma'am, just as you say."

I understood now because of Caroline's warning that I could no longer just play, like an innocent, in the surf on the beach. From this point forward, somehow I will have to learn to remember everything, every occasion, and every person. No longer can I breeze in and out of life, following Raymond. After all, I am a mother with a huge responsibility for two other lives."

***

We landed on Grand Island. Ray's driver was waiting for me. I was wearing my gold-rimmed aviator glasses. Raymond always had the lenses tinted in my favorite shades of pink; a deep rose color along the top edge, then fading gradually into a soft shade of pink at the bottom. Properly positioned, they hid the hot tears welling up in my eyes; I would have been mortified if this driver knew how devastated I was to see him and not Raymond. The puffy top of my cheek met the gold wire frame, keeping any errant tears from rolling down my face. I was acutely aware of the salty taste as the tears that—through some mysterious exercise of will, I was able to keep from brimming over--ran down the back of my nose and into my throat.

Where was Raymond? I panicked. Had we become just another couple of pieces of luggage to him?

"Ma'am, I've been sent here to take you to your husband, just a short boat ride from here." said the driver. The air steward was already carrying my luggage to the waiting car. Sean was perched atop my hip, as always.

"Can I help you with the baby, Ma'am?" asked the driver.

No, you can't help me with my baby. His father should be here helping me with his baby. I thought.

The non-stop echoing of Caroline's words added mental strain to the already tedious flight. And Sean, with nothing better to keep him occupied, continued to pull and tug on me the entire flight. He finally found the shiny zipper of my sweater to keep him busy. Up and down and up and down on the zipper pull. It wasn't possible to nap. I was exhausted.

On top of all that, I now had to take a car to a waiting boat. I wondered, did I have a "husband"? If I did, would he be there waiting for us? Or would another set of shiny white teeth beaming out from another ebony-complexioned face be there to greet me and take me to yet another location?

Climbing aboard planes, into cars, and down into boats with a baby on my hip was now adding to my exhaustion. If I had any common sense at all I would have made the phone call to my mother or Aunt Esther and, choking on humble pie, gotten on the next plane off the island.

Finally at the waiting boat, the first thing I heard that sounded vaguely familiar was, "Conch Ma'am? Twenty-five cents. Thirteen for a quarter." the Bahamian man said.

Looking down at him, I said, "No thank you."

The tide was low. The small footbridge was just high enough to allow the fisherman to stand barefoot, balancing his weight while the shifting tide rolled his skiff back and forth. He would pass up a string of fresh, sweet conch meat to the people passing over. Just as you might expect to read in a tourist brochure, I observed tourists disembarking from the cruise ships and Chalk Airlines. They were entering into a symphony of Bahamian delight. Delight for the fishermen and an opportunity to make money. Delight of the tourists witnessing a way of life foreign to them. There was another group of fisherman balancing barefoot in their Boston Whalers, the ever-present sea gulls swirling around their heads, diving to scavenge any waste thrown overboard.

As the sun struck their glistening skin, it had a prism effect. Their leathery, weathered hides threw off fractured shades of a rainbow as the tourists and passersby reached down to collect the string of conch meat. The tourists' skin was in stark contrast; a milky white. They came to the island from places such as Minnesota, Iowa, and New York. It was a beautiful, almost harmonic play of sea, sun and humanity.

The fishermen had been given Boston Whalers many years ago, as part of a contract deal with England and the Bahamian government. These boats, wood by design were now old. The paint jobs were faded and crackled, showing more raw wood than color; the worn wooden slats allowing in all of the sea elements.

If there was anything to bring me some joy in the midst of the chaos, it was this very scenario of natives; native life intersecting with the gawking tourists

We were making our way to another bright, shiny powerboat to head over to Lyford Cay. The baby and I stayed down in the cabin of the Chris Craft to keep the salt spray from making us feel stickier than we already were. When the captain said we were getting close to the dock, I peered out the porthole and strained behind my rose-colored glasses; looking for my strawberry blonde man among all the dark islanders.

I had started to believe that he was a figment of my imagination. Would the baby and I be jetted all around the world, picked up by strange faces and delivered to out-of-the-way hotels? All of our needs catered to by the servants of Ray's entrepreneurial friends, while they were busy making "deals".

Raymond was there! It seemed almost surreal.

Whenever Ray held me—regardless of how angry I was at him—my heart skipped beats, my stomach rolled and parts of my body quivered. *Always!* And it happened again this time as he hugged me tightly.

"Hey Baby, how was your trip? How's Sean? Let me have that boy." He swung Sean up in the air and got giggles *and* that long string of baby drool. That's what happens when you tilt a baby just a bit too far above your head.

He scrunched up his face in utter disgust and started to say, "Ah shi…" but stopped in mid word, not wanting to anger me for fear of losing his opportunity later that night for a lusty roll in the hay.

Instead he forced a smile and handed the baby back to me. He pulled his handkerchief out of his back pants pocket and wiped the spittle off his face.

Taking my hand in his, he pulled me along saying,

"Come on Baby, I've got something to show you."

We walked away from the dock, down a short block, and around a corner. We stopped in front of a stucco building the color of an orange creamsicle, trimmed in white. It was a motorcycle/scooter dealership. The building was turquoise, pink and royal blue. In a grand gesture, so typical of Raymond, he swung his arm toward a cotton candy pink motor scooter and pointing at it said, "Look what I got you Baby. Go get on it, see how it feels."

"What do you mean?" I asked.

"Well," he said. "You know we're here on business this trip. I won't have days to spend with you so I hired a Bahamian Nanny for the baby and bought you this motor scooter. Now you can go around the island doing all the things you love to do. And look Baby, its pink!"

Hanging from the handlebar was a white glossy bag with aqua blue lettering. It read Sophie's Boutique.

"Go on Baby, get on it and see how it fits. Oh by the way, see the bag." He said.

Hesitantly, I walked over to the motor scooter, straddled it with the kickstand down and took the hanging bag off the handlebars.

"What is this Ray?"

"Well just look inside the bag Baby."

"Oh my goodness, it's beautiful Ray." Inside, wrapped in white lacy tissue paper was a bikini swimsuit. It was the same cotton candy pink as this motorized bicycle with over inflated tires. I was supposed to accept all of this as a peacemaking gift for being left behind and chauffeured around by strangers, I thought.

Baby. I always thought that was an endearment. To me that was something very special. Ray seldom called me Gabbi or Gabrielle. The word Baby to men like Ray is a convenient moniker for *women*, to a man who has had so many. God forbid he call me by the wrong name. *Chickies* came in and out of his life; some for short periods, some for longer periods; but *never* forever. Baby was not an endearment. I missed being called Baby. Damn it! I didn't care why he called me Baby.

I looked in the bag again and then I looked over at Ray. He was beaming from ear to ear. He didn't get it. I didn't want a new swimsuit. I didn't want a pink motor scooter. I didn't want a wallet filled with money to spend any way I wanted. I wanted to be with Ray. I wanted to be part of Ray with our babies. That was what I always wanted. It was becoming harder and harder.

"Where's yours? Where's your motor scooter? Is yours pink, or is it blue?" I asked with sarcasm.

He pointed to the scooter next to the one I was sitting atop and beamed.

"How do you like peacock blue with silver fleck?" He said, followed by one of his sexy, silly giggles.

"You mean to tell me that's yours?"

"Well you don't think I'm only going to buy one? What's the point of buying just one scooter? We do everything together, don't we?"

I answered under my breath, *"No, but I wish we did."*

There was a salesman standing in the doorway of the establishment. Ray waved him over to us. After instructing him to get them road ready and legal, we headed back to his driver and the waiting Lincoln.

"Don't forget your bathing suit." Ray called out. He retrieved it from the handlebars and held it high, passing it to me with a mischievous glint.

What was I supposed to read from that?

***

The leather gunmetal gray bench seat felt cold, soothing and refreshing under my sticky body. The driver had the air conditioning on high. "Where would you like to go now, boss?" he asked, glancing at us in the rearview mirror.

"Home." said Ray.

We wended our way around the narrow streets passing hammocks of Banyans and Live Oaks draped with Spanish Moss. The musty odor hung in the air, thick with decaying wood.

There were many three sided wooden shacks, barely standing. They were seemingly held up by the native standing in the doorway, arms outstretched, hands resting on either side of the door jambs. I saw a smoking barbecue grill on an old worn picnic table. I asked Ray to have the driver stop. Heavily scented smoke wafted from under the domed top. My mouth watered. Jerk chicken was just what the doctor ordered!

"Oh, are you hungry Baby, I'm sorry, I didn't even think about that." Ray said.

"Yes, I'm starved. Buy several servings and let's get home. We're exhausted and Sean needs to nurse. This way we'll have food to just stay home, relax and enjoy each other." I said.

The dark skinned woman with kinky salt and pepper colored hair was beaming as we drove away. Ray was generous in paying for the magical Caribbean chicken dish prepared with a cacophony of exotic and aromatic spices.

***

Sean was resting peacefully under the white gauze sheet of mosquito netting hanging above his crib.

The paddle fan overhead was set on low to keep the thick, humid Bahamian night air moving.

There was always a supply of wine, Remy Martin, Mumm's and assorted whiskeys, ryes, and liqueurs stocked in the pantry. We ate our jerk chicken and rice accompanied by several bottles of St. Pauli Girl beer.

Finally, he uttered the words I'd been waiting to hear.

"Come on Baby," he said as he extended his arm, waiting for my hand to join his and steal off in the dark, over cool terrazzo floors to the master suite.

We never made it!

A pounding broke the silence. As if severed by cold hard metal, our hands were separated.

"What's that? Oh my God, the baby!" I whispered coarsely from the back of my throat.

With a push to my shoulders, Ray guided me into Sean's room and instructed "Stay here until I return. Don't come out under any circumstances!" he said sharply and closed the door.

That shocked me out of a trancelike state of mind that the St. Pauli Girl, nighttime breeze heavily scented with Gardenia and the sound of the breaking waves had eased me into. Thank God, the baby stayed asleep. As my eyes were adjusting to the dark, I pressed my ear against the bedroom door. I was straining to hear and get some hint of what was happening.

At first, all I could hear was the sound of muffled voices; definitely Bahamian. At one point I thought I understood some Patois, then back to English.

Cocaine? Guns? Bricks?

Next I heard a horrible crash. Was it the huge vase on our round mahogany entry hall table shattering on the tile floor? I gasped and jumped back from the door. I stood frozen and couldn't catch my breath. The baby whimpered from his crib. I spun around in the pitch dark, praying he wouldn't break into a full-blown cry. I hadn't heard Ray's voice at all and I didn't want these men finding us back here.

As I eased over to his crib, I realized Sean had just made a typical sleeping baby sound. Inhaling as much air as my lungs would hold, I made my way back to the door. I was terrified, but put my ear against the door again. What were those sounds? I could make out footsteps. They were getting closer; I now heard Raymond's voice.

"Put that gun down maan!" bellowed a voice I couldn't identify.

The living room had very tall ceilings. One wall was all glass. There was really nothing soft in the room to absorb the vocals I was trying to identify. Ray's voice was not deep enough, his tenor not loud enough, but I knew he was communicating with the mysterious intruders.

What is that sound? I thought to myself. *Oh my God, it's the sound of me breathing. Please, God, please don't let them hurt Sean...Our Father, who art in heaven, hallowed be thy...*

I felt the doorknob beneath my waist start to turn. My body slid along the wall to the left of the door so that I would be behind it. As the light began to fill the void, I saw a fair-skinned arm reach in, searching out the light switch on the wall.

"Raymond!" I gasped, throwing myself against his chest.

He held me and then cupped my chin in his hand, bringing my eyes up to meet his.

"Don't cry Pet. It's okay, I've got you. They're gone."

My knees began to buckle. The front of my body slid down the front of his until I puddled like a ragdoll on the floor. When I'd been trapped behind that door, the adrenalin rushing through my veins had held me up. But no more; not now.

Raymond knelt down and scooped me into his arms. He lifted me off the cold terrazzo, holding me securely against his chest, my head tucked in the nape of his neck. We left the baby's room and finally made it to the master suite.

Ray didn't stop to switch on a light. As he made his way over to our bed he had already unfastened his trousers. We stripped each other naked. He laid me down and allowed my listless body to meld into the pure white linen duvet; my head nestled into the down filled, king-sized pillow. One part of my mind was trying to release the pent up terror I had been feeling. The other was filling with dopamine as he began kissing my neck and easing his tongue into the hollow of my ear. In a flash of ecstasy the dopamine won the battle. We rolled in each other's arms back and forth over the king sized bed, as a child might in a meadow of thick luscious green grass. He hadn't stopped to put on our paddle fan. The sound of sweat built up to a crescendo as our bodies smacked together in a frenzied passionate thrust to meet each other's needs; a need to erase the terror that had just happened.

Later, as we lay there side by side, I waited for my heartbeat to return to normal. When I caught my breath, I asked, "What gun?"

The sheets were soaked in perspiration. I turned and looked at Raymond; his eyes were still closed. The corners of his mouth were turned up as he lay totally spent. But he owed me an explanation.

"What gun Ray? Who were they? What happened last night?" I asked, surprised at myself; I was daring to enter that territory that I'd been told—repeatedly—*was not my business.*

As I watched his face intently, I saw the blissful look disappear.

The "be seen and not heard" little girl who stayed behind at Old Baldy would be shocked at the utterance of these questions. Always in the past, I risked being smacked or hit or punished in some manner for crossing this line. I took his chin in a pinch between my thumb and first finger, drawing his head closer to mine to look at me. I patiently and bravely waited for an answer.

"How can you ask me those questions at a time like this?" he murmured.

"It's easy Ray! Sleeping in the other bedroom is one of our sons. I want answers." I said.

I lay there staring, gazing at him. I could see in his eyes that he was searching for a "creative" answer.

"No honey, stop spinning your wheels, I'm not asking for a fairytale."

He said nothing. Just as I expected, his life, the happenings, would remain a mystery.

I sat up and swung my legs over the side of the bed. I sat there for a moment, naked, twirling my string of pearls. Something was different as I looked at my body. My legs were tanned and toned. My breasts were youthful, but had more definition. My nipples were no longer just to pleasure my husband. Now they were the conveyor of life sustaining sweet milk for Sean. My body was changing, getting stronger; maturing. At least that was my perception. And so too was my psyche. I was feeling strong in all ways. The metamorphosis was continuing.

I grabbed my thin terrycloth robe and put on my slippers. I shuffled out of the room to attend to the needs of the baby. We had set up an old wicker rocker on the veranda facing the ocean. Remembering the events from the night before could affect the milk flow.

Cocaine? Guns? Bricks? I remembered Caroline's question, *"Don't you know what you married into?"*

Stop it Gabbi! The baby needs to nurse. I allowed my mind to escape with the dolphins and porpoises, playing and chasing schools of fish in the wide expanse of ocean beyond the veranda.

***

The sun had come up, beaming a swath of gold on the turquoise water. I sensed someone behind me.

"I've got to go now." Ray said quietly.

I turned my head and looked up over my shoulder. I never tired of looking at him. He was magnificent. I loved his sharp, chiseled features; the light spray of freckles across his cheeks, the thick wavy strawberry blonde hair, never one out of place. He was wearing a cotton candy pink, guayaberas shirt. These shirts originated in Cuba and were lightweight cotton. They came in pastel colors, with fine handwork woven into the fabric. And Ray had one in every color. This type of shirt kept the men cool in the heat of the tropics.

Bending over my shoulder, he kissed the baby, rubbed up against my cheek and then put his finger to my lips. No need to talk. He was telling me don't ask; no questions.

"You and the baby go down to the beach. Don't forget your Coppertone, my little Coppertone girl! Silvia will be here soon. Make sure she adds the Boraxo to my shirts. Oh, and her brother's coming to clean up the foyer. You're not to worry your pretty little head over last night. That nonsense was just a business misunderstanding; everything is fine now."

"Will you be home for dinner?" I asked.

"I don't know, but don't worry, Silvia will be here. She'll bring provisions. You and the baby have a fabulous day and don't get into trouble." He smirked.

Sean had satisfied himself and fallen asleep in the crook of my arm. I eased out of the rocker and off to the nursery to lay him down for a nap.

Ray was gone and the baby was napping. I tried hard not to look in the direction of the foyer. I went to the teak entertainment cabinet that housed our LP collection; this would be an Abbey Roads kind of morning. Finding my brave always seemed a little easier with the familiarity of 'Here Comes the Sun'.

Silvia arrived a short time later with her brother. After some introductory small talk, she did Ray's laundry as instructed and then the baby's and mine. Her brother had the foyer cleaned up in no time and left.

Once Sean was up we headed down to the beach where Silvia served lunch in our cabana. We had a platter of mango, watermelon, cantaloupe and several cheeses. It was all served with a small pitcher of sweet tea. Sean and I played in the ocean; he loved the water. I slathered him with Coppertone and when he began turning pink, I put a shirt and floppy hat on him.

That evening I couldn't eat the curried goat and breadfruit that Silvia had prepared. I had no appetite. Yes, we were in a beautiful place, but I wondered if this was going to continue as life had for us in Miami and Wyoming—days spent alone with Sean and a nanny while Ray was missing in action, doing who knows what?

Sometime later, after I had bathed Sean and put him down for the night, I was lying in my bed, mosquito netting down. I was reading a book when I heard a clicking sound at the front door. My heart felt as if a huge hand had reached into my chest; wringing it tight, squeezing the life out of me. Had the boogeymen from last night come back looking for Ray? I held my breath. I thought if I didn't breathe no one would know I was here.

And then I heard *his* voice.

"Hey Baby, it's me."

I could breathe again! I rolled over to the center of bed and sat up Indian style, waiting for him to come in. As he did, I said, "Ray, don't talk, don't say anything. Just come over to me. I patted the bed beside me. "Look at my face; look into my eyes. You must see that I'm very serious right now."

The only light in the room came from my small bedside lamp.

As he climbed onto the bed, I continued. "Don't make the mistake of not taking me seriously Ray."

"But…"

I covered his mouth with my other hand, stopping him in mid-sentence.

"Be quiet; it's my turn. You'd better listen to me now."

Whether he could sense the level of urgency in my voice or see the intensity on my face, I didn't know.

I'd made the decision and I wasn't turning back. "Life with you is a mystery and I think I'm better off keeping it that way."

"A mystery about what?" He said.

I raised my hand and covered his mouth again. "Shhhh! You are not talking now, I am."

My heart was skipping, my mind racing. He was going to hear me out. I sensed his body grow tense. "I'm not sleeping in this house for one more night."

I raised my hand and held a finger up, warning him not to speak.

I rushed on, "What happened here last night could have cost us our lives. It terrified me; I don't believe the baby was safe. My gut tells me to get out!"

I heard him inhale, wanting to jump in and stop me, but I forged ahead. "Ray, you have two choices. One, take the baby and me back to Miami for good." Letting out a little sigh, I continued. "That isn't what I want though. You know I love these islands." I said a bit softer now. "Your other choice is simple. You can get your checkbook, your hidden bags of money…" I didn't need a brightly lit room to see the startled look on his face. "That's right Ray. I don't know how you pay for things. Ever since you came to me in Miami, you've bought us cars, provided beautiful places to live; what's missing from the equation? Where the hell does the money come from? Whenever I've broached the subject, you've shut me up. But look around us Ray. All of *this* represents big bucks. I'm not stupid!"

"Do you remember when you tendered Gill and me off the Yacht in Bimini?"

That grandiose yacht was 138 feet long with gold fixtures and faucets; a galley larger than the kitchen in my house in Miami. And it even had a library. There was a captain, a steward, a cook and a first mate.

"Ray, I was seventeen when I met you. I didn't question us owning homes in other countries and limos and yachts. I'm in my twenties now, and not as naïve. I know this isn't most peoples' reality.

I didn't pause to let him answer. "Well, Gill and I took a long walk on Bimini. It's quiet, charming and sparsely populated. I was enveloped with the feelings of tranquility. Ray, I saw houses for sale there. They're not as large or opulent as this one. They're quaint and charming. It's secluded and I'd feel safe there. I'd love it!"

"Can I talk yet Gabbi?"

"It depends on what you want to say."

After a moment of silence, I heard him take in a deep breath, "Is it on the water Baby? Are you sure you would be happy living there?" he looked at me.

"I'd have to find you a new housekeeper, unless I could get Sylvia to move with us. I'm sure for the right amount of money she'd be willing."

By now I had my arms wrapped around his neck. I squealed. "You mean you're not saying no?"

"I'll send somebody over there tomorrow morning and see what's available. I can't promise that you can move in tomorrow. But I give you my word, if it's possible to make it happen, I will do it for you Baby."

As Ray got up and left the room, I laid back down. Outside our bedroom window, the moon was reflecting off the ocean. I remembered so clearly the day Ray tendered Gill and I off the yacht for his secretive business rendezvous.

I'd never felt a need to share with Ray that I had met The Bread Lady and my new friend Alan, besides, he'd either not care or be insanely jealous.

On that day, I took off my flip flops and ran in the white surf. The sand was like powder, it felt good, exhilarating. To my right, congregated under the thick leaves of an old sea grape tree, on weathered stumps, with roughhewn makeshift plank table tops, sat the local contingent of elderly Bahamian men. They gathered in camaraderie, to play heated games of dominoes, solve local political issues or resolve family disagreements; always siding with the men's point of view; that was the Bahamian way of life. The amazing canopy of the sea grape tree protected them from both the hot baking sun and predictable afternoon showers. Inevitably there would be groups of children building long lines of dominoes, tipping the first, laughing as they all tumbled in a snake like movement; the domino effect.

To my left, a few yards down from this ritualistic scene, nestled under a group of Royal Palms, was a chickee hut. Bamboo poles supported its thatched palm roof, and under that protection sat a stack of old wooden crab traps. I couldn't smell crab, so I was curious to see what was in them.

"Come on Gill, let's go look." I shouted, running up to the chickee hut.

As I got there, I saw a tall thin woman. "Hi. What's in here? What are you selling?" I asked, smiling at her.

This woman didn't have an ounce of fat. She braided her kinky hair close over her scalp. A few wisps escaped the weaving, revealing the beginning of middle-aged gray. She glistened in the morning sun. Her skin was the most magnificent shade of ebony I'd ever seen.

"Hi my sweet." she said "Welcome to The Bread Lady." She swept her arm back, directing my attention to the loaves of bread and baked goods inside the crab traps.

Crab traps, slats worn and splintered, no longer able to hold the crustaceans that scooted along the Caribbean floor, were now repurposed for holding safe from the diving sea gulls the sweet treats and breads of The Bread Lady.

"Oh it smells yummy. Show me more."

She reached into the traps and brought out several varieties of homemade delights.

I turned and smiled at Gill, after all, it was late morning and we hadn't had breakfast.

"Gill, did Ray give you any money?" I asked.

"Yes Ma'am, we can have anything we want."

The Bread Lady sold us some morning delights and offered us tea from a glass jar she kept steeping in the sun. As we chatted I noticed her batiked sarong and its shades of blue, green and yellow.

"Oh my! Is that batik?" I exclaimed.

"Yes my dear. You be familiar with Batik?"

"Oh yes, I love the technique. But I've never had the experience of doing it myself. I'd be afraid that I would ruin the fabric."

"Oh my sweet, it's no problem. You be here tomorrow morning at the same time and my daughters will take you to my house and you will learn Batik!"

"Oh, but I don't know if I can ever come back, let alone tomorrow morning. But you are very kind to make such a wonderful invitation."

I turned and looked at Gill and said, "Did you say he gave us enough money that I could have anything I want?"

"Yes Ma'am." he mumbled.

I spun around in the sand on the balls of my feet and looked at The Bread Lady and pointed my fingers and said, "How much is that?"

"How much is what my dear? This sweet cake?" as she held up one delicacy.

"No." I said. And with a sweeping motion I indicated *everything* in her cases.

As she excitedly worked her pencil stub on a scrap of paper, figuring her numbers, I turned back to Gill and said, "Gill, we'll take this back to Raymond and his guests and the steward and the captain." and then as I put my finger to my chin I said, "Do you think we'll have enough?"

We'd been there for about half an hour, when I saw a man walking up the beach. He wore khaki shorts, a silk turquoise colored shirt with epaulets. His legs and stride reminded me of a thoroughbred. he was walking through the white powdery sand in his bare feet. *Oh be still my heart, this man is beautiful.* Old enough to be my father I'm sure, but beautiful none the less.

My ear was accustomed to the cadence at which the Bahamians spoke. It sounded pretty. He first spoke to The Bread Lady with a cordial good morning. And then with a puzzled look on his face, threw his two hands up in the air and said,

"Sold out! I'm here too late?"

Seizing this as an opportunity to speak to this fine man I said, "He did it, look! He bought them all. There's none left for you, and none left for me! Let's jump him." I pointed to poor Gill loaded down with the breads.

Gill stood looking shocked.

We all burst into laughter.

"Mr. Howell", she said, "Let me introduce you to my new American friends.

Thrusting my hand forward, I said, "Hi, I'm Gabrielle!" I said in a very animated manner, seizing the opportunity to touch this man. "And this is my friend, Mr. Gillie."

"How do you do?" he said, reaching out to accept my hand. "Please call me Alan."

"And you may call me Gabbi."

Alan turned to me and asked "Are you staying on the island?"

I explained that Gill and I had been brought to the island in one of the Zodiac inflatables, while my husband tended to business.

"Well then…" Alan exclaimed, again throwing his two hands and arms high above his head, beaming the most beautiful smile I'd ever seen, "…may I ask you to be my guests for the day?"

I turned to Gill and said "Please carry our sack of goodies, we're going with Alan."

I saw the concerned look on Gill's face and said "Come on Gill let's all go and see what Alan has in mind for us."

With that, I turned to my new friend Alan Howell and said, "Lead on kind sir." in an almost flirtatious voice.

As we walked my new friend did most of the talking. He pointed to a shanty structure and shared who lived there or told me of the family that had been born in *that* house. He identified fauna and foliage. Before I knew it, we were standing in front of a charming and lovely cottage. It was stucco that had once been painted a vibrant lime green. It was now a pale mossy color, dulled by the effects of wind, rain, hurricanes and the hot piercing sun.

"Well…" he said, and threw out his arm pointing to the structure, "…won't you please come into my modest home? I'll have the house boy make us some cold refreshments."

"Oh Alan, how delightful!"

Alan was dark skinned. His absolutely brilliant smile in the right circumstances, I thought, could turn any woman into his plaything.

As we sat and enjoyed a platter of mango, star fruit, cheese and crackers, I admired how nicely appointed the room was. Casual yet elegant, there were rich mahoganies, tiled floors and Bahamian shutters over every window to direct the daily breezes.

Gill gently squeezed my arm and reminded me that it was time to go.

I thanked Alan for his hospitality.

"Alan, have you ever met somebody that you just *knew* was supposed to be a part of your life; not just somebody you meet on a beach, to never see again?"

He approached me and extended his arms. We shared a hug that implied 'until we meet again'.

***

Ray handled all aspects of buying me the new house *and* even worked out an arrangement with Sylvia;

she'd be with me and Sean five days a week. Her cousins would fill in on her days off.

On those magical days when Ray didn't leave for business, we would fish, swim, make love, play with the baby and explore the island. Sometimes we'd go to the old Grand Hotel for cold beer and fresh Conch Fritters. Memorabilia of Ernest Hemmingway, Howard Hughes, Diane von Furstenberg and other colorful characters adorned the walls.

When Ray did leave for "business" I'd meet up with Alan at the Bread Lady's for afternoon tea.

Our relationship was very unique. I was in my early twenties and guessed him to be in his forties or fifties, simply because he had a lifetime of stories.

"Gabbi, do you know very much about politics?" Alan asked me one afternoon at tea.

His question made me feel uneducated. I didn't want to act or sound stupid, but I didn't know anything about politics.

"Well Alan to tell you the truth, I stay so busy with Sean and Ray…"

He interrupted with a chuckle, "Maybe dear Gabbi, that's a blessing!"

He told me stories of corruption and payoffs. He talked about the United States Congress. There were stories that took place at the famous Willard Hotel in Washington DC.

"Have you been to the Willard in D.C. Gabbi?" Before I had a chance to answer he said, "You are such a breath of fresh air! Oh, of course you've never been to the Willard. Well, my little dove, most of what I will share with you in the days to come won't make any sense to you now, but I'll venture a guess that there will come a time in your life when you will understand who your barefooted friend in the Bahamas was."

I listened intently. My role in our relationship went beyond friends who walked the white sandy beaches of Bimini. He told me once that he didn't understand why, but he trusted me more than anyone else he knew. He explained to me that he had been accused of illegal activities. There was one particular day we were sitting on the beach at the water's edge watching the sailboats, the occasional power boat and the sea gulls.

He turned to me and said, "Gabbi, do you know that I'm hiding out here? Do you understand that I can't go back to the states?"

Before I could answer he cupped my cheeks in his hands; I recoiled back, afraid he was going to kiss me. That reaction was a throwback to my teenage years, remembering how my adoptive father's incestuous abuse had left me with such disdain for the male touch. But instead he rested his forehead against mine and began to weep.

"Gabbi promise me that you won't leave the island without telling me where to find you." He pleaded. "I've grown to love and cherish our friendship more than I can express. I'm sorry." he saw a puzzled look on my face and continued, "I'm sorry because I've told you things that don't make any sense to you. Truth be known I've been very selfish with you." he sighed. "I've needed to say these things and talk about them for years. In the beginning, my career was exciting, fun and deviant; all that I was raised knowing was morally sinful. Until meeting *you*, my little dove, I've had to keep it all in. There's one thing I want you to know Gabbi, I don't think that any harm will come to you from knowing me. But for your sake and mine, promise me the secrets I'm sharing will stay with you, me and the seagulls above our heads."

When he stopped weeping, I squeezed his two hands, looked him in the eyes and said, "I've been amazed and mesmerized listening to all of your tales. You are right. I don't understand most of it; I can't relate to it. Maybe someday I will. You've given me a gift and I don't know if this will ever happen to me again."

"A *gift* dear girl? What *gift* have I given you?"

"You've given me honesty. You've told me who and what you are, we have no secrets."

"Now why are *you* weeping?" Alan asked.

I shifted my gaze back from the water, looked at him and said, "I sleep with a man every night; I have two sons by him. I don't know who he is. I don't know what he stands for. I don't know when he's telling me the truth or when he's lying. Until meeting you Alan I didn't know that *this* is what loving and caring about someone should be. You're my friend. I will always let you know where I am! I'll take your secrets to my grave. I'll cherish our friendship for all of my life!" I exclaimed

During the many hours that we walked the beach resting under a stand of palms or sitting in the shallow surf, he told of people using cocaine. He spoke about his disdain for the years he wasted doing drugs and partying with unscrupulous politicians and wannabes. I sensed his torment. He seemed comforted to have found in me, a confidante to whom he could express his remorse. I was exalted in the knowledge that this might save him.

The symbolic *treasure chest* he found in me held the secrets of his life. Under the safety of our imaginations, we held up the key that locked the chest and threw it far out into the deep blue Caribbean Sea.

***

"This is the story of Alan HOWELLC. Howell, who lived in exile on the island of Bimini."

Whoa! That shocked me to pay attention to the commentator. I was now forty-eight years old, watching a PBS program. Alan told me that someday I would understand just who my barefoot friend in the Bahamas was.

That was the first time I knew the true meaning of all of the stories that Alan had shared. I finally understood why it was so important that everything he told me remain in it's watery Caribbean grave.

Alan was a complex man, living a complex life, who had found peace and tranquility with a Coppertone Girl, while having a cup of tea at The Bread Lady's on Bimini.

Sometimes in life we think we know a person, but never really do. On rare occasions someone can come into our lives for a short period of time and show us their true selves; a glance into their soul and the feeling of knowing them a lifetime. That is how I would sum up the relationship with *my* Alan.

Chapter Eighteen

Most days in my new Caribbean paradise started the same. Ray kissed me passionately, smacked my rear and said, "I'll be back later. You and the baby have a wonderful day."

This had become his signature goodbye. It meant have fun; don't worry about anything *and* don't ask me any questions.

***

The surf was a little rough, so I was teaching Sean how to build sandcastles on the beach. We always had the beach to ourselves, as our part of the island was very secluded. Tourists had no reason to wander down this far. Off in the distance I saw two men coming towards us. At first I continued with Sean, showing him how to drizzle water on the sand to make it mold for the sandcastle. Then that sixth sense said, *put the baby in his playpen inside the cabana.*

"Madame Fortier?" said one of the men.

"Yes. How can I help you? And how do you know my name?" The hair on the back of my neck began to prickle.

"Madam you need to come with us. We are officers of the Royal Bahamian Police and have been sent here to escort you to Headquarters."

By their khaki shorts and white shirts, I knew these "uniformed" men represented the police. I wondered why they were on my part of the beach, how they knew my name and why they wanted to take me anywhere. This was all incomprehensible; I couldn't wrap my mind around this scene.

"I'm sorry, I don't know you!" I said in the strongest voice I could muster. This was no time to fall apart. I wasn't in America. I was alone with the baby. Dig deep girl.

"What are you doing here? I'm not going anywhere with you. Are you sure you're not looking for my husband?" I looked away from them and down to my feet; my toes clenched in the sand, as if taking a stand: I will not be moved! Then I turned and pointed to Sean, "I can't leave my baby."

The shorter of the two fellows walked over and smiled at Sean. He clapped his two hands together and cooed, "Come, Baby."

Sean babbled in return, extending both his little arms straight up in the air, inviting this stranger to pick him up.

"It will be okay, Madam." he said, "Please, get your shoes and robe and come with us."

Maybe cooperating would be best, safest, I thought. I would go with the men. Perhaps by doing so I'd gain answers to mysteries in my life with Raymond.

If I smiled and was amiable, might that help shield me and Sean from harm? I did as I was told.

***

At Police Headquarters we were taken into a small office with one large, old wooden desk. There was a paddle fan on the ceiling made of thatched palm fronds. The office was sparsely appointed with several wooden chairs. Large openings were cut in the walls. It was common in the Caribbean, that these would not be covered with glass or screens. This primitive window opening was secured only by the Bahamas shutters which could keep out inclement weather and allow in the revitalizing tropical breeze.

Behind the desk sat a Bahamian man dressed in a guayaberas shirt and long khaki pants. The plaque on his desk identified him as Inspector General D'Clute.

"Please, Madam, have a seat."

Have a seat?! I know I'm not here for tea and crumpets! I was taught growing up that you get more with honey than with vinegar. But this "politeness", glossing over an implicit menace as it did, was testing the limits of my genteel manners.

"Why am I here? I need you to tell me why I'm here; right now!" My hands folded in my lap, to prevent me from pounding fists on the desk.

"Yes Madam, I will tell you. May I ask the Matron to take the little one to another room where he can have some sweets and be more comfortable?"

"No, you cannot! My baby is not going anywhere without me." I said hugging Sean closer to me.

"As you wish Madam. Now then, we will start." His manner was almost hypnotic.

From his desk, he picked up an eight-by-ten glossy photograph. He stood up, walked around the desk; dragging a large straight-back wooden chair and sat next to me.

"Madam, I have here a picture that was taken this morning. I need to warn you it is an unpleasant. However, I must ask you to take your time, study the face, and tell me who this man is."

You want me to look at a photo? You want me to identify somebody? What is this, a joke? I thought to myself. However, it was an official setting, so I complied.

I reached up and took the picture from him. I had detected something in his voice and mannerism; he was trying to prepare me. But there was no way to prepare me for the horror I saw in the picture. I sucked in a deep breath; my hand fell open, allowing the picture to flutter to the floor. I had only glanced at it for a second. *As I sat there with my eyes squeezed shut, the image of a grossly deformed, bloated face and body floating in neon turquoise water was indelibly etched in my mind.*

I know who that is! It was Hammi Hamilton.

Two years earlier at the Flagler Dog Track in Miami, I had helped the FBI identify him so they could deport him back to Canada. This man was ruining our lives. Hammi Hamilton was dragging Ray to the tracks; dogs in the day, flats in the evening and Jai Lai at night. I overheard them talking one day about how Hammi had crossed into America illegally and some other illegal activities. I knew that to save our little family, I had to do something to get him the hell away from us. In fact, there was one point when I thought the only way he would disappear from our lives was if he was dead! *I* wanted to kill him. Now it appears that I wasn't the only one who wanted him dead!

As D'Clute bent over to pick up the picture, he motioned to the young officer who was sitting behind me in a corner of the room. "Ramsbottom, go quickly and bring a cold, wet cloth for Madam's head." Eager to please, the officer scurried off.

"Madam," he reassured, "If you'll just breathe deeply and have a sip of the cold sweet tea, you will be fine."

I raised my head to look into the inspector's eyes. *"Please, somebody…wake me up. This must be a horrible dream."* I murmured. My mind was spinning. The temperature outside was ninety-eight degrees and the humidity was ninety-seven percent. The air inside of this office was stifling; so thick that I couldn't catch my breath.

As Ramsbottom returned to the office, he handed me a cold, wet wash cloth.

"Please Madam," D'Clute said, "I must have answers, take a look at this picture again. Do you know this man?"

His cadence had changed. Now he was being deliberate, paced, and almost monotone. His effort at keeping me calm failed. I detected danger!

"No, I don't…and I don't know why I'm here." My tone was angry and belligerent.

I sensed that D'Clute wanted to take his fist and slam it down on the desk; instead he maintained great control and calmly said, "This man's body was found floating underneath the Paradise Island Bridge this morning."

Unable to speak, I sat frozen in my seat.. The inspector went on to explain a situation that was happening on the island. "A small militant group of natives is strongly opposed to the new two-dollar toll fee that is being instituted to cross the bridge. This bridge provides access to the casinos, hotels and restaurants. The locals are the labor force. This is *their* island; *their* ocean. It angers them that the white tycoons have the audacity to charge them to cross the bridge to get to the jobs they need, while lining the pockets of the "outsiders". There have been rumors lately about this group. We were notified that a quantity of dynamite had come up missing from one of the local construction sites. So, this morning I instructed several officers to go under the bridge to see if anything looked amiss. And that, Madam, was when we found the body."

If not for that one little rumor, Hammi Hamilton's body may well have been dinner for the sharks and other sea creatures.

Why did he connect me with this body found floating under the Paradise Island Bridge?

"Take your time answering this question. The look on your face tells me that you recognize the man in the picture."

"Yes." I said. "That's Herman Hamilton. They called him Hammi." I heaved a sigh.

"All right. Now we're getting somewhere. Did you know this man you call Hammi, was in the Bahamas?"

"No."

"Did you know your husband…"

My husband? Those words hit me like a scorpion sting.

"…and this man were engaged in illegal business here?"

God help me! How should I answer this question? Do

I answer like the girl from Miami with the Coppertone tan and pigtails? Or should I answer as the young woman who evolved and learned to speak up for herself?

"Officer?"

"*Inspector.* Please call me *Inspector* D'Clute."

"Sir. What makes you think my husband has anything to do with this man? What illegal operations are you talking about? My husband is a business man in the United States."

"But he's Canadian, correct?"

"Yes, but... Why? What does that have to do with--"

"If you will help us, Madam, you and your child can go home to Florida. That is where you live isn't it?"

I nodded. *But truthfully, I wasn't sure if I even had a home. Wyoming, Bimini, Pennsylvania, Lyford Cay, Miami, Montréal.* I thought to myself. *Where is home?*

"There was a third man with them. Last evening we observed this man and your husband at the craps tables in one of the casinos. He had a stockier build, reddish hair and a round face. Do you know who that person might be?" he asked.

"It sounds like my brother-in-law, but--"

"You thought he was in Canada, right?"

"Yes."

"These three men have been on the island for several days." he informed me.

"My husband is here on legitimate business with another American." I hastily added.

"Yes, that's what he wants everyone to think. We believe that is simply a cover for the real reason these men are here."

At this point I stood up from my chair and walked over to one of the windows. A bright yellow sunfish with turquoise numbers was sailing by. I wanted to yell out to the man in the boat, in desperation, *I don't know who you are, but please come back for me.*

Whisking that thought from my mind, I returned to my seat and faced the inspector.

"I had no idea Hammi and Philip were here." I sighed with resignation. I would cooperate. "I'm never included in conversations regarding the business my husband does. He doesn't feel it's anything I should know." Caroline's words to me in that Wyoming tent are coming back to haunt me now, sitting in this Bahamian Police Station. *As much as you love this man, be aware, you are sleeping with danger.*

"At this moment Mrs. Fortier, some of my

officers are at your home on the island looking for evidence."

"Evidence? Evidence of what?" I said frantically.

"Drugs, quite frankly. Drugs and weapons."

"Please take me home! Where is my husband?"

After a pause, he asked, "Is your husband's name Lawrence MacDonald?"

"What? Larry MacDonald? He's a friend of my husband. What does he have to do with this?"

"We have your husband, he's here."

"For God sake, what is going on? My head is spinning. First, you show me the picture of a dead body and then you tell me you are searching my home. Now you are questioning my husband's name."

I stood up. "His name is Raymond Fortier! You've made a terrible mistake! I'm leaving. I don't belong in this office and your men do not belong in my home."

"Sit down Madam! We are not finished!" he ordered.

Sean had been toddling around the office and was now crawling into my lap; getting up and down and whining, "Up, up mama."

"Surely you see the seriousness of this? We will be here all day. *Now* may I have the Matron to take the child to another room to play and have refreshment?" D'Clute asked with his British comportment.

"Yes, please take him out of this room and keep him happy and safe, until we go home." I used those words "go home" to convince myself that *we were going home.*

An attractive, ebony-skinned young woman came in. She had a stuffed bear in her hand, and had no trouble using it as bait to lure Sean. He willingly took her hand and toddled out.

Drinking the sweetened cold tea eased my senses into the moment. "You see, you're confused!" I said defiantly to the inspector.

"Mrs. Fortier, have you ever seen your husband's passport?"

Close to hysterics, I said, "Of course not! *Money, paper work, adult things.* I was not privy to any of that. I don't think I should be talking to you. Where is Ray? I want my husband right now. Do I have to stay here? I want to leave *now!*"

After what seemed an eternity, D'Clute got up from his chair and called an officer into the room. "Madam is ready to go home. Have we finished searching the residence?"

"Yes sir, they have just returned." said the young, very thin policeman.

"Fine. Please have a car and driver come around."

"Yes sir."

D'Clute turned to me and said forcefully, "Madam, your husband's name is not Raymond Fortier. Not according to official paperwork acquired from Canada by the Bahamian Government. It is Lawrence MacDonald, of Burnaby, Vancouver B.C. I would strongly recommend that you ask your husband for the facts. Perhaps you are telling me the truth. Perhaps you do not know about these men and their activities on the island or how this man Hammi came to be dead in our waters. If you are telling me the truth, it is time you get the facts--in order to protect yourself and the child. Remember Mrs. Fortier, this case involves murder."

If Inspector D'Clute's intent was to instill terror in me, he had succeeded.

"Mrs. Fortier, as of an hour ago I have set in place officers to observe your home and your husband. Since there is no police station on Bimini, I have been in contact with the Lerner Marine Laboratory. For your safety and convenience, I have set up an office there. This facility will accommodate your needs during the next days and weeks."

Days and weeks? I thought.

Chapter Nineteen

Boarding the boat for the return trip, I notice Sean's little sunglasses on the seat. I yearned for this day to be over; to be back at my quaint little home on Bimini. The officers insisted upon escorting me into my house. As we approached the little screened-in front porch the young willowy officer asked if he could carry the baby into the house for me. I didn't hesitate.

"Yes, that would be very nice of you." I said, being physically and emotionally spent.

When I stepped inside the front door, there was no sign of Ray. Where was Sylvia? I called out but got no answer. I looked at my Gucci watch. I'd squealed with joy when Ray brought it home several nights ago. Whenever he came home at two a.m., he never came in empty handed. I knew it was a peace offering.

Silvia should be here, preparing the evening meal and finishing up the days chores. Where was she? I walked around the corner, and gasped at what I saw. The room had been ransacked; drawers were hanging out of the chests, pillows and cushions had been swept off the sectional sofa. Magazines and books that had been neatly displayed on my sleek, teak cocktail table were strewn all over the floor. I felt sick; like I'd been physically assaulted. The two officers hung their heads; they looked embarrassed. Had they known I would encounter this when I walked in? Is that why they'd insisted on coming in with me?

"Madam, would you like us to stay and help you put back together your things?" The unusual Bahamian phrasing brought me back to the reality of where I was and who they were; standing in the middle of this chaos. "I'm so sorry Madam." He said. As he handed Sean back to me, the baby immediately clung to my neck.

"That would be very kind of you." I said. "I need to feed my son." I wasn't sure if I wanted to sit down and sob, or scream, but the kindness in his voice eased my nerves.

Get grounded, this was all so surreal. In order to bring myself back to reality, I needed to walk around and touch my belongings. I smelled the sweetness of the mango from this morning's breakfast. I had to erase the insanity of the last several hours. I took Sean out to the veranda and sat in my favorite wicker rocker as I did every day. I had to relax to meet this most important responsibility in my life. As he suckled, I allowed my mind to float away with the dolphins. I could see them gliding through the turquoise waters and wanted to follow them toward the setting sun. Please God, help me escape this hell.

I don't know how much time had passed when one of the officers stepped out and told me they were leaving. He kept his voice low when he saw that Sean was sleeping.

I nodded and whispered "Thank you." It was long after I heard them close the front door, that I was able to finally gather enough energy to get up and take Sean to his crib. I was spent from the ordeal at the police station—and the crushing anxiety. Where was Ray? When would I see him again? Was he still in custody? What was going to happen to us?

After I settled Sean, I returned to my rocker. As if on cue, the dolphins and porpoises appeared. They were playing, chasing one another, seemingly without a care in the world. I would join them, even if only in my imagination.

I pleaded with the turquoise green waters of the Caribbean to provide, for my mind, an escape from the day. I needed the horrific vision of Hammi's body, chalk white, bloated and disfigured, erased. The slow rolling waves, the tranquility and the clouds diffusing the brightness of the moon lulled me to sleep.

***

By the light of the moon, I recognized his finely chiseled features, awakened by him lightly tapping my shoulder. Illusion or not, I followed him.

Shaking, I threw myself into his arms. "You're home. Where have you been? They said you'd been arrested. When did you get home?"

"I wasn't arrested. I was taken in for questioning only. Now shhh! Don't wake the baby."

"But…"

"Shh! Quiet!"

With his touch, my body responded; my breasts tingled, my tummy flip-flopped. It didn't make sense that after that kind of terror I could feel such passion. Frantic I said, "The police said they had you; Hammi is dead. They said they had you in custody!"

"Shhh!" He swept me off my feet, carried me to the bed, tore open my blouse; buttons flying everywhere.

"But…Raymond…but…"

He squelched my "buts" with kisses, passionate kisses; he kissed my earlobes, my neck and my breasts.

Passion was preventing the questions; delaying the answers.

His body looked austere. His angular physique was marred only by the fist sized tattoo on his upper arm; a rose. Rose, the first love of his life would apparently live throughout eternity with him.

"But, the police?"

A menacing look flashed across his face. I knew all too well that his temper could surge from passion to anger. The light of the moon illuminated our bodies, as I stroked his high cheek bones down to his squared jaw.

"But Ray, the police said…"

Rolling and thrashing around, the sucking, smacking sounds of our sweaty bodies had a welcomed familiarity. In such moments of passion I found pleasure in the salty, sticky build-up of moisture on my body. His tongue flicked in my ear and turned my knees to jelly. I wanted this passion. Now more than ever I needed to feel connected to some sort of reality. There had been nothing "real" in this day. In the darkness it was safe to be Gabbi from Coral Gables.

He whispered in French:

"Vous Etes mon amour, vous ma vie, vous etes mon tout."

("You are my love, you are my life, you are my everything.")

This was when I glimpsed the very soul of this man I loved and *once* trusted with our lives. He was a dark and heavily tormented man. Once I was thrilled with my new life; now, I had no idea who had just made passionate love to me.

I also knew that when this love-making ended, I'd be assaulted again by the realities of Sean's needs, the questions from Inspector D'Clute, and the mystery of Hammi's body floating in the Caribbean.

It was not long after our last kiss that Ray was breathing heavily and evenly; I knew even in the darkness that he was sound asleep, his arm flailed out across the pillow. I, however, could not sleep. My thoughts immediately jumped back to those grueling hours at Police Headquarters. *Answers.* D'Clute needed answers. *I* needed answers. Was now the time? Should I be asking Ray to show me his passport? There was so much at risk. I knew that once I crossed *that* line, things would never be the same between us. I quietly slipped from the bed and hurried into the baby's room with a juice bottle. I felt sure that would keep him quiet and calm for a little while.

Some of the monikers I had worn to this point in my life were wife, lover and mother. But getting the answers would require a new hat, a new moniker; sleuth, detective, spy.

Ray was now lying on his stomach, arms stretched up over his head, his face buried in his pillow. In my new role as spy, I stealthily crossed the room where Ray's pants lay in a heap. Other than the sound of the waves crashing on the beach, the only noise to be heard was Ray's snoring.

You owe this to your children I thought. Get the answers!

Slipping my shaking hand into his trouser pocket, I tried to calm myself. Slowly and deliberately I removed his wallet, wondering what price I would pay if he woke up and caught me. As I clutched his wallet close to my chest, a little voice in my head said run! Run now! I headed down the hallway to the laundry room; he wouldn't come looking for me there. That's right; there was a bizarre irony that this was the last place he would come looking for *me*. On my tiptoes, I hurried across the cold, hard floor. Nothing could prepare me for the consequences of my actions.

***

The next day, I handed Inspector D'Clute a piece of paper.

"What is this Madam?"

"Inspector D'Clute, at great risk I believe to my own life, I did as you urged. The information on this piece of paper is copied from two forms of identification that I found in my husband's wallet. The first is Ray's Florida driver's license. The second is a Canadian Birth Certificate."

The inspector's hands were smooth. He had the long thin fingers of a piano player, lots of stretch between the thumb and the pinkie. If I were to describe him, I'd say that he reminded me of a star fruit, prickly and unwelcoming on the outside, but on the inside, sweet with a bit of tartness—just enough to take him seriously.

As he began to study the information I provided, he slid his reading glasses back down onto his nose. I guessed him to be in his forties. My father once told me how annoying it was that once you reach age forty you need reading glasses.

For what seemed like a lifetime, D'Clute said nothing. I wanted him to tell me what the information that I had given him meant. Finally he rose from his chair and came around the desk to sit next to me. With two of his shiny, slender fingers, he pushed his reading glasses back to the top of his head, looked me in the eyes, and took one of my hands into his.

"Madam", he said, "where we go from here will not be easy for you. At this time I would ask your permission to call you by your given name. May I?"

There was no need for me to speak the word yes; I just nodded.

"Gabrielle, do you know who your husband is?"

Oh my God! I've heard this before? Is it me? Why do I continue to cling to this delusional state of bliss with Ray? They say love is blind, but I must remove the blinders.

Officer Ramsbottom was sitting attentively in the corner of the room; I turned and ask him if he would kindly bring me a tall glass of their wonderful sweetened iced tea. After he left the room, Inspector D'Clute began speaking.

"You are very young Gabrielle, with the responsibility of a young son. I will speak to you now as though you were my daughter."

I gave him a half smile, my way of saying it's okay I'm ready.

"Four days ago on Chalk Airlines, three men came to the island. The purpose for their visit was stated as pleasure. The driver of the cab said the tall skinny one with the cigar asked where they could rent a small powerboat. The driver says he questioned them as to the knowledge of our local waters; he also asked if they wanted to rent this boat at night or in the day?"

"The one with the cigar was very abrupt and told the driver, that's not what he'd been asked. He said he just wanted to know where he could rent a small powerboat. Rather than going straight to their hotel, they wanted to be taken to the pier. The driver is the husband of my sister. He has always fancied himself as a detective. It's uncommon for visitors to the islands to rent a boat after dark. These men were not dressed in fishing attire and had no fishing gear with them. So my brother-in-law felt the need to bring this to my attention after dropping these three men off at the boat rental shack. I agreed with my brother-in-law and thanked him. I told him he had done a good job and to keep his eyes and ears open. I also decided to send two of my officers down to the pier, to observe only."

"I must tell you, you and your baby are not safe!"

I felt the blood rush from my limbs. It was sticky and hot in his office, yet I suddenly yearned for my down-filled comforter.

"Arrangements must be made to get you off the island."

"What? This is too fast! Leave the island? Without Ray?"

"Okay." He held his hands out as if to keep me calm and keep me in the chair. "This information you have brought in confirms what my investigators have found. These men--and your husband, we believe--are drug runners. Are you aware of the airstrip in Homestead, Florida, used by your husband?"

"No."

My mind was racing, trying to grab at all the possibilities of what this could mean; discarding them as fast as I came up with them. I was trembling. What did all this mean? How would it affect Caleb and Sean? Was something horrible about to happen? Should I have brought the baby with me?

No! No. I'm just panicking. Calm down, I commanded myself. As I fought for control of my emotions, I lowered my head into my palms letting it hang supported by my hands. The weight of all of this was becoming unbearable. D'Clute touched my shoulder, patting me gently until I looked back up. I'd have to face the truths that Inspector D'Clute laid out before me. I looked at his almonds shaped eyes and saw the look of concern. I was fighting the urge to plunge into hysteria. He offered me his monogrammed cotton handkerchief to absorb the tears now escaping my eyes. The urge was to get up out of the chair and run, just run. But where? To whom?

Officer Ramsbottom returned with the cold tea, and the two men waited for me to drink half of it before D'Clute began speaking again. Ramsbottom went back to his place in the corner, although he sat on the edge of the chair as if he was going to need to jump up at any moment.

"We must find out who murdered this man," the inspector said, and he stretched out one of his long fingers to tap on the photo of Hammi's corpse on his desk. "And we must put an end to this drug-running business in Bahamian waters." He walked over to me with a yellowed chart.

"I want to show you something." He ran his finger over the map, starting at Nassau and moving down to St. Lucia, passing Barbados and Martinique and finally stopping at St. Vincent.

"From what we can tell so far," he continued, "the drugs are brought up from someplace near Caracas, with the first stop-off point being the sparsely populated island of St. Vincent. From there local islanders, who know the currents in these waters and when to avoid the head winds, are using old, unsophisticated Boston Whalers until they get closer to Barbados. There they are met with 'go fast' boats."

"But I don't know how I can help you." I interrupted. "How can I possibly provide information to help?" This was all draining me.

"My dear girl, take some more sips of this refreshment. I can assure you, you know more than you think you do. Please Gabrielle, allow me to ask you methodical questions. Are you comfortable now, this will take some time."

No, I'm not comfortable. I thought. *Would I ever be again? Comfort was the furthest thing from my mind.*

"Ok, go ahead." I sighed.

"First, does your husband have a gun?"

I took a deep breath as my mind flashed back to that night when I hid in the baby's nursery. "I have never seen a gun." I said, but then I shared with him the events of the home invasion.

"Very good." He was sitting more erect in his chair. I could sense a building up of excitement in his manner. Oddly, I was beginning to feel a twinge of strength. Inspector D'Clute had been educated in London, England. I think to this day that his genteel British accent and mannerisms helped to keep me calm and to do as he asked. I was beginning to understand the need he had to pry information from me about my brother-in-law and Ray's friends from Canada.

"May I tell you a story, is it okay?" I asked.

"Certainly my dear." He signaled to Ramsbottom, pointing to my empty glass.

"Ramsbottom, Madam needs…will it be iced tea or would you prefer fruit juice this time?"

The formality was almost comical, that's the way it is in the Bahamas; very British, very formal.

"Oh, some fruit juice would be welcomed. Thank you Officer Ramsbottom." I can remember vividly when I addressed Officer Ramsbottom by name he almost swooned at the personal attention. He would smile and his eyes would become two little slits on his face. *Smiling could be hazardous to his health,* I thought as he shuffled out of the room. *Stop smiling officer; you may bump into a wall or something.*

"Yes, tell me the story please." he urged.

"When we were living in Montréal with Ray's mother, I didn't know that I was pregnant, but I was very ill. I couldn't even keep liquids down. One evening, Ray told me to put on my boots and my winter coat. We were going to visit his friend, Larry MacDonald. Larry lived in a penthouse apartment with a huge patio that wrapped around the living room and bedrooms. There was a swing; its design enveloped your body like a cocoon. I loved sitting in it. It faced downtown Montréal. I would swing, enjoying the panoramic view of downtown. Montréal was, to me, like being in Paris, France and Manhattan, New York, all wrapped into one. The gentle motion of the swing seemed to ease the nausea I had been experiencing twenty-four hours a day. I was quite content to take my place on the swing and remember shopping trips at Place Ville Marie and the many fun dinners with friends at Ruby Foo's Restaurant, up on the hill.

"That particular night, Ray, Larry and several other men were sitting at a large round kitchen table; there was an exposed bulb light fixture dangling above their heads. As I headed into the bar area to get a ginger ale, the words I heard next made me freeze in my tracks. Robbing. Robbery. Armored Trucks. Weapons. Furs. Department stores. I decided I had a choice, ginger ale for the nausea or instant death for overhearing words never meant for my ears. I did an about face and headed back to the swing."

Dredging this memory up is causing a great deal of discomfort. I gripped the smooth arms of the old mahogany chair; smoothed, I imagined, by many other people needing to grasp hard, to keep the room from tilting from the weight of their stress, sitting in D'Clute's office.

Ray came out onto the patio and draped my fur coat over my shoulders and said, "It's time to get you home."

I stood up, not making eye contact with him, knowing without a doubt that my "fairytale" life in Canada was over.

"So you were never suspicious about your husband's activities before that night?" the inspector said.

"Oh, I'd been suspicious about Ray for a while. The thugs he was chummy with, and the rolls of money he always had in his pockets never made sense to me because he wasn't "working".

My eyes scanned the charts of the Caribbean waters, still open on the desk. I'd come to believe what Inspector D'Clute had told me. No more guessing, wondering or justifying; Ray was, in fact, a very bad and very dangerous man.

"This is proof that my life with this man has been a complete myth. We've taken so many trips to St. Lucia, to Barbados, to Martinique. On each trip, we stayed with or at the homes of some of his very affluent friends. I had been led to believe that the owners of these homes, many built up on the mountains with walls of glass, overlooking Pigeon Island, or other small islands, were successful businessmen."

"Oh, they've been successful until now, my dear. And it is a business—a most diabolical sort of business; drugs and gun-running. Please focus now, Gabrielle. Is there anything else you can tell me? Any names you recall in particular, perhaps people your husband had frequent contact with?"

I stood up and began pacing the room. I was feeling strong again and my mind was clearing. "I want to ask you a question." I said. "I need these answers desperately. If I help you further, will my "husband" be going home to the States with me?" I knew it was perverse, and I was disgusted with myself, but I still wasn't ready to give up the warped sense of love and security I thought I had with him.

I was standing beside the window. D'Clute got out of his chair and came toward me. "My dear, I'm asking you to help us find some very evil men. There's no direct evidence against your husband at this point. But I'm afraid if we stop now, if we end this meeting, you may be traveling home with your son alone."

"Now Gabrielle is the time you must share everything you know, please I implore you. Possibly it will clear your husband. Perhaps we'll find that he is not directly involved with the dealings of these men. His involvement may simply have been peripheral. I can only say that there is a possibility that your husband will be allowed to join you. Now, however I cannot make any promises."

I sucked in a long breath, filling my lungs with the heavy, salty air coming in through the window and I forged ahead. I supplied Inspector D'Clute with the names of everyone I could remember that had ever been associated with Ray. Finally, reaching deep inside my hippie knapsack, which had remained in a heap under his desk all these hours, I removed a piece of paper. On it I had copied part of Ray's little black book. I'd found it while sitting on the floor of the laundry room, rifling through Ray's wallet.

"I think now Inspector D'Clute, the information on this piece of paper will be more than what you expected from me. I'm praying that he is not as deeply involved as you think. I love him. He is the father of my sons and the only man I've ever loved. I want him back. We met when I was eighteen, he was twenty-eight; he was the adult that replaced my parents. If I help you to catch all of these bad men…"

He got a very pensive look on his face. My bronzed hand was trembling as I held out the wrinkled wad of paper I'd almost destroyed, rather than turn it over.

When he took it, it was as though everything kicked into slow motion. I watched him lower himself into his chair; he exhaled and slowly opened the piece of paper. I hoped he now held the proverbial golden nugget that might buy our freedom and change so many lives.

We made eye contact, both of us knew this could be the defining moment as to whether Ray would be allowed to come home to me.

I was filled with guilt, betrayal and a sense of impending doom; what had I just done? Would my actions force Ray to live the *Square's Life*?

A Square gets up, goes to work, comes home, just getting by, never getting ahead; that's Ray's definition, and Squares were chumps! But a Rounder, that's altogether different. A Rounder lives for the thrill of the deal. No two days are the same.

"Baby, don't you know the palms of my hands get sweaty? My arms and hands tingle at the mere thought of "putting together a deal". It's an adrenalin rush. It's like I'm a junkie and the "deal" is the drug that produces the high. It's a way of life."

That's the answer to my question; it's an addiction, it's the thrill. He could never conform to the Square's Life.

It may be a way of life but I knew that I wouldn't raise my sons in that environment.

"Inspector, I know it sounds sappy; the happy husband and wife, a couple of kids, the white house and picket fence. Daddy goes to work every day and Mommy makes cookies for the kids after school. I'd give up *this* extravagant lifestyle to have *that* with Ray and our boys, in a New York minute."

"Inspector D'Clute, as I see it, I've already crossed a line. Take this information that I retrieved like a thief in the night from the man that I love. But I'm not leaving this office; I'm not getting out of this chair without some answers. I'm going back to Miami.

I'm going back. I want Ray and my baby. I looked D'Clute in the eyes.

"I'm not Mrs. Fortier!" Those words rushed out of me like a body being sucked out to sea by a strong undertow; freeing my soul from this life of constant deception. "I now understand that I must tell you the whole truth if you're to get me and my babies out of this situation. Ray lives the *Rounder's* life. *That* does not include marrying all the women he impregnates. I know for a fact there are at least three other children, in Canada, whose mothers he never married." I was feeling dirty and used.

"Are you aware that I have another child?" My voice was getting louder, the pitch getting higher. The words were rushing out of my mouth. His brow wrinkled and his eyes focused as he knelt closer to me.

"No Gabrielle, tell me."

"My first born son is in Miami." He looked puzzled. "If you have time, I'll explain it to you now."

"Gabrielle" he said, "this is the beginning of a journey that you and I have committed to. Yes my dear, I have time to listen. This will not be a brief encounter. I need to know everything about you. What do you prefer I call him? His face looked pained. There was empathy.

His name is Caleb. As all mothers do, I thought him to be the most angelic baby. Six weeks after his birth a blood vessel in his brain burst. The entire left side of his brain was destroyed. Because of that, the son I love more than life itself now lives in a private nursing facility. He requires medical care around the clock. That's where my heartstrings are tied."

Salmon colored walls in my peripheral vision, seemed all at once to be moving. *No silly, the wall isn't moving that's just the setting sun casting shadows.* Sunrise and sunset in the Caribbean are special. So special in fact, that they are followed by a celebration. I didn't want to talk anymore. Yesterday I thought this man was destroying my life, perhaps I could find solace that he is trying to *gift* me the chance for another Miami sunrise.

The inspector said nothing, but when he raised his head I could see that his piercing dark eyes were brimming with tears. I walked over to him, stood on my toes and hugged his neck. In that stark silence, I realize that Caleb's story was too painful for anyone to hear.

As D'Clute raised his ebony hand and gently whisked away the moisture from his cheek, he summoned Officer Ramsbottom, who was sitting outside in the hall.   "Ramsbottom," he said, "it's time to see Madam home. You are to see that she is safe. I want her comforts seen to. Do you understand?" I never tired of listening to the Bahamian sing-song manner of speech.

"Oh yes, Inspector. Yes sir."

I felt the inspector's long, sinewy arm stretch around my back and gently guide me.

"What's next?" I asked anxiously.

He forced a smile. "We will know when Ray has left your home tomorrow. When my officers are sure he is gone, you will be brought here to my office to continue this journey. Ramsbottom, didn't you tell me that you know the family of Madam's housekeeper?"

"Oh yes sir, I do. In fact she's married to a cousin…"

"Splendid! Before you come back to headquarters, I want you to go to her home and inform her that she will be picked up and brought to Madam's home tomorrow morning. She's to stay there with the child until Madam returns."

"Yes sir, I'm sure this will be no trouble." He was happy and almost giddy that he would be seeing to my needs and comforts.

Chapter Twenty

There was an urgency to continue searching out the truth, having committed to helping Inspector D'Clute. Ray always carried a black leather satchel, a gift from Mr.Bontoni on one those mysterious trips to Italy. And of course there would always be some fabulous gift for me. I always loved Ray's bag, made of the softest, most pliable leather. I'd always assumed that the contents were papers that dealt with his business interests. I'd thought legitimate business; now I realize spurious business. I decided that this black bag and I would make a duplicitous trip down the hallway to the laundry room at the very next opportunity.

When Ramsbottom delivered me home, I found Sylvia sitting in the rocker which had so many times offered me comfort and tranquility from the long stressful days. She was rocking Sean, I chose not to interrupt this tender scene. Instead I went straight into our bedroom where I witnessed the brilliant golden orb, the sun, ready to make its plunge into the ocean.

I remember asking Ray once while sipping a demitasse of espresso, "Honey, use the second hand on your watch and tell me how long it takes the sun to slip beneath the horizon."

"Thirty-eight seconds!" he exclaimed. "It took thirty-eight seconds for your sun to escape the heat of the day."

Ramsbottom had gotten me back home just in time to witness the splendor of another Bahamian sunset. I'd love to lie down now and take a nap but I was on a mission.

Where to begin? There was a deep, long walk-in closet that Ray had had cedar lined. Several of his custom made tailored silk suits, hung on wooden hangers spaced two inches apart. There were nine pairs of shoes lined up like little soldiers waiting for action. I was always fascinated by his stories of flying to Europe; spending two or three days with Mr. Bontoni and his family.

"But honey, why can't I go with you? I would love to meet Mr. Bontoni and his family. Don't you want me to go along and learn to cook some of your favorite Italian dishes?"

He grabbed my hand, pulled me close to him and said, "No my Pet, my trips to Italy don't allow time for such fun."

The luxurious Bontoni craftsmanship could not be found anywhere else on the planet according to Ray. *The pockets!* I've never dug through his pockets. As I went from suit to suit to suit, it was difficult to enjoy the rich softness of the handmade suits when the task at hand was so dastardly. When I touched the fourth or fifth jacket, I heard a paper rustle in an inside pocket. Wait! What's this? It's a receipt! I recognized *that* before I even removed it from its secret hiding place. I wasn't trembling this time. I slid it out and carefully held it up to my eyes. I hadn't dared to turn on the light in the closet. It was a receipt; not in English. At the very top I understood and recognized the name *Bontoni*. I read further down on the receipt and saw that it was made out to *Lawrence MacDonald*. Oh my God! D'Clute thinks Ray *is* Larry MacDonald! He isn't! He's just using his name! I need to make sure D'Clute understands this, I thought as I crumbled the receipt in my hand and ran back into the bedroom. I tucked it into the little Fendi coin purse which always stayed at the bottom of my large leather hobo bag. It would be safe there.

I fell asleep that night wondering how many of his trips to Europe for custom suit fittings and meetings with his cobbler were guises for the sinister Ray; or, was it Lawrence? In my poor pea brain, I still couldn't get a grip on who was who. The facts were all too bizarre; dates, cancelled airline tickets, family calendars, hotel reservations…D'Clute would have to resolve all of this. Just then I heard a man's voice and the door slam closed. It was Ray. My heart sank. I wouldn't be snooping anymore tonight. I didn't think the little receipt from Bontoni was going to be worth anything to Inspector D'Clute. I needed more time.

"Baby I'm home."

I didn't care who he was, what his name was, where he'd been or what he'd done. I wanted to be in his arms. I wanted to be his little Coppertone girl. That's who ran down the hallway. I jumped into the arms of the man I didn't even know; all I wanted was the passion that would follow.

***

We awoke to the glow of God's spectacular sunrise. The glorious paint-to-canvas, created by Monet, hanging on the wall was a close second.

Ray left our bed, showered, dressed and went into the kitchen to prepare us a continental breakfast. Neither of us enjoyed a heavy meal first thing in the morning; fresh fruits and croissants was the special way we celebrated morning. I went into the nursery and attended to Sean. Ray had set a bright and cheerful breakfast table on the veranda. There was a medley of orange sections, grapefruit halves, sliced banana with heavy cream, a luscious bowl of ripe strawberries, his favorite chocolate chip croissants from The Bread Lady and a sterling silver carafe of his famous steamy café con leche`.

In the center of the table in a beautiful Waterford vase, were fresh cut double bloom peach colored Hibiscus flowers. The blooms were so large, he had only cut three.

He came into the nursery and scooped the baby out of my lap. I loved his hands. They were smooth, no calluses, large but not menacing. The backs of his hands were lightly freckled and just like the rest of his body had just enough masculine strawberry blonde hairs. These were the hands that caressed me and brought me great pleasure. It seemed impossible that those same hands that now placed our baby in the satin bunting in the pram, had been involved with murder and other illegal activities. I had to shake that thought off. I wanted to soak up every minute with him. I couldn't bear to allow those thoughts of gloom into my mind.

We had a custom made, antique British pram for Sean. It was white leather which sat on larger than normal tires; the inside was lined with luscious hand-embroidered, satin bunting. He gently placed the baby on the luxurious white satin bedding and pushed him onto the veranda to join us.

Looking at me Ray could tell that in my mind I was far away. "Hey Baby, where are you?"

"Well, for a split second I was off with that school of porpoises chasing their breakfast in the turquoise waters." *They never went too far to feed; the tasty meal they sought would not be found in the colder darker waters of the Caribbean. I can remember allowing myself at times, to pretend that these mammals of the sea were my friends; that at any moment they would turn around and look at the veranda and say, "Hey, aren't you coming out to play with us today?"*

"Okay Baby, I hate to leave you but I have business to take care of. When Sylvia gets here today tell her to see about of my laundry, I don't think I'll be back in time for dinner. Are you still reading your Hemmingway book?"

"Yes." I knew what that meant, *The Old Man and the Sea*, would be called upon to entertain me for the day.

Chapter Twenty-One

"I doubt if this is anything important." I chirped as I handed D'Clute the receipt from Mr. Bontoni's Leather Shop.

He raised his hand signaling, please don't speak. As was his normal British formal manner, he would never just tell me to be quiet. I enjoyed that he treated me with adult respect; one equal to another.

With the aid of his two fists on his desk, he pushed himself out of the old wooden chair and walked over to a tall rusty metal filing cabinet. He pulled the top drawer open, retrieved a file and extracted one sheet of paper. I could tell that he was trying to decide whether to hand it to me or share the information with me at all.

"Wait a minute!" D'Clute said as he turned and faced me, "My brother-in-law came to me last year. He had a generous repeat Italian customer. I had Ramsbottom take down all the information; days, dates and times. The man's name and country of origin and as best as Pieter could provide, any known associates. We've kept that file open in the event anything developed. "

It was a good sign as he tentatively extended the paper out for me to read. I needed to know that this man was working with me, not against me. My life with Ray had always been like a thousand piece puzzle, missing the cover picture. Looking at this paper, additional pieces of the puzzle were now falling into place.

"What does this mean? Why does it matter?"

"You see my dear, Ray and these other men are low players on the totem pole of the organization. We know and have known for some time that the money which feeds this frenzy, is coming out of Europe. What we didn't know until you presented this receipt, was how they were transporting the funds."

"How? What funds?"

"My country, unlike the U.S. and Europe is very tiny. Do you remember my sister's husband, the cab driver?"

"Yes. I remember you telling me that he picked up Raymond and his friends off of a Chalk flight."

"That's correct. I told you before, Pieter imagines himself to be an investigator. For over a year now he has had a steady repeat customer; a man from Italy. He always had something special for Pieter and his family; candy, trinkets and such. It escalated to things that are *more substantial.* It was when the trinkets became items of real value, such as jewelry, the red flag went up for Pieter, as you Americans would say. No one gives such valuable gifts without an ulterior motive, e.g. 'see nothing, do nothing, say nothing!'

And, Pieter was told to be available to the man anytime day or night."

"One evening Pieter dropped his Italian fare off at the home of a very prominent Bahamian business man, who by the way," D'Clute continued, as he pulled his glasses further down his nose and peered over the lenses, "is the builder of *go fast* boats; in the States you know them as high powered speed boats. Being a small country we are all related somehow and pay close attention to foreigners."

"I'm beginning to understand the *business* aspect of all of this." I said. "It's becoming obvious why Ray had the need to own nine pairs of custom made Italian shoes."

"Correct!" exclaimed D'Clute. He felt, the more I understood, the more I could assist him with this investigation.

"Nine pairs of shoes…" I said.

"…nine trips to Italy!" D'Clute finished my sentence. "Yes Madam. And each of the nine trips represents close to one million dollars in cash, being smuggled out of Italy and into…"

"You mean he brought that money back to our home in Miami?"

"No. This is where it gets tricky. Each time your husband returned from Italy he flew into Miami

International Airport. From there, he would make a connecting flight on Chalk airlines to the Bahamas. Pieter has corroborated that his *very special Italian customer* was also on the island for every one of your husband's brief visits; some of which were only several hours long."

I was smiling; this wasn't something to be smiling about. But, I was beginning to see the bigger picture.

"So..." I jumped up out of my seat and paced back and forth over the terra cotta floor and continued,

"...he would fly to Italy saying the purpose of the trip was to get custom-made shoes. That always made perfect sense since his suits were also custom made."

"Yes, that would never draw attention to him as it was his normal pattern; custom shoes, custom suits." D'Clute clarified. "Now you're getting it my dear."

"Okay. Instead of coming home to Miami, he takes the forty-five minute flight here. He then meets with the cab driver's *Italian Customer*."

I stopped pacing; I was out of answers. "Please, fill in the blanks for me."

"You are on the right track. Pieter's customer would meet your husband at the Chalk Terminal. From there the two men would have Pieter take them to the estate of the man who builds the *go fast* boats. Pieter says he was always told to be back in two hours."

"Oh my goodness." I was standing next to the open window looking down at my hands. They felt cold, wet and clammy. My heart was pounding wildly in my chest. My adrenalin was flowing as fast the information being swapped.

Slowly I pivoted back to face D'Clute. My brow was wrinkled. I now had a whole new set of questions. "But Hammi? How and why…why do Raymond's identification papers say Larry MacDonald?"

"Ah ha." said D'Clute, dragging out the aaaah. "Can you see now Gabbi why every small, seemingly insignificant memory or piece of paper *isn't* insignificant? Your husband simply used MacDonald's name so that in the event papers such as these came to light, he would never be implicated."

He continued, "I can see that you are still confused. Listen carefully to this time line my dear…

- Ray makes the trips to Italy
- Ray smuggles money into the Bahamas
- Ray meets with Pieter's Italian customer
- Ray hands over money to Italian
- The Italian man goes to *go fast* boat builder

…does that help?"

"But what about Hammi? How and why did he end up dead under the bridge?"

"That, my dear, we hope to find out today. We are interviewing a possible *witness* this evening. But, for now I'm afraid I cannot answer you."

"I just pray that Ray was nowhere around when that happened. It's one thing to think that the father of your children is involved in smuggling, but…murder…"

D'Clute gave me a warning look, as though saying, be prepared for anything.

***

I had a sleepless night. Ray didn't come home and as usual he didn't call. I thought perhaps the *witness* had implicated him. No, I was sure that inspector D'Clute would have called me.

***

The next day the short ride to D'Clute's office was anything but comfortable. As I slid into the car I noticed the cracked and chipped red leather of the seats which had been abused by the tropical sun. It's brittle, prickly surface had a therapeutic value; it kept me in the present.

"Good morning Madam." said Ramsbottom.

Wow, his aura of innocence that I so admired was now replaced with a worried and pensive look. I'd always felt that this typically genteel officer would be better suited as a manservant or houseboy; he seemed to derive great personal pleasure from seeing to the needs of others.

"Ramsbottom, this bright and sunny morning is not reflected on your face. What's troubling you my new friend?" I inquired.

"Well, Madam, um…"

"What is it? Has something happened? Isn't D'Clute waiting for me? Speak up! I can see by your demeanor that something is amiss."

"Yes Madam, the Inspector *is* waiting for you…but…um…with…"

"Dear man, please speak up right now. Stop hesitating! *Who* is waiting with him?"

"Madam, it's not my place…well…"

I thought my heart would jump out of my chest. It was all I could do to keep from reaching forward and placing my two hands around his scrawny neck to squeeze the information from him.

I leaned forward and slapped my hands down on the back of the seat, making his shoulders jump and he blurted out, "There are two men in business suits with the Inspector; I believe they are from the States; under their suit jackets are guns."

"Ramsbottom take a breath, breathe." I encouraged.

"I wasn't introduced to them, but...well..."f

"If you say *well* one more time I'm going to strangle you! *Who are those men?*" I almost screamed.

"Wel...um...F.B.I.! They are from the States and I think F.B.I men!" he finally said.

Ramsbottom delivered me to D'Clute's office and inquired as to my preference of a beverage.

"A sweet iced tea would be fine."

Standing with my feet firmly on the terra cotta tiles, I affixed my eyes on D'Clute's face and said, "Who are these men? What are they doing here?" *I had the audacity for the first time in my life, to demand answers. And, from of all people, the Inspector General of the Royal Bahamian Police.*

"Calm down Gabrielle," he said as he placed his hands on my shoulders; holding me at arm's length, he said, "Take a few deep breaths; calm yourself and I will explain everything."

He directed me to take a seat in the chair.

Two can play this game of cat and mouse. Bring it on big boys, I thought.

"Madam Fortier I would like to introduce Agent Saunders and Agent Blakely." said Inspector D'Clute.

I guess he saw the blank look on my face and continued.

"First let me assure you these men are not here to bring harm to you."

Without even taking a breath, I demanded, "Well then why am I here; what do these two men have to do with me?"

It was agent Saunders who spoke first. "I'm glad to meet you Mrs. Fortier. Allow me to apologize for making you uncomfortable. I'm sure this cannot be easy for you. I won't waste your time; let's just get to the facts; just the facts ma'am."

Who does he think he is, Joe Friday from Dragnet?

"Agent Saunders, as we say in the States the clock starts ticking now." *Wow, did I just say that?* "You've got the floor Agent Saunders. Either I get straight answers now, or I'm walking out of this office."

Saunders was a short man. His hair was carrot orange. He wore freckles like a mask on a raccoon with a smile that I imagined was useful in breaking down barriers. I needed his smile at that very moment. My heightened state of anxiety was causing my body to feel tingly. Breathing had become difficult. I'd had that sensation before in my life and found the safety of the roots of an old banyan tree to protect me. There'd be no protection in this room. I must maintain the "I'm in charge attitude."

"May I sit down next to you?" Saunders said.

I shook my head yes.

From the corner of my eye I watched Blakely cross the room to sit in the chair most often occupied by Officer Ramsbottom.

I understood that this was a matter of life and death. I looked at the agent and said, "Look! For the past week I've came to trust and believe Inspector D'Clute. I need to speak to him now, *privately*."

Chapter Twenty-Two

Sean and I were in danger; no one was sugar-coating anything! I realized from this day forward my whole life would change—and my life might no longer include Ray—I folded. So much for the bold, in-command Mrs. Fortier who'd come in demanding answers.

I dropped my head into my hands and began to sob. D'Clute pulled that straight-backed wooden chair next to me, as he had done so many times before; wrapped his long, thin arm around my shoulders and let me weep. Over the next hour he spoke to me as a loving concerned father might speak to a daughter. He told me that once he had called the United States and gotten the FBI involved, he was no longer the decision maker in the case. He further explained the role these two men would play in my life from this day forward.

"I'm sorry that I didn't take the time to explain this to you better. But as I see it time is of the essence. There are agents already in Europe and Italy rounding up the moneymen. We have good reason to believe you are not safe in the Bahamas for even *one* more night. "

I nodded, sniffing and wiping my face with the handkerchief he'd handed me.

I was very upset that I couldn't say good-bye to Alan, and I asked D'Clute if he would get a message to him, when he came back in a few weeks.

"He's been my only friend here, Inspector. It would mean so much to me."

"I will tell him that you were called away due to an illness in your family, my dear."

I turned in my chair to face D'Clute one more time. "Dear friend do you have a crystal ball? Is my destiny to live one illusion after another? Will I ever have my dream of the Squares life?"

"My Dear, I had no idea how your life would be altered the day I sent my men to your beach."

"Listen   Inspector   D'Clute,   my   new confidant…" *my only confidante*, I thought to myself,

"…when Peter asks Jesus, how many times do I forgive those who sin against me, seven times? Jesus says maybe even seventy times. Well, I've turned my cheek for Ray for the very last time. I cannot live with a man and allow that man to raise these children, our children. He is a thief and most likely a key player in murder. For all these years, I've had my suspicions, but now the FBI and that picture of Hammi's dead, bloated body are absolute proof."

D'Clute with his long sinewy fingers, slid the picture of Hammi Hamilton's body into his desk drawer and closed it gingerly; a symbolic confirmation of my decision.

I stood up and walked over to Ramsbottom. As I stroked his cheek I said, "Ramsbottom my glass is empty and my mouth is dry. Might I trouble you to get me a tall sweetened iced tea? Thank you. While out there, you can tell *those men* they can come back in."

My stomach flipped as I prepared to relinquished all control over my life. Once the "suits" returned, I pivoted to face them and said,

"Gentlemen, I want you all to sit down and listen to me. I don't understand any of this. But I have to believe in somebody. So I'll do as you say for the sake of my children. Alright, I'm ready to play this game and it's obvious that you have the ball, so please, continue."

"Inspector D'Clute tells me that he calls you Gabrielle. I'd like your permission to do the same." asked Saunders.

"You have it!" I said curtly.

***

We would be whisked away to the United States, in the Witness Protection Program. The Feds had everything planned. All I had to do was fill in the blanks for them. What were my hobbies? What kind of jobs had I had? Was I interested in furthering my education?

After I'd answered their questions for another hour, they went into a huddle and came up with Nashville, Tennessee, as an excellent place for us to live. There were good hospitals, good schools; in fact, it was called the *Little Parthenon*.

As I look back on those few days prior to leaving the island, I had very little to do with making the plans for our new lives. Not surprisingly at the time, I thought that normal. Until now I'd had no input into my life; either as a kid in my parents' home, or as Ray's wife. Wife? That was sounding even more foreign than usual. No one had ever asked for proof that we were married. Most had referred to him as my husband and I never corrected them. Unfortunately the whole thing was a fairytale, made up in my mind. I believed that living as husband and wife was good enough. But good enough doesn't build a strong family foundation. In my case, good enough never was.

***

Fill me with your never ending power; your renewable energy. I'll not only survive, I will thrive! I thought as I gazed from the cutout window of D'Clute's office. The ocean had always fueled me and filled me with the energy to continue. This wasn't going to be easy. I understood how urgent it all was. The image of Hammi's dead body was enough of a lesson to convince me the Feds were right. This was a matter of life or *death*.

There weren't programs on television educating young girls about the dangers of living with a man who on one hand professes love and with the other beats the tar out of you. Of course in later days, even mental cruelty was taught to young women and girls as a type of abuse. I had met all the criteria for being an enabler to a beast. I was so starved for love and affection that I bought it; hook, line and sinker. I had zero self-esteem. He was a "professional" at saying what I needed to hear in order to be molded into the puppet of obedience he desired.

Perhaps getting a college education and studying psychology, I could learn why I had been so easily led into hell, thinking it paradise. I continually went back to this abusive man. My beloved friends in the Pocono's tried to warn me; my parents tried to warn me. His abuse of me was one thing, but murder, drug running and God only knows what else was another. It's no longer just my life at stake; it's the children as well. By taking advantage of education maybe I wouldn't end up a statistic of the American battered woman. Psychology was the path I'd take. Maybe, just maybe I'd be able to help other young women and girls in their fight to escape such abuses. I was emotionally spent. I sat there and hung my head.

Nope, not gonna do it. The verses of an old song that I'd sung so many times on stage, contained life lessons...*wisdom born of pain...been down there on the floor and no one's ever gonna keep me down again...* Amen Sister!!!

I'd have to learn to stand on my own two feet; be a decision maker. More importantly, make the right decisions. Okay, I'll go to Tennessee. But when? *Now,* was the answer. I'd never go back to my beach home on Bimini; never to my beloved home in Miami. As I sat there, the adrenalin had taken over. I was feeling oddly strong, secure and capable.

***

They got into specific details as we sat there and designed my new life like architects around a drawing board. The house had to have three bedrooms, and one had to be on the ground floor. Carrying Caleb up and down stairs was out of the question. (Yes, I would finally have my beloved angel with me again!) It was to be, not too far or too close to town. The hospital needed to be no more than a five-minute drive. I'd need a car.

"What type of car would you like?" Agent Saunders asked.

"Well, I don't know...we've always had Cadillacs, and once—"

"*Mrs. Fortier,*" he interrupted, "you must remember, do not duplicate anything from your past. No Cadillacs! How about a Volvo?"

"A Volvo...I love Volvos; they're very safe. And they bring back some fond memories."

He was on the phone now to the U.S. Into the phone he said, "Make it a Volvo 245 wagon. Ohhh, not more than five years old. And she'll need a live-in caregiver for the first year, at least. Set up a neurologist to take care of Caleb, and make sure he has all the child's records."

I panicked. "But how will I transport him?"

"Do you trust us?" Agent Blakely asked.

What should I say? Was I supposed to trust these strangers I'd only known for seven hours? I'd trusted Ray and look at me now.

"Mrs. Fortier, you must trust the people who are going to protect you. I understand it isn't easy. You're confused and in shock."

Shock? Was that what this state of calm and control was called? I wasn't scared. My heart wasn't racing. "Is that what I'm in, shock?"

"Yes, it's the brain's way of protecting itself. We have a man and a woman who will travel with you. Now listen carefully. In an hour, a day, a week, the shock will wear off. Then you may well fall apart. That's common and we will have professionals in place to pick up the pieces. We'll be there to insure you stay on track. We have years of experience transplanting people and creating new lives for them."

He continued, "I think when your mind is ready to wrap itself around all that's happened to you in such a short period of time, you'll be amazed at just how much we will do for you. The biggest key is you must never—I repeat, never—tell anyone about your past. I know that seems impossible at this point, but I'm sure you'll comply, knowing that the lives of your children are at stake. Fortunately your children are so young there's no chance of them slipping."

"Slipping? What if I slip?"

"For the first six months you will be meeting with counselors from the agency, experts who'll guide you; they'll teach you how to create your new identity. You won't be alone, and we won't allow any harm to befall you or your children. You will have bank accounts with funds enough to take care of your basic needs and essentials that arise, a new Social Security number, driver's license, and voter registration card. And you'll have a new passport. For the first year, we will be your husband, parents, preacher, confessor, spiritual guide. We will provide whatever it takes for you to successfully morph into *Katrina Dillard*."

"*Katrina Dillard?* Who's that?" I asked.

"That's you!"

Chapter Twenty-Three

To our new Nashville neighbors on Lakeshore Drive, we were the Dillard family: Katrina (Mrs. Dillard) and her two sons, Jeremy and Kyle. And of course our family pet Valeska (Leski), a Borzoi. There was no Mr. Dillard because sadly he'd been killed in a tragic accident.

Agent Saunders had recommended we have a fairly large dog, "the best security system you can have.", he'd said. I immediately asked if it could be a Borzoi, a Russian Wolfhound and Saunders looked puzzled. He'd never seen a Borzoi and continued to refer to my requested pet as a "Bourgeois".

As for what I was to tell friends and neighbors about my missing husband, the Feds had that story down pat. "When anyone asks you about your husband you will refer to him as Liam," Saunders said. "And here is your story: 'He was killed in a motorcycle accident while crossing the Miami River Bridge. He lost control of the motorcycle and it slid under the front end of the car behind him. Liam was thrown into the murky river and the strong currents there swept him away. His body was never found.'"

"The good thing about death Katrina is that it's final. People will accept this explanation and in fear of hurting you or bringing back sad memories, most people will never broach the subject again."

According to my day planner my classes at the University of Tennessee started at 9 a.m. I'd pick up Sean…uh, Jeremy, at day care at 4:00, then head home for dinner with Oliver (my new love). My singing gig at the Captain's Table in Printer's Alley was at 9 p.m.

Kyle (Caleb) was having a bath. His live-in nurse, Hope was a blessing. She had fast become a *real* member of our family.

There was a knock at the door. It still startled me when someone knocked. First of all I hadn't established many friendships since moving to Nashville and the few friends I did have wouldn't come over without calling first. I tiptoed over to the door so that whoever was there wouldn't hear me, and peered through the peephole. Valeska was right beside me, barking and growling.

Hansen's Delivery. Hmm, I thought. *Who's sending me a package?*

"Leski, quiet now!" I took her by the collar and pulled her back and away from the door. Through the closed door, I said, "Yes? How can I help you?"

"Good morning, ma'am, can I get you to sign for this package?"

I opened the door as far as the chain would allow with one hand and pulled Valeska back with the other.

"Oh my God, lady, what is that?" He was looking almost eye to eye with Valeska.

That poor young man's eyes got big as dinner plates.

"I'll sign for it; give me the package."

After I watched him leave, I closed the door, checked the locks and smiled at Valeska. "Girl, you are the best alarm system I could have. Come on, let's get you a cookie and see what this package is all about. You're such a good girl."

Leski had curled up on the wonderful, comfy sofa I'd found at a thrift shop—a down-filled Thomasville treasure. I'd managed to furnish the whole house shopping at thrift shops, church bazaars and Salvation Army stores. With the modest stipend given me I'd managed to make our home not only comfortable but filled with quality pieces. My Oliver, or Olive Oil, as Jeremy called him, had set up a beautiful little bar area in our formal living room.

Oliver and I met one night after I finished my set at the Captain's Table. Jake Foster, manager of the club, came up to me and said some people would "like to meet you". He and his friends had heard about a new singer in town. It was common practice that entertainers would often go and check out new acts.

"I'd be happy to." I said.

He escorted me over to a table with four men. As he started doing introductions, I recognized the guys as "The Baron's".

"I've heard of you fellas! You lead the country club circuit." I said, smiling.

"Would you like to join us? May we buy you a cocktail?" asked Oliver.

"Oh, I would love a *Kir Royale*, thank you."

The one who introduced himself as Oliver held out my chair. It didn't matter if the others were Tom, Dick and Harry; from that meeting forward it would be Oliver and Katrina. Over the next few months Oliver and I fell madly in love. For convenience sake and to help me with the kids, we decided that he would move in. Oliver was a complete departure of what I was used to from a lover.

I felt like I needed some extra courage before I sat down with this envelope. I know *liquid courage*. "This Miami girl loves her grapefruit juice; and Stolichnaya vodka has no taste. That's the ticket!" I said aloud to myself.

I went into the kitchen and mixed the drink. I carried the envelope and my morning cocktail upstairs to Oliver's study. I sat in his tapestry covered, wing back chair and pulled up the big paisley ottoman. Somehow sitting in his chair helped me to feel a little braver.

I took a deep breath and opened the package. In it was a stack of newspaper articles clipped together; on top was a letter. I opened the letter first and glanced down at the signature. "Uncle Tommy", it was signed. That's the name used whenever I got something from the Feds.

Dear Mrs. Dillard,

I hope this letter finds you in good health and spirits. The material I've enclosed for you will help to answer many of the questions you had prior to your hurried departure. I want to personally commend you again. I find you to be one of the bravest young women I have ever known. You showed a courage and wisdom far beyond your age. I dare not say more. I'll end by saying burn this material when you have finished reading it.

Sincerely, Uncle Tommy

I skimmed through the various newspaper clippings from papers in Miami and the Bahamas. There was even one from an Italian newspaper, which I couldn't interpret.

I closed my eyes and rested my head back for just a minute. I allowed my mind to transport me back to the blue green waters, the voluptuous orange/yellow sunrises and my rocker on

my Bahamian veranda. Nope! I can't do that. It hurts too much.
No escaping, even in my imagination. Maybe in a few years when
more of my life with Ray becomes a distant memory. But not
now; it was all still too new, too raw.

I didn't know what I would find when I began
to read the clippings. The only thing Uncle Tommy had
told me—by phone two months after we got to
Nashville—was that Ray had sold out all of his
comrades in crime in exchange for a deal with
WITSEC, the federal prison system's version of the
Witness Protection Program. I had no idea when he
might be walking the streets again; and I didn't want to
know.

The grandfather clock in the corner with the
crescent moon face chimed eight times. The morning
was quickly slipping away and if I planned to make my
first class I would have time to read only one of the
articles.

I sat my drink down and started reading the
newspaper article from the Miami Herald. It told the
story of marijuana and cocaine smuggling from Central
America through the Bahamas, eventually being
distributed in Miami, Florida. The United States
Attorney's Office had extradition agreements with the
Italian Polizia. The case had been cracked when the
discovery of a dead body under the Paradise Island
Bridge led the Bahamian authorities to a small group of
men; three Canadians, two Italians and one Bahamian.
Credit was given to Inspector D'Clute, a man named

Pieter LaRue and other unnamed sources for busting this Cartel.

Deals had been made to allow the Italian *players* to be extradited back to Italy, for naming the murderer of Herman Hamilton. They had provided evidence about a Bahamian businessman named Joseph Tomlinson. He was a builder of *go fast* boats and provided them as the means of transport for the drugs from a small island in the southern Caribbean to the Bahamas, with the final destination of Miami, Florida.

Mr. Tomlinson hired a worker from his boat yard to murder Mr. Hamilton. Mr. Hamilton it seems had been overheard at a Bahamian casino describing the hollowed-out hulls in Tomlinson's boats. Hamilton had been drinking heavily and bragging about his smuggling activities. His night of partying and heavy drinking had resulted in his death.

An autopsy determined that Mr. Hamilton's body had six bullet holes and had been in the water approximately twelve to eighteen hours, thus proving that he had been murdered shortly after his "scene" in the casino. His murder led to the investigation that covered three countries. Powerful businessmen, legislators and even the highest levels of the judicial systems of two countries were snared in the vast web of corruption, violence and murder.

The actual triggerman in the Hamilton murder was a Bahamian; Jackson Smith. He had been sentenced to life in prison in the Bahamas. The money